MW01134940

HER LYING DAYS ARE DONE

Liars and Vampires
Book 5

Robert J. Crane
with Lauren Harper

Her Lying Days are Done
Liars and Vampires, Book 5

Robert J. Crane
with Lauren Harper
Copyright © 2018 Ostiagard Press
All Rights Reserved.

1st Edition

Chapter 1

I'd always wondered what it would be like to introduce my boyfriend to my parents. Never having had a real boyfriend before, it was something I'd only imagined. I pictured a pleasant scene, a family dinner where we'd sit down over garlic breadsticks and pizza and share a meal and a conversation. My dad would be smiling, pleased with my choice in men. My mom might even crack a grin at some funny thing he said, all of us laughing at some witty joke. I could imagine myself sitting back, serene, watching it all go smoothly.

I'd also like to have been involved in the decision of inviting said boyfriend over to the house to meet dear old Mom and Dad. That way, I could have been the one to agree to disagree at my own leisure.

But that wasn't the way it had happened. I'd come downstairs and there he was, no choice, no control. And here I was, left sitting across from my parents and my boyfriend at the dining room table, chewing awkwardly into the silence, wondering how I was going to explain that my boyfriend was a vampire. No easy feat for any normal teenage girl, trusted by her parents.

But it was especially difficult when you're known as a perpetual liar.

The food was starting to get cold as we were sitting there, the four of us— me, my boyfriend Mill, Mom and Dad, around the old oak stained table that Mom actually really hated but brought with us to Florida when we moved, as a memento

1

of our home in New York.

The garlic knots filled the air with a tantalizing aroma. I wanted to sink my teeth into their warm, soft, salty goodness, but some of my appetite had sort of jumped out of the window when I had decided that it was time—finally—to spill my guts.

About everything.

All eyes were on me on me, as if they could see it written all over my face that I wanted to say something. That I was bursting to say something, really. My mouth hung partially open, and not for a garlic knot. My palms, curled up into fists in my lap, were slick with sweat. The knot in my chest was tight and uncomfortable, lacking any garlic joy.

The wooden chair was uncomfortable, hard against my legs and my back, and I wondered if Mom had cranked up the air conditioning. I was freezing, goosebumps appearing on my bare arms, a chill raking up and down my spine. It didn't have anything to do with the fact that everything was about to change when I finally chose to open my mouth.

Nope. Definitely not that.

I brought a shaky hand up to my forehead. I was so tired, I closed my eyes for just a second. I'd just spent almost a week in Faerie with Lockwood, caught in the middle of a war between two kingdoms...but barely fifteen minutes had passed here on Earth.

I took a deep breath, trying to steady my racing heart, the adrenaline surging through my veins like I was hooked up to a pure caffeine drip. Pulling my hand back from my face, I looked around the table.

Mill was watching me, his gaze sharp yet questioning, his head slightly cocked to the side. His forehead was wrinkled as his eyebrows knit together in one line. His mouth opened, and wordlessly he mouthed, "Cassie?"

I looked away.

Mom and Dad were looking at me, waiting, Mom's eyes surprisingly hawk-like, Dad's soft and questioning. My heart skipped a beat, and a moment of doubt caused me to rub my fingers against my sweating palms.

I, the compulsive liar, was seriously contemplating telling my parents that I was dating a vampire. Madness was not— as far as I knew— hereditary in my family, which meant maybe I was setting a new trend.

No. Lying was not a new trend. Not for me.

I was done running.

I was done hiding the truth.

"Mom? Dad?" I licked my lips softly, my tongue running dry over them. I looked back at Mill. I hoped he would forgive me for what I was about to do. "There are vampires in the world."

Crickets.

No, seriously, there were crickets outside, chirping happily in the warm, late spring night.

Mill's eyes grew wide, thick brows arching so high they were nearly lost underneath all his dirty blond hair.

Mom's face was blank. Dad sighed, looking down at his hands that were knotted together on the scratched table top.

I drew a shaky breath. "Mill? He's one of them."

Mill, still as a statue, gaped at me, his gaze unwavering, as if he wasn't sure he had heard me right.

Well, he should have told me that he was coming over, first. We could have planned this better, something a little more in line with my adolescent fantasies of how this boyfriend/parents meeting should have gone, dammit.

Besides, once I told him everything that had happened in Faerie…well, hopefully he'd understand my need to turn over a new leaf.

My revelation about Mill's true nature was greeted by more silence. It was like the school library in here, minus the smell of old books and the hissing of the librarian, Mrs. Greene.

Mom's brow was slightly arched, her lawyer face passive and unreadable.

Dad's face had fallen, and I could see the confusion lingering in his eyes behind his glasses.

Well, this was about as well I could have expected it to go, in all honesty. It was about how well I took it when it first happened to me, and I was being chased by one. Even when I saw the dents in the steel door, I couldn't believe it.

Kinda like how my parents looked right now.

Mom was the first to move, folding her arms over her chest,

and letting out a mighty sigh. "Cassie…we really hoped you were past this lying thing."

Mill ground his teeth together, unnoticed by my parents. He was probably biting his tongue so hard that I half expected black blood to start oozing out of the corner of his mouth.

"I'm not lying," I said. "…This time."

Mom flinched, blinking a few times.

"Here, let me prove it," I said. I was on a roll. I had to keep going, and I wasn't lacking for experiences to help illustrate the point. "That guy who was stalking me? Who kidnapped you and locked you in that wine cellar out by the bay? Totally a vampire."

Mom and Dad exchanged a look.

"Remember when, a few weeks ago, I got busted sneaking back in at daybreak? And I told you I fell asleep at Xandra's house? Yeah, I actually went to Miami, and started a vampire war with Mill's help. Sorry."

Mill blanched. Mom's eyes narrowed, her red acrylic nails tapping against the table, and Dad started looking at me over the top of his glasses, as if he wasn't hearing me right.

Emboldened by their lack of reaction, I went on. "The New York thing? Where Uncle Mike got attacked and our house burned down? Vampires. Mill and I had to burn down the lodge where they were hiding to get rid of them."

Mom pinched the bridge of her nose. "You're confessing to arson, Cassandra?"

Uh oh.

She only pulled out the full "Cassandra" on me when she was really mad.

"I—"

Dad cut in. "What happened with that guy in the mansion here in Tampa?"

"I killed him," I said without thinking.

That one landed with a thud. "And murder, too," Mom said, throwing her hands up. "Cassandra, I don't even need to hand you a shovel. You're digging your own grave."

Dad looked at me like I had suddenly grown another head. "I can't even believe this," he muttered under his breath.

"Um, Katherine—" Mill started.

"It's Mrs. Howell, thank you very much," Mom snapped, giving Mill the most fleeting glance. She was so chummy with him before. Guess her daughter admitting to arson and murder killed the goodwill, too.

Mill hung his head ever so slightly. "Mrs. Howell... Byron was undead. Soooo... He can't technically be *murdered*..."

Mom looked over at Mill. Dad just shook his head.

Mill cleared his throat. "You know what? Maybe I'll just stay out of this one."

Mom gave him a daggered look. "Excellent idea, hotshot."

I nodded, pointing at Mill. "Killing a vampire isn't murder. How can I be arrested for killing someone who's already dead? There isn't even a body. I mean, you're the lawyer and all, but I'm pretty sure there's a thing about habeas corpses—"

"It's 'habeas corpus'," Mom said through gritted teeth.

I shrugged. "He was going to kill you guys, and me, if I didn't stop him."

Mom was totally done with me. Her expression was suddenly blank as she sat away from me, placing her arms like a castle wall in front of her. It was like I was some client, completely off my rocker. She'd told me stories about those sorts before; they were the ones she refused to represent.

Dad was staring at his plate, his shoulders sagging.

The looks they were giving me suggested they were just about ready to send me away to the local asylum for some time in a padded cell.

After all this time, after moving from New York to Tampa, giving up everything I'd known my whole life for a fresh start...

They still thought I was the world's biggest liar.

The worst part was that I had just confessed to everything—*everything*—that had caused them so much strife the last few months. Every situation where I was in danger, every time I'd fibbed to hide the crazy truth of this world, and every instance where I had lied to protect them from the vampires and fae and paranormal madness flooding my new life.

In one five-minute conversation, I had confessed it all...

And they didn't believe me.

It was as though every muscle in my body died, and I just sat there, still. "You don't believe me," I said.

"Can you think of any reason we should, dear?" Mom asked, in the least affectionate tone she could have possibly used. "Given your history?"

Mill wouldn't even look at me, his eyes glued to the table.

"You know," I said, almost let out a quiet chuckle of complete, forlorn desperation, "I actually thought about telling you when Byron first started stalking me. This…was exactly what I thought would happen. That you wouldn't listen rationally to my tale of a super stalker, that you'd skip right to, 'Let's chain Cassie up and throw her in the loony bin'!"

"Tempting," Mom said. "Very tempting at the moment." I could see her anger building in the redness of her cheeks. She was distancing herself from me, emotionally, the lawyer in her coming to the fore.

"Cassie…" Dad said, leaning onto the table with both elbows, voice soft, almost pitying. "I thought we were past all of this. I thought you were done telling lies. But…" he sighed, shaking his head. "Here you are, telling us that all your problems come down to…vampires? Cassie, what are you trying to do here?"

"I'm not trying to do anything—"

"Do not interrupt your father!" Mom said, glaring icily at me. She was done with me.

"Vampire wars? Your boyfriend, a vampire?" Dad asked, raising a hand to wave at Mill. "What do you think of all this?"

Mill's mouth moved up and down a couple times, no sound coming out. When he finally spoke, it was a gentle stutter. "I… uh…"

"Even your boyfriend won't back up your lies this time," Mom said, shaking her head. "There are no such things as vampires, Cassandra. You know that. I don't even know why you're trying to pull this nonsense. What's your game, here?"

I averted my eyes, staring down at the water mark on the table where I set down my glass every time we sat at this table, like a reflection of every night of my life. "I don't have a game."

"We thought that Tampa was going to be good for you," she

said, the contempt just welling out of her voice. "That things were getting better, in spite of the...setbacks. But...it seems like we were wrong. That it's worse than ever..."

Bile rose in my throat. I tried to swallow it away.

"These friends of yours… they're just enabling you," Mom said. "Is Xandra in on this, too? This... vampire lie?" Her arms were clamped tightly around her midsection. "Because if so, I don't know how comfortable I am with you spending time with her anymore." She looked at Mill. "With any of your new friends."

I looked at Mill, who was now sitting rigidly in his chair.

I had told the truth, at last... And I'd failed.

Mom was right. Things really were worse than ever. I had a hard time imagining how they could have possibly gotten any more terrible from here—

But then there was a shattering sound, and glass from one of the windows behind Mom gave way to something orange and glowing, about the size of small pineapple that tumbled into the room. It hit the ground and shattered, a bottle filled with gasoline and flames, breaking into pieces and igniting the carpet on fire.

Oh.

Well.

Question answered.

That was how things could get worse.

Chapter 2

The fire blazed on the carpet behind my mother, throwing off immediate heat that turned my sweating palms into a furious river of perspiration down my hands and the back of my neck. My heart was beating rapidly in my chest, and there was a sharp ringing in my ears from the shattered glass. I rose to my feet, knees feeling like jelly, and I winced as I banged my thigh on the bottom of the table as I stood.

This couldn't be happening. Not again.

All thoughts of my leg pain were forgotten as I looked across the table. Flames were rising behind my mother as she stood there, framed by a rising fire in the background, like some sort of hellish portrait. She wasn't even looking at the imminent danger at her back, though, instead staring at my father, her finger rising to point at him, shaking slightly, her mouth hanging open.

Wheeling to follow her finger, I saw Dad on the floor, trying to roll on the carpet in the narrow space, the sleeve of his sweater singed and smoking. He didn't even make a sound, he just stared at his arm, trying to beat at it with his bare palm.

I snatched one of Mom's good cloth napkins from the table, along with my half empty glass of water. I knelt beside him and doused his sleeve in the water. The fabric hissed, and I took to it with the napkin. Sorry, Mom. I know you got those as a wedding present.

My gaze shifted upward at the sign of movement. The edge of Dad's chair had caught fire, and the carpet was smoldering where he landed on the ground. The splash from the Molotov cocktail had gotten him.

"Dad, are you okay?" I asked.

He didn't answer; his eyes were rooted to the fire behind my mother.

The edge of the curtains over the windows were slowly being engulfed in flames, too. The room was brighter than it ever was even in the middle of the day.

Mill had leapt the table and was dragging Mom away from the window. She stared at the fire as it continued to crawl up the walls, not resisting him as he pulled her away. "We have to get out of here," he said.

"Obviously." I seized Dad by the sleeve he hadn't singed, pulling him toward the door.

"Where's the fire extinguisher?" Mom asked, clinging to Mill. Maybe she thought he was Dad. "We have to find it— we have to stop this—"

The fire alarm had started to shriek, the sharp beeping overhead making me want to cover my ears. I didn't let go of Dad, though.

"Fire extinguishers are for when your skillet goes up while you're cooking, Katherine," my dad said, voice a little scratchy. "This is way beyond us. We need to get the hell out of here."

"The man knows what he's talking about," Mill said as my mother did a double take, looking up at him. "Closest exit?"

"Pool door," I said, ducking to avoid the wood carving Mom bought in Costa Rica that was burning as the fire licked up the walls, the flames sending off waves of heat. Thus far the splash of gasoline had mostly confined itself to the curtains and carpet behind Mom, though some had gone astray, hitting around Dad and even making it to the wall behind where I'd been sitting. Several feet of fire blazed across Mom's art, though, spreading rapidly.

Mill nodded, and with my mom's arm wrapped around him, started toward the back door.

My eyes stung, and as I looked up, smoke was billowing into the air, hovering along the ceiling like a dense, dark cloud. It had been gathering in stringy whorls, but now it was becoming dense as the flames fed it.

How was it that both of the houses I had ever lived in were set on fire? And while I was in them, no less?

Mill was dragging my mother through the haze of smoke, just ahead of me. I still had my dad, whose bare, slightly crisped arm could be seen underneath the new hole in his shirt, all pink and blistered already.

I tried to cover my mouth and nose by burying them in the shoulder of my shirt sleeve. I was starting to get lightheaded, and the room was beginning to sway in front of me. I glanced over my shoulder, and my eyes widened.

The whole dining room was now on fire. The table, the chairs…all of the food was engulfed in the glowing flames.

RIP, the garlic knots. We hardly knew ye.

"Come on, come on," I urged Dad along, hoping that he wouldn't look back and see what I had. It wouldn't have broken his heart like it would have Mom's, but still…

This was our home.

My head was splitting by the time we reached the sliding door, and Mill smashed it with his fist, and the glass just shattered like somebody had just thrown a Molotov cocktail through it. Too soon?

I didn't hear any complaints from Mom or Dad as he stepped through and pulled Mom out after him. When I reached the door, the hot, smoking room at my back, Mill grabbed Dad and helped him through before turning to me, gently grabbing my hand and helping out over the threshold.

I collapsed onto my hands and knees, gasping for breath, hacking all of the smoke out of my lungs. It spewed from my mouth as if I had taken up vaping. I was going to get lung cancer before I was twenty, at this rate.

Dad hobbled over to where Mom was, sitting next to a lawn chair instead of in it, and wrapped his arm around her shoulders. He was sputtering, but his burn was already forgotten. Mom was trembling, her arms tight around herself. She didn't even notice Dad was there.

I was taking in great gulps of the air, chill and flushing into my lungs like a soothing balm to the fiery pain that the hacking had produced. It was almost like I was drowning, like I'd gone a few extra steps and toppled into the pool by accident.

Flickers of flame glowed in almost all of the windows of the living room, now, and if not flames, the bright amber glow of the fiery beast growing within.

Mill, not needing to breathe, knelt calmly in front of me "Are you all right?" He brushed some stray hairs out of my eyes.

I nodded; trying to talk sent me into another fit of coughing.

"What…" Mom was gasping for air. "Was…that?"

"That was a—" I started, but dissolved into another barking coughing fit.

"Molotov cocktail," Mill said. "It's gasoline in a bottle, with—"

"Yes, thank you…for the science lesson," Mom said, coughing once more. "But I'm wondering *why the hell a Molotov cocktail came through MY window?*"

I forgot what I was going to say as my eyes adjusted to the darkness around. My heart sank, and I grabbed Mill's arm for support. "…Mill? Do you—"

"I see them." There was a quiet determination.

Through the screen of the lanai, silhouettes slowly sauntered across the yard. A dozen? Maybe more? They all walked with a deliberate slowness, but were graceful, supple…predatory.

Vampires. A whole lot of them.

Their fangs seemed to flash as they caught the light flooding out from the fire inside. I thought I recognized a few of them even in the dark. I had seen more of the vampires of this local clan than I ever wanted to. I caught a few malicious grins pointed in my direction.

Draven's people. These were his vampires.

I had fallen for this again. They had literally smoked me out of the house, except this time, I wasn't alone. Mom and Dad were involved now, too. We were like bees, and they were trying to take our honey…or rather, our lives.

Draven, the Lord of the Tampa vampires… He'd finally found me. Tracked me back to my own house, which meant…

Now he knew I wasn't a vampire.

He knew who I was, really.

My last great lie fell off the board.

The circle of vampires closing in on the lanai was like a wall descending between me and safety. My old, peaceful, human

11

life was now gone, over with, and the danger that lurked just outside the screened porch reminded me of sharks circling a weary swimmer. They loomed in the darkness, shadows with ill intent, every one of them exhibiting a hunger that would have been terrifying on anyone's face.

But the one that made my heart stop was the slender girl with the pretty face and the braided hair, standing right in the midst of them all, her arms folded across her chest, and a wide, wicked smile on her face.

Jacquelyn.

My best friend from New York.

Chapter 3

I guess life doesn't always turn out the way we want it to.

I, for one, would have really liked to have lived a Draven-free existence, where I could spend my days in Tampa like an ordinary teen. Minus the vampire boyfriend thing. That wasn't ordinary, but I wanted to keep him.

Life, however, doesn't follow the rules that we think it should. It likes to wind up, sock us right in the teeth, all while pulling the rug out from underneath us. And so, we lie, tasting blood, toothless, rugless, on a bare floor wondering what just hit us. It was life, the sucker-punching bastard.

That's what it felt like, seeing vampire Jacquelyn standing there in front of me. Like life had sucker-punched me. Again.

Mill helped me to my feet as I stared through the screen at her. He didn't let go of my hand.

She looked exactly like she always had. She was even wearing a jacket that she had borrowed from me before I had moved away.

Did she remember that? Was she doing it on purpose just to spite me?

"Jacquelyn, what...what are you doing here?" I asked. My breathing had turned into wheezing, and I tried to stifle the coughing that threatened to start again.

Jacquelyn cocked her hip out the way she used to as a kid that annoyed the heck out of me and gave me the look; the look she used to give the other kids on the playground when they did something stupid or weird. Now I was on the receiving end of it. A smug grin appeared on her face, and she flashed her pointy, vampire fangs at me. "I came to town looking for you, Cassie…but when I stopped in to pay homage to the local lord… as one does in the vampire world… I ended up running into some of your friends instead." She opened her arms wide, gesturing to the group around her.

Low chuckles came from some of the vampires, like barks from a pack of wild dogs. Mill's hand gripped mine.

"Lord Draven's got a bone to pick with you," Jacquelyn said. There was a dangerous glare on her face now, and every trace of a smile disappeared.

My blood had turned to ice, and my stomach fell, as though dropped out of a fourth-story window.

"Is that…?" Mom asked, her eyes wide, face paling. She leaned forward, staring out into the darkness. "Jacquelyn Gustafson? Sweetie, is that you?"

"Oh, hi, Mrs. Howell," Jacquelyn said in a falsely sweet, high pitched voice. She bent over, her hands on her knees as she peered into the lanai like we were some kind of exhibit at the zoo. "I just love your new house. It's so… You."

"On fire is us?" I asked. Jacquelyn ignored me. Mom was looking between us. It was as if her heart had been ripped out and stomped on. Appropriate reaction to seeing your daughter's childhood friend standing in your backyard, apparently unconcerned about the burning building just a few feet away.

"Did you know that your daughter ruined my life, not once, but twice now?" she said, still carrying on that disgustingly sweet voice. She cocked her head to side like a child, her braids swinging. "First, when she lied and made me the laughing stock of the school in New York. And again just a few weeks ago."

She did a twirl like a bride trying on a wedding dress, even giving us a little curtsey as she came to a stop.

My stomach twisted in knots. The sarcasm was washing off of her in waves.

"What's she talking about, Cassie?" Mom asked, looking up at me. It freaked me out to hear the tremble in her words.

"She's a vampire now," I said. Better to not beat around the

14

bush. If I was committing to this whole turning over a new leaf, then I might as well go all in, right?

"Vampires," my mom muttered under her breath. "Your boyfriend's a vampire, your best friend's a vampire. Everybody's a freaking vampire. Are your father and I vampires, too, in your mind?"

"Well, you're kinda sucking right now, but no, you're still human, so far as I know," I said. I gritted my teeth, my eyes fixed on Jacquelyn, who was grinning a wide, toothy grin back at me.

My mind flashed to the lodge burning, and how she had tackled me. We had tumbled down the hill together, so fast that it was like we were caught in a dryer, flipping end over end. I remembered the wet scent of the earth, like my grandmother's garden I had helped to weed when I was little. I remembered the scrapes and cuts on my bare arms, the stinging of the smoke in my eyes. She had bashed my head against the ground again and again, all the while the stars hung sparkling above us.

I wondered if she knew how truly devastated I was that she got dragged into this mess.

How heartbroken I still was.

"Seriously, what is with you and all this vampire nonsense?" Mom asked, her eyes narrowing.

"Mom, I think that you're focusing on the wrong thing right now," I said.

"You told your parents about vampires?" Jacquelyn said, her hands on her hips. "Wow. Kinda like the 'broken clock is right twice a day' thing, I guess even you manage to spit out a truth between the lies every now and again. Probably by accident." She tossed back her head and let out a barking laugh.

I cringed as her verbal blow hit home.

"You know what happened after you left, Cass?" Jacquelyn asked. "I got chased out of town. Like something out of a monster movie, can you believe it? When I went home, my parents kicked me out because even they knew something was wrong." Her eyes narrowed, her lips a taut line. "I tried to get them to understand that I was just a little changed. But do you know what my mother did? She threw a knife at me. Called me a demon, said I was possessed. She screamed that she didn't have a daughter anymore. That her daughter was dead."

Mill tensed beside me. I wondered if any of her story was hitting home for him.

"Well she was right…" Jacquelyn smiled. "I am dead."

It struck me just how similar our lives were all of the sudden. I had been chased out of New York, and now she had been, too. We were both running from our pasts. Our new lives were completely saturated with vampires. Her parents had written her off, just like mine had.

At least mine hadn't kicked me out yet. Or thrown dangerous objects at me. Again, yet.

I tried to swallow around a dry throat. With a sinking heart, I realized ultimately that we both had to leave Onondoga Springs because of choices that I made. Terrible choices. Choices that had hurt a lot more people than just me.

Where had she gone after they'd kicked her out? What were those first few days like? I couldn't help but wonder how terrified she had been. What was she going to do? She'd had all of eternity stretching out before her now…with no one to help her.

"But I don't understand…" It was Dad who spoke this time. "What are you doing here in Florida?" He had an earnest look behind his glasses. "Especially if you're a vampire. You realize this is the Sunshine State, don't you?"

Oh, good, it sounded like at least one of my parents was coming around on the vampire thing. Yay for progress.

"Oh, that's easy," Jacquelyn said with a shrug. "Because everything that has gone wrong— everything I've lost, every single person who's turned on me, hated me, every piece of my life that's been shattered to shards... all of it... every last thing... is Cassie's fault." She pointed a black-nailed finger in my direction.

It was like she was a lion in waiting, watching for the moment when I let my guard down. It was like she had known that what she said would back me into a corner. It did. It hit me like a bat, and I felt my heart breaking all over again.

She was right to be angry with me.

It *was* all my fault.

"Cassie."

It was Mill's voice, low and gentle. He could probably see the strain on my face, see the tension in my stiff shoulders.

He had been with me in New York. He had seen everything that had happened between us. He'd watched as I struggled my way through that misadventure, protecting my family, my home, my friends. He'd seen what she'd done to me, physically and emotionally, and had carried me away from that fight as I was broken and bleeding.

"This doesn't make any sense," Mom said, shaking her head.

"It makes a lot more sense if you start to consider that vampires are real," my dad said. Yay Dad.

"Too complicated for you, Mrs. Howell?" Jacquelyn asked. "I'll spell it out. I thought I'd come here and pay back Cassie for everything she did to me. I figured since she burned down my entire life... that burning down your house was a nice place to start."

My heart did a somersault.

Jacquelyn laughed like she had just heard the best joke of her life, and with a wave of her hand, vampires had started edging closer to us. Some were right up against the lanai, their beady eyes peering inside, fingers pressed against the screen. Others were still hopping the fence into the yard, as gracefully as the hunters they were.

"Don't kill her," Jacquelyn said, flipping one of her braids between her fingers. "Draven wants her alive. The rest of them..." She shrugged. "Bon appetit."

I felt as if a bucket of ice had been dumped over me. Mill tensed beside me, and a low snarl sounded deep in his throat.

"Who is Draven?" Dad asked, apparently missing that Jacquelyn had just rung the dinner bell on him and Mom.

Yeah…now was not the time to be explaining all of *that* right now.

"Cassandra," Dad said in the tone he only used when I stayed up too late or went over our data on the cell phone bill. "Answer me."

The fires inside the house were still roaring behind me, crackling and snapping. I tried to find an answer that would make sense, but nothing came to me. Smoke was starting to accumulate in the lanai, held back just enough by the screen that a billow was beginning to cause that scratching in the back of my throat again, as though I were going to choke.

"Oh, he's just the Lord of the Tampa vampire territory," Jacquelyn said, giggling, when I didn't answer. "Cassie stepped on his toes, big time." Her eyes focused on mine, and it was like staring into endless pools of darkness in the dead of night. "Cassie... I want you to hear this and know what's coming. We're going to kill your parents, and then your boyfriend. Slowly. In the worst ways you can imagine. Then I am going to take you, kicking and screaming and crying— I hope, for the funsies of it— to Draven." Her smile was low and malicious, and there was no joy in it, only the promise of pain— pain that she wanted to inflict on me, pain of the sort that seemed infinite, endless— the kind that her smile suggested she would enjoy every single moment of. "He's expecting us."

Chapter 4

Every time I thought that my life couldn't get any worse, it surprised me.

It had never occurred to me that Jacquelyn hated me so much that she would track me down, halfway across the country, to literally set my house on fire and then threaten to kill those people about whom I cared the most.

It was like something out of a movie. Not as though the rest of my life since moving to Florida wasn't already like a movie.

The vampires were starting to get antsy now. A few had crawled up on top of the lanai, staring down from its metal frame between the screen panels as if we were some kind of exhibit at the Busch Gardens Zoo.

Some were gnashing their teeth. Others were licking their tongues over their fangs, grinning viciously.

The fight was inevitable. My heart started to race, beating like it was trapped in the same sort of cage that I was. I didn't see a way out. I had enough experience. Mill, Iona, and Lockwood had all been there to help me learn to protect myself.

And this time, it wasn't only to protect myself. It was to protect Mom and Dad, too. It was such a hopeless situation.

I was ready to fight anyway. Thankfully, it seemed, Mill felt the same way.

Taking a deep breath, I fell back into the fighting stance that he had taught me. I bent my knees, put one foot behind me to brace, and held my hands up in front of my face to block any attacks to my neck.

Mill did the same, and we stood between the flimsy door of the lanai and my parents, who were completely unaware of what was about to happen. I figured it was best not to tell them.

My heart thundered against my chest. Mill could hear it for certain. There was a dull roar in my ears as I faced death head on once more. I wished that I hadn't left my stakes upstairs to burn. I wondered if they would survive the fire. If they did, I should sleep with those in from now on, ignoring the possible punctures to the skull.

A loud crinkling sound startled me, and some of the other vampires as well. I thought maybe they had broken down the door, but it was intact, Jacquelyn and two others still standing behind it, barring our escape.

A cat call echoed from somewhere in the backyard, followed by the hissing scream of pain from a vampire.

What the hell?

Out of the darkness, silhouettes moved over a fallen figure. The screams ceased, and into the fire light came—

Gregory and Laura, my neighbors and friends from school, standing over a slain vampire in front of Mom's blood red hibiscus bush in the side yard.

Laura, the ever-popular cheerleader, looked as good fighting vampires as she did doing her classwork. Her blonde hair was tied in a tight knot on top of her head, and she was wielding bottles filled with holy water in each hand.

Gregory, a gangly sort of boy, stood beside her, a stake raised in front of him like a sword. The firelight glinted off the lenses of his glasses.

"Cassie, you okay?" he called, his voice shaking only a little.

"Been better," I said, moving closer to the screen, a little wash of relief running over my skin as though I'd just taken a dip in the pool. Nope, not from swimming. Just sweating like a pig from nervousness. "You?"

I was torn about seeing them. On one hand, I couldn't have been happier to see the cavalry, seeing as we were trapped like deer surrounded by a pack of wolves. But they were out there with all of those vampires and had just outright attacked them.

That definitely was not destined to end well.

There was another crinkling sound, and I realized it was coming from Laura's water bottles. She chucked one like a pro softball pitcher, and as it spun through the air, water spewed out and splattered the vampires nearest to Jacquelyn. She managed to duck out of the way as her bodyguards collapsed into screams.

"Did you bring holy water?" I asked, my eyes widening as the smoke rose off the vamps outside the screen door.

"No," Laura said, tossing another bottle at a vampire who was charging her. "I'm just really keen on hydrating after cheerleading practice, and these guys are allergic to Gatorade." She flashed a smile through the darkness. "What do you think?"

"That in spite of your grades, you're kind of a genius," I said. "And that I now see why every boy in school is in love with you."

Gregory was in front of her, and as a vampire ran at the two of them, he whirled aside, drew his hand back around, and slammed the stake right between the vampire's shoulder blades. The vampire tumbled to the ground, screeching as it started to turn to goo.

Gregory withdrew the stake from its back and turned on the other vampires like a gladiator facing his opponents.

A ripple of hesitation ran through the vampires in the yard. Laura and Gregory looked like a couple of crocodile hunters, calm and collected.

"Cassie, not sure if you know this, but your house is on fire," Gregory said. "Being your neighbor, I thought I should come and check it out. And given your history with vampires—or our history, rather…"

Another vampire approached, and Gregory leapt into the air and slashed the stake across the vampire's face. It shrieked, and then Gregory sank it into its chest, black blood spurting onto his wrist.

Laura threw the bottle into the air, which drew the eyes of the vamps. While they were distracted, she pulled a water balloon that I hadn't noticed hanging from a backpack she was wearing and tossed it at the chest of the vampire closest to her. It exploded like a wave crashing against a rockface.

That vampire, and the two beside it, fell to the ground, their skin already starting to peel off. The acrid stench of vampire blood reached the inside of the lanai, overriding the smell of the burning house.

"Oh, God... What is that?" Mom said, clamping her fingers over her nose.

Mill took off in a rush of wind. He kicked open the screen door and charged at the vampires just outside, using their surprise as a chance to sink a couple stakes of his own into their chests. He then charged on, leaving them clawing at their chests in helpless horror as they sank to the ground.

Mom let out a shriek as I grabbed her hand and pulled her toward the door. My dad followed without me having to say anything, the heat from the housefire finally driving us forward now that Mill had cleared the way.

It probably sounded like we were having a wild backyard party to others in the neighborhood, but it was more like Halloween Horror Nights at Universal Studios with all the screaming. Vampires were leaping into the air, so fast that I couldn't keep track. Mill was keeping them distracted, moving in a blur, drawing their attention away from my family and me.

Laura and Gregory were back to back, pulling off moves that Kim Possible would have been proud of. A pile of water bottles lay at Laura's feet, and she was lobbing water balloons like there was no tomorrow. Gregory's sudden acquisition of ninja skills seemed to be paying off; or maybe it was his crush on Laura and desire to impress her that was giving him the strength to fight like a guy on steroids.

Jacquelyn hung back, eyes wide, her wicked grin gone. I recognized the look in her eyes; it wasn't that far off from how she'd looked when all my lies had come crashing down on the both of us. Her bad girl demeanor all wrapped up in disappointment and crushing defeat, her lips pressed together in a tight pout. With a shaky hand, she pointed at me, but looked at the remaining vamps circled around and upon the lanai. "If you let her get away, Draven's going to stake you to the fields at Raymond James Stadium an hour before sunrise and park his limo on the fifty-yard line so he can hear you scream your last."

One vampire threw himself right at me without any

hesitation, through the open gate to the lanai. Mom and Dad screamed behind me, but I was able to duck just as he reached me. Good thing I anticipated it.

I fell backward to the ground, rolling, keeping my neck well out of his reach and latching onto his grasping hand. With the momentum of my legs and of his charge carrying us both, I planted my feet in his chest and shoved, sending him flying over me and into the window behind me.

Ka-Ching. Field goal.

It shattered as he struck it, and he sailed into the burning house, disappearing amongst the flames behind the glass.

"Cassandra!"

I scrambled to my feet. Mom was staring at me, eyes wide with horror. Dad was looking past me through the broken window.

"Mom," I said, "vampires."

Her eyes looked like they were about to pop out of her head. "That is your answer to everything!"

"Not so," I said, turning back to the yawning lanai door. Beyond it, the vampire fight was raging on and Jacquelyn was looking at me with pure malice in her eyes. "My answer to homework is 'burn it'. Which is kinda my answer to vampires, too, though, so there's a symmetry at work in my life, at least."

Mill had left a trail of bodies behind him, all of them turning to a black goopy mess on the lawn. Dad was going to *love* that. He was peering at it, even in the dark, brow furrowed beneath his glasses. "Living is priority now, Dad. Focus on lawn care later."

"I... was definitely not thinking about the fertilizer properties of vampires," Dad said, blinking in surprise.

"What is happening to those people on the lawn?" my mother asked, staring into the dark. "It's like they're melting."

"They're secretly the wicked witches of the north, east, south and west," I said.

My mother stared at me in the dark, fire reflecting off her eyes. "Really?"

"No," I said. "Vampires, Mom. Keep up."

She made a grunting noise deep in her throat and I grabbed her hand, dragging her toward the door— and Jacquelyn.

I was feeling entirely too trapped inside the lanai, just watching Gregory and Laura and Mill out there with weapons. Jacquelyn's posse was dwindling, and she was slipping away, moving behind a wall of them that was at least three bodies thick.

"Hey, Jacquelyn," I said, the anger flushing through my body as I surged forward, pulling Mom with me. "I don't think this career you've got planned as a supervillain is working out very well. Maybe you should stick to something you're good at. Probably not cheerleading, because you sucked at that, too. Or dance, because you have white girl rhythm." I frowned. "Actually... Thinking back... Was there ever anything you were *actually* good at?"

She glared at me, her eyes flashing dangerously. "I'm getting pretty good at burning down your houses."

"Well, I'm fresh out of those, so unless you're planning to buy me another one to burn down," I said, striding forward, "I'd say you've about run out of use. Especially since your services as 'bestie' are no longer needed."

Jacquelyn stooped behind her offensive line of vampire muscle, her brow an angry line that probably needed some plucking. She let out an angry hiss and motioned toward me, sending a couple vampires at me.

"Cassie, heads up!" Mill tossed a stake onto the ground just outside the lanai for me.

One of the vampires that was a little closer saw it, and we made eye contact for a fraction of a second over it.

Then we both dove for the stake.

I threw my body across it, and the vampire flung herself on top of me, knee catching me in the ribs and knocking the wind out of me. I squirmed to pull my arm, and the stake, from beneath my chest. She was trying to roll me over, hands dragging at my side. I let her win that one, using her movement to dislodge my arm. As I came over, I thrust the stake through the middle of her chest.

Her eyes bulged, and when she coughed, she sprayed my face with black blood. It speckled my cheeks and eyebrows, and I flinched as it spattered me. "Oh, *gross...*" I shoved her off, yanking the stake free. "Why can't vampires turn to something nice when they die? Like bath beads?"

I furiously scrubbed at my face with my sleeve. A sharp, piercing wail sounded in the distance. It took me a second for my brain to register what I was hearing. Living in the city of Tampa, or any city in general, really, there are certain sounds you always hear.

Car horns.

Slamming doors.

And sirens. Generally, not as close as these, which were getting nearer with every passing second.

The vampires who were still standing perked up like cats hearing a rustle in a nearby bush. Almost as one, they turned and looked at Jacquelyn.

She seemed lost, too. Or like she *had* lost.

Because she had. They'd failed.

"Ha," I said. "You monologued too long."

Jacquelyn stood behind her line of vampires, staring between two muscly shoulders at me. "This isn't over, Cassie."

"You're right about that," I said. My face darkened. "Get out of here."

Jacquelyn stared at me for but a moment before letting out a snarl. Then she took off, disappearing around the side of the house as the sirens grew louder, her vampires fleeing behind her.

My adrenaline seemed to leave me the moment she was gone, my knees, already weak, giving way as I hit the lawn, palms striking the sawgrass like jagged, pointy blades. I turned my head to look—

Flames were rising out of the roofline, now, billowing into the night sky. The first flashes of red and blue lights fell along the sides of the house to either side of ours, mingling with the orange cast of the flames.

It felt like all the life had left me as I knelt there in the shadow of my house. It shouldn't matter; we were safe, after all. Jacquelyn and her vampires had left. With the help of my friends and my boyfriend... We'd won.

But somehow none of that mattered, and it consoled me not at all as I stayed there on my hands and knees as my house, my home, burned before my very eyes… Again.

Chapter 5

A shock blanket. That was what the firemen had called the soft, bright orange cloth that they had wrapped around my shoulders. Somehow it was supposed to give me comfort like a swaddling cloth around a baby. How was a blanket supposed to help me deal with the emotional trauma of yet another one of my houses burning down? Was the orange supposed to be distracting? Was it supposed to warn everyone to stay away that wanted to come near me and ask me how I was feeling?

The police showed up shortly after and started asking us questions. They also asked about the flecks of black... whatever it was all over us.

"Oil," Mill said. "We were changing the oil in our car before dinner. Hadn't had a chance to wash up when everything... Happened."

Dad, Gregory, Laura and I gave Mill a look. Dad then looked at me like, *so your boyfriend is a liar, too?*

Ouch.

Mom was catatonic, so I told the police, with Dad's help, that we had been eating dinner when a Molotov cocktail was tossed through the dining room window. I knew that the forensics would turn up the bottle as what had caused the fire in the first place. There was no reason to lie about that. If I hadn't already just sworn off lying.

"Do you have any idea who could have done it?" the police officer asked, his silvery moustache twitching as he spoke. This guy had seen some stuff in his time. His scrutinizing gaze didn't faze me, though; I was used to Mom's lawyer stare.

"I know who it was, actually," I said. "A girl I used to know when we lived in New York…she seemed to have a real grudge against me…and also to sunlight, for some reason. Can't imagine why. Grunge fan, maybe—"

The police officer had been scrawling my response down on the tablet in his hands, and hesitated, staring up at me.

I shrugged.

I heard Mill sigh beside me.

The officer left us with a promise to investigate, but I knew it didn't matter. Jacquelyn would be untraceable as a vampire. It was the same thing with Byron. That was why I hadn't given the police her real name.

Why did this have to be so messy all the time?

It didn't take the firemen long to put the fire out, which was good, all things considered, but they made it very clear that we were not allowed to go back inside. There was the chance that it could reignite, and they would need to ensure that it was safe before we could get the insurance company in there to assess the damage.

As to the damage… it was considerable. I couldn't even see how bad it was, but the skeletal frame of the attic beams was visible where the roofing tiles had been burned away.

The firemen told us we could keep our shock blankets. It was really hard not to laugh at the sight of Mill wrapped snugly in fluorescent orange. If anything, I thought he looked downright adorable, though I doubted he would appreciate me saying that out loud.

The firetrucks left shortly after the cop cars, and we were alone. All of the neighborhood onlookers who had been snooping on their lawns had come and given their condolences before returning to their own warm, well-lit, still intact homes.

"It's good to know that the house isn't a total loss," I said, staring up at the charred building. There was black soot outside of the dining room, and water dripped from the broken window. It was probably going to be a long time before we could move back in, but at least we still had a house when I thought we had lost everything.

"Well," Dad said, "I guess I should start calling hotels, seeing if they have any availability..."

"That's not a good idea," Mill said, shaking his head. "The vampires are going to go looking at nearby hotels for you. It wouldn't be safe." He turned to look at me. "I'd suggest my place, but...."

"Yeah, Draven will be looking for us there, too," I said, crossing my arms. "You probably can't go home now. Sorry."

He shrugged. "I didn't really love any of that stuff anyway. Except the Roomba. That was kinda cool."

Mom was sitting on the ground, the blanket wrapped around her shoulders, staring off into the distance. She wasn't contributing to the conversation in any way.

I tried not to get lost in worry about her mental state in that moment. We had to get to safety, first. Then I could have a freak out if I needed to.

"You guys can stay at my house," Gregory said.

"Or mine," Laura said, her perfect hair still perfect, even after a fight with vampires. "My family isn't even home right now."

I looked at Laura and the whole trip to Miami came flooding back to me. I had literally traveled across the state to protect this girl. I was not going to let anything happen to her now by turning her home into a vampire magnet. I shook my head. "Laura, I hate to break this to you but…you should come with us. Because they're going to be looking for you, too." I looked pointedly at her and Gregory. "Both of you."

Gregory shrugged. "Thanks for the offer, Cass, but I can't. My parents are here, and it would probably be best if at least one of us stayed around here to keep an eye on things, you know?"

I didn't like that answer. "Gregory, I'm not sure that's smart."

"Did you see me tonight?" he asked. He twirled the stake in his hand, stained black, like a drumstick. It tumbled out of his grasp and he scrambled to retrieve it as it clattered on the asphalt. "Just ignore that. I totally have things under control. I've got more of these, and some holy water, just like you had suggested. I'll be fine."

I sighed. He had done pretty well. And it wasn't like I could force him to come with me. At least, I didn't think that it would be smart to pressure him. Besides, he was right. His parents were here, and if we were to leave them unprotected, they could end up getting hurt. "Just…don't be stupid, okay? If they show up again…please get out of here, okay? You and your family."

He nodded his head. "Don't worry. I'll be in contact every step of the way." He looked at the stake in his fingers, then sort of brought it around behind his back, as though I'd just forget about it. "I won't do anything stupid. I promise."

That should have been a relief, but since I had no idea how long this ordeal was going to last, it only just made me worry about leaving him in the first place. If I didn't have eyes on him, how could I be sure he'd be safe? That any of them would be safe?

And why did I feel so responsible?

Because like Jacquelyn said… It was my fault.

If Draven knew who I was…did that mean I was going to be running forever now? I had a target painted on my back by the most powerful vampire in Tampa, and it was totally my fault.

But I couldn't think about that right now. Life needed to become manageable steps, and the next one in front of me was getting everyone to safety.

"Okay, well, make sure to text Laura, because, you know…" I pointed at the house behind me. "That's where my phone is. Hopefully it's good and crisped and not sitting up there, streaming episodes of *Pretty Little Liars* and burning through my data plan, uh… literally." Because Dad had been through enough this week.

"This is just too much…" Dad said, holding his head. "Everything that I've seen tonight…"

I put a hand on his arm. "I know, Dad. It's okay." I looked up at Mill. "Hey…if they know you and I hang out…do they know about Iona?"

Mill's eyes got wide.

Yeah…I was afraid of that.

"We need to get to her…like, right now," Mill said.

29

"Can you call her?" I asked.

His eyes darted. "I don't have her number."

I groaned and pointed at the house. "My phone."

My mind drifted to Xandra and how all of this danger might affect her as well. She wasn't involved in this situation, and Jacquelyn wouldn't know about her…right? She was probably fine. At least for now.

I made a mental note to reach out to her later.

Mill was looking around. "How are we going to get there?"

"My keys are in the house," Dad said. "Also, my car." The garage looked just as burned as the rest of the house, and the door wasn't going up anytime soon, not under its own power.

Mom didn't reply. She was still staring into the distance.

"I can drive," Laura said. "I'll go get my keys. Meet me at the curb in five."

"Okay, just hurry," I said, already feeling like time was starting to speed up. Jacquelyn was somewhere out there, with her new vampire friends, looking to do me harm and fully aware that Iona was part of my crew…

We had to get to her before they did.

Chapter 6

The Prius that Laura drove was the perfect example of a teenage girl.

She had pink, tropical air fresheners crammed into the vents on the dashboard. A small garland of flowers hung from her rearview mirror. There was a coiled clamp for her phone that hooked up to her stereo system so she could play her jams. And the back seat was littered with empty sparkling water and kombucha bottles.

I had somehow ended up crammed in the back seat between my father and Mill, holding my own elbows because of the lack of room. The fake flowery smell was giving me a headache, and Dad constantly leaning around me to give Mill the stink eye was doing anything but make me feel at ease.

"Okay, so where are we going?" Laura asked, turning onto one of the main roads leading toward Tampa.

"Head for the interstate. We're going to turn just before it. She lives on the Hillsborough River." Mill replied.

"Wait, that close?" I asked.

Mill nodded. "How do you think she was always able to get here as quickly as she did?"

"Well, you don't exactly live close," I said.

I got a death glare from Dad. Yeah…probably shouldn't have mentioned going to my boyfriend's house unsupervised.

I sighed and leaned back against the headrest. Which I quickly realized didn't exist in the middle seat. My neck snapped back, which caused me to wince and rub the already

31

stiff muscles.

"Ugh…" I groaned. "I am sooo tired."

"It's been a crazy day," Mill said. "First the accident, then the fire."

I snorted. "Wow, I totally forgot that all happened today."

"Even for me, it feels like a long day," he said.

"No," I said, lifting my head. "I mean that it actually was like a week ago for me."

"What?" Mill said, arching a brow.

"I just got back from Faerie with Lockwood right before I came downstairs and found you standing there in the kitchen. Way to warn me about your visit, by the way."

"Wait…what?" Mill said, blinking.

"Faerie?" Laura asked, her eyes meeting mine in the rearview mirror.

"Yeah, there's a world of fae," I said.

I got mixed reactions. Dad just shook his head, like he couldn't handle any more. Laura seemed to be in awe, her eyes wide and twinkling with wonder in the rearview mirror. Mill was glaring at me, stiff and stern as I'd ever seen him, like he was jealous or something.

And Mom. She found her voice at last, much to my chagrin.

"More lies?" she said, shaking her head. "This is a psychosis level of crazy, Cassandra. Faeries? Vampires? I'm really starting to worry about you, young lady." She craned her neck around to glare at me from the front seat.

"Yeah, you really don't have any room to talk, Mom," I said. "You are fully swimming in a river in Egypt here. Come out, Mom."

Her eyes narrowed. "What?"

"Denial, dear," Dad said under his breath. "De-Nile, see? The Ni—"

"I got it, thanks," she said, cold glare fixed on him now. Which was sort of a relief, because it was off me, at least for the moment.

"You went to Faerie, and you didn't take me with you?" Mill asked, because I didn't need a chance to take a breath and simmer down before someone else started volleying questions at me. Nah, I was good. Keep firing, people.

"It wasn't like I had a chance to tell you," I said. "Lockwood showed up in my room asking for help. Remember the pixies? They were coming after Lockwood to kill him so he didn't go back and expose the truth about—You know what? Never mind. We can talk about it some time when we're not being chased and having Molotov cocktails thrown at us and whatnot." Which, if Draven had his way, would be *never*.

"Wait, I want to hear more about this Faerie place," Laura said, pouting her lip.

"Later," I said.

Mill rattled off a few more directions, but his attitude toward me had cooled, which annoyed me. It wasn't like I would have been able to talk to him about any of this, since the first time I had seen him since getting back was when he had sprung the truth about us on my parents, and I had to deal with all of that drama.

"Our house..." Mom's voice cracked in the newly settled silence. "And Jacquelyn...she used to be such a nice girl... when did she become a compulsive liar, too?"

"Mom," I said. "She's. A. Vampire. How many times do I have to say this before you believe it?"

"How many times are you going to lie before you tell the truth?" Mom asked, her voice rising.

"Katherine..." Dad said. "Please."

Mom looked at Dad, her cheeks flushed. She turned back around in a huff.

"So, Lockwood really took you to Faerie?" Mill asked again.

I glared at him, wondering why - why - why? Was I dealing with everyone being snotty at once? "I thought I said we'd talk about this later."

"Yeah, but...why did he take you?" Mill's brow was furrowed like he was puzzling through something particularly heavy. "Isn't taking humans to Faerie a no-no?"

I frowned. "He needed me to lie for him."

Dad perked up. As did Mom. Go figure they would want to hear about me lying to give themselves more ammunition. This was just peachy. "Which I did not, okay? And let me tell you, Faeries lie *way* more than I do. That whole idea that they can't is just a load of bull."

33

ROBERT J. CRANE with LAUREN HARPER

"Yes, I know, I've caught Lockwood being a little deceptive a time or two," Mill said.

"Where exactly are we going?" Mom asked, staring out of her window in the front seat. Her arms were firmly crossed in front of her.

"Iona's house," I said. "Come on, Mom, we've said it at least three times."

"Who is this Iona?" Dad asked. "Another of these friends that we didn't know about?"

"Yes, Dad, another of my secret, special Super-friends," I said. "A.K.A *vampires*."

"I should have come with you," Mill said. "Lockwood should have known how dangerous it was for you to go."

"Yeah, you have no idea," I said. "But I think he said he couldn't bring a vampire to Faerie for some reason."

Mill's face darkened with concern. "That's what he said about humans, too, but he brought you."

"Well, he needed the right tool for the job," I said.

"And what job was that?" he asked more firmly.

"I told you, lying," I said, blowing air impatiently between my lips.

"Do I take a right, here?" Laura asked from the front, having stopped at a stop sign.

"Yes," Mill said and then turned back to me.

"Do Jacquelyn's parents even know that she's here?" Mom asked.

"Mom, Jacquelyn is a *vampire*. Didn't you hear her say that her parents had kicked her out? Swore that she was dead to them? Didn't you hear her blaming me for all of that, plus her hamster dying in third grade?" I asked, my heart beating uncomfortably in my chest. I hated knowing that she was right to be angry with me.

"Wait, you killed the girl's hamster?" Laura asked, looking at me in the rearview with wide eyes.

"No," I said, "I loved Mr. Giggles, but I figure since she's blaming me for everything else crappy in her life, she's probably throwing in a few unrelated disasters to further stir the pot."

Laura was pulling down a narrow road, and I could see the

34

reflection of her headlights off to the left on glimmering water. The river. The sky was as dark as ink, but the light pollution from Tampa ensured that only the brightest of stars could be seen. This far off the main roads, it was quiet and there were very few street lights.

"It's right here," Mill said, pointing out of his window.

We had reached the end of the road.

There was a small house just off the street to the right. It was a small, aged bungalow. The front porch light was on, revealing the chipping, peeling yellow paint on the exterior. A brand-new, bright red, Volkswagen Beetle was sitting in the dirt driveway. Planter boxes were scattered all over the slightly overgrown yard, and there was a swing strung up in one of the large, old, oak trees.

All of the lights were on inside, spilling light out onto the grass and circular stone path leading up to the door.

"Oh no…" I said, my stomach plummeting, the hairs on the back of my neck standing up straight.

The bright blue front door stood ajar.

Someone had beaten us here.

Chapter 7

"Laura, stop the car," I said, my hand already reaching for the door handle, my palms sweating. My eyes were fixed on the open door. How had they had found her already?

She hit the brakes and I narrowly missed mashing my face against the seats in front of me. I shoved Mill to get out, desperate to reach the inside to find Iona.

"How did they get here before us?" I asked as I crawled out after him.

Mill made it to the front porch in the blink of an eye, staying outside of the pool of light flooding the lawn in a narrow beam. Without stopping to wait for Mom and Dad, I ran to catch up with him. I still had the stake that he had given me, and he had pulled another one out from... somewhere? I had started to wonder if he had a utility belt or something. Maybe I was dating the vampire Batman.

He was hovering near the doorway, peering around the frame into the house like a secret agent, ready and waiting to throw himself into the thick of it.

A putrid smell wafted out the door, like spoiled meat or rotten produce. I plugged my nose. "Holy…what is that?" I whispered.

"I have my suspicions, but I'd rather be certain," Mill said. "Are you ready?"

"Ready." I said.

"Okay, on three. One…two…"

We both dashed inside, Laura's running footsteps rustling

on the grass behind us. She must have parked the car.

We stumbled into the small living room, and I blinked against the sudden bright light. The television was on, too, playing *Mean Girls*, at some point halfway through the movie. There were bookshelves packed beyond capacity on either side, with others spilling out onto the carpeted floor, or stacked in leaning towers on top.

The sofa looked like something straight from Ikea, grey with slightly squished and worn cushions, and some throw pillows with encouraging sayings like *Adventure Awaits* and *Because when you stop and look around, this life is pretty amazing.*

Everything looked…normal. Undisturbed. And that's what made it so eerie.

There was a desk beneath the window with a laptop at least ten years old on top, and poster hanging above it. Was it…Hanson? That boy band from the nineties? A trio of long-haired blond dudes stared back at me.

There was a clink of something metal in the kitchen. My heart leapt into my throat, and Mill crouched down. He gestured to me to be quiet.

I nodded. Like I was going to make any sudden, stupid moves after that.

Laura appeared a moment later and stared between the two of us. I nodded silently toward the kitchen, and she nodded in response. I was glad that she understood it wasn't time to play twenty questions.

There was definitely someone in there. Something ceramic rattled on the counter as we crept across the small living room. Each sound made my heart jump, and my chest burned with anxiety.

Mill glanced over at me and waited. Why was he waiting for me to give the signal? I was the rookie here, wasn't I?

Mill leapt into the kitchen, and I followed quickly behind, wielding my stake out in front of me like a dagger, expecting a fight as soon as my feet hit the floor—

And there was Iona, standing at the stove, wearing a frilly pink apron with a wooden spoon in her hand.

"What the—" Mill started, getting to his feet, his thick eyebrows knitting together in one, angry line.

Iona blinked at us, way less surprised than I would have thought she'd be at the fact that three people had just appeared in her kitchen. "Um…" she said, staring between us, her eyes narrowing. "What are you doing in my kitchen, Forehead?"

Mill and I both exhaled heavily as I stood up straight. The relief was great, but annoyance quickly took its place. My knees began to ache as the adrenaline left my body for the umpteenth time in the last few hours. Was it possible to completely exhaust your adrenal glands? Because between the fae war and my house being attacked by vampires, if such a thing was possible, I had to be close.

"We thought you were kidnapped, or dead, or something," I said, glaring at her. I knew it wasn't her fault, but I had to blame someone for making me get so worked up over her door being opened. "We thought Draven's minions had gotten you."

"What?" Iona asked. "What are you even talking about?" She glanced at Laura as if just noticing her.

"Hey, Iona," Laura said awkwardly.

"Hi…strange girl? I can't remember your name," Iona said.

"Laura," she said with a smile. "The Miami fiasco? Remember?"

"Yeah, I don't actually care," Iona said, turning to glare at me instead. "You know, it's a little rude to show up at someone's house unannounced. Why didn't you call first? Or at least text me?"

"I lost my phone—" I said.

Iona rolled her eyes. "Likely story." And she turned back to the stove.

The acrid stench was lingering, and as I got another strong whiff of it when a breeze passed through the back door, also wide open, I nearly gagged. I realized that the smell was emanating from the metal pot on the stove.

"Iona, what are you cooking?" I pinched my nose. Laura covered her mouth, too, her eyes watering.

Iona looked at the pot and then back at me, her face passive. "I'm boiling blood."

Laura made a gagging sound beside me.

"What?" I asked. The bile was definitely climbing up into my mouth.

Iona's eyes widened as my parents walked into the kitchen, and she shifted a glare to me. "What is this? A family outing?"

Mom was clearly ready to scold me, but as soon as she opened her mouth to speak, she covered her face with her hands, face turning green. "What is *that?*"

"Oh, for heaven's sake," Iona said, and she turned the stove off.

"That smell," Mom said. "It's terrible. What are you making?"

"Stew?" Iona said. She lifted the pot and started pouring it into a series of mason jars. The dark red liquid, moving with the viscosity of maple syrup, was steaming.

"It's blood," Mill said. If he was trying to get on my parents' good side by telling them the truth about everything, he better start multiplying the compliments and hope they would outweigh the negatives he was starting with.

I had to look away from the filled jars. It was too gross.

It was clear that my parents were horrified, too. Mom was cowering behind Dad, and Dad's face was the color of Mill's skin; papery white.

"So why do you boil it?" Mill said.

Mill, why did you have to ask?

"It changes the flavor profile," Iona said as she drained the rest of the pot into the last mason jar.

"Really?" Mill asked, folding his arms. "That's interesting. How so?"

"I like it, reminds me of a hot cup of tea when I was still human," Iona said.

I probably would have been even more disgusted by the image if I hadn't caught the slight remorse in Iona's tone. Which was rare, for Iona.

"I'd rather have mine ice cold. Especially AB," Mill said.

"I prefer O, myself. It has a better shelf life," Iona said, capping the jars with metal lids.

"I think that's a myth," he said. "But that reminds me of the vegetarian that I got stuck with not long ago. Ugh. Talk about low iron count—"

"You guys," I said. "This is disgusting. Stop. Like, now.

We're not here to swap cooking tips. You can exchange recipes when we aren't around."

"I think they really are vampires…" Dad said under his breath.

I turned around and glared at him. Now? He was going to choose now to believe me? "Aww, thanks, Dad," I said, my smile tight, not even trying to hide my sarcasm. "For finally believing in me."

Iona picked up her jars and placed them inside another pot that was partially filled with water. It, too, was steaming, a roiling boil inside. "Yeah, so…" Iona said. "Why are you here, exactly? What was all of that about Draven?"

I was grateful that she had sealed the lids on the jars. The smell was becoming less prominent now that they were submerged in the simmering water. I wished she'd rinse out the pot in the sink, though. Seeing the blood dripping down the sides was reminding me way too much of a scene in *The Strangers*. At least no one was wearing a mask, but Iona's house sure was remote enough.

"Draven's crew showed up at Cassie's house while we were eating dinner," Mill said.

"Thanks for inviting me." Iona's face split into a smirk. "So… they know about you two?"

"Mill came over to tell my parents about the car accident that we were in," I said. "With Lockwood. Pixies attacked us. I'll tell you about that later. Anyway, while we were sitting there, someone lobbed a Molotov cocktail right through our dining room window, setting the whole place on fire."

She paused as she placed a lid onto the pot of boiling water.

"This sounds awfully familiar," she said. "Were they waiting for you when you got outside?"

"It wasn't a highly original plan of attack, if that's what you are implying," I said.

Mom and Dad were standing squished together near the door and fresh air, and also easy escape, and Laura was staring closely at a shelf covered in old wine bottles.

"All right, everybody out," Iona said, waving us away from the stove. "I may not be living anymore, but that doesn't mean I don't get claustrophobic surrounded by mouth-breathing meat bags."

"Gee, I wonder why we're breathing through our mouths," my mother muttered under her breath.

We made our way back into the living room, and I breathed in the fresh air flowing in through the front door. The smell of the blood had made me sick to my stomach, and I was glad to be out from under its stinking cloud.

Now that I knew that she was safe, it gave me a chance to really look at her living room. It was painted a pale blue, trimmed in white. There were windows on every wall, all of which were uncovered for the time being. A tropical ceiling fan hung in the middle of the room, spinning lazily.

Her collection of movies was impressive; she had both regular DVDs and Bluray discs, and I also saw a few VHS tapes tucked away on the end of one of the bookcases. I blinked; they were all the oversized white boxes indicating old Disney movies. She also had candles scattered around the room, all of which had been lit. She had a basket full of flipflops near the front door, all brightly colored.

Her walls were plastered with paintings of the beach, and of open fields bathed in golden sunlight. I imagined it would be easy to miss the sun when it was impossible to ever be near it again.

It looked like an ordinary teenager lived there. It was almost like Iona was trying to hold onto her humanity in her personal life. I smirked. Iona was actually an unironic hipster. She had Emily Dickenson and Douglas Adams side by side on the shelf together. Beanies hung beside a gorgeous sun hat tied with a pale blue ribbon on pegs next to the door. I saw a stack of vinyl records on the corner of her desk, and I recognized the wooden box beneath the window as a record player.

She had all of this stuff before it was cool.

Iona was untying her apron as she followed us into the living room.

"Don't you get, like…swarmed with mosquitos?" I asked. "You're so close to the river."

"I don't worry about mosquitos. They want human blood, not vampire. I just wanted a breeze," she said. She looked around to us all. "Okay, everyone not in my kitchen? Good.

41

Sit."

"We don't have time to sit," I said. "That's why we came here. We have to leave. You have to come with us."

"Okay, but why?" she said. "They came to your house and attacked *you*. This is not my problem. Witness my house, still standing and not on fire."

"You keep boiling that blood and someone's going to have to burn it down just to get the smell out," my mother said, opening her mouth and making a glottal stop sound, like a preface to retching.

"No way is she getting her security deposit back," my dad said, and my mom nodded, sticking her finger under her nose.

I sighed. I really wished that she would just take my word for it and we could leave. I didn't know how much time we had before they came to search her house, too. "Do you remember Jacquelyn?"

"From New York? The crazy one that hates you?" Iona paused in thought. "The one whose life you ruined?"

"You can remember her name, but you can't remember mine?" Laura said quietly from off to the side. "Laura is five letters. Jacquelyn is like…sixteen."

"Who taught you to count?" Iona asked. "Is this the Tampa educational system at 'work'?" She made air quotes with her fingers.

Mom flared up at the same time. "How do all of these people know Jacquelyn?"

"Mom, not now," I said. "Iona, Draven knows who I am now."

Iona frowned slightly. "Then he knows that we've been helping you too."

"Yes," I said.

"It's likely," Mill said.

"I'm going to have to leave all this blood behind, aren't I?" she asked.

I groaned in exasperation. "This is what you worry about? Yes. Yes, you will."

She darted from the room and was back in less than a second with her car keys, a black jacket to cover up her Japanese cat shirt, and a pair of combat boots.

"Really?" I asked as she plonked down on her couch and started pulling them on.

"What?" she said. "You said Draven. I need to be ready."

"Good movie choice," Laura said with a grin, eyeing *Mean Girls*.

"Thanks, I guess," Iona said, giving Laura a confused glance.

Aww, two teenage girls doing girl things.

She stopped when she caught sight of Laura's car. "Yeah…I am not going to fit in there." She counted all of us with the tip of her finger. "And it doesn't look like you all will either."

Mill and I exchanged a look.

"I can take someone else with me in my car, and just follow you," Iona said.

"I think it's safer if we all go together—" I said.

She held up her hands. "I am not getting into another trunk."

I looked at Mom and Dad, and then back at Iona. They would be safe with Mill, and they could watch over Laura. "I'll go with Iona," I said.

"No, you will not," Mom said. "Why don't the vampires ride together?"

I raised an eyebrow at her. Did she actually just let the word vampire pass between her lips? I caught Iona and Mill glance at each other for a second, and then look away.

"That's not gonna work," Iona said.

"Why not?" Mom asked.

"It's better if the vampires are split up—" Mill said in an even tone.

"I hate him," Iona said.

I sighed heavily.

"I hate him like I hate the taste of fresh human food," Iona said, "or like a dog hates a mailman. I hate him like General Patton hates the Germans. I hate him like Harvey Weinstein hates the word 'no'. I hate him like—" Iona said.

"Okay, I get it, Lady Shakespeare," Mom said, rolling her eyes. I could see the exhaustion in her shoulders and the lines near her eyes. "Fine. I'll ride with you," she said, suddenly timid, as if enacting a great sacrifice on my behalf. "I…I should be fine, right? It's just a car ride, after all."

"You'll be fine," Iona said. "I haven't had a chance to boil your blood yet, after all."

"Give it a car ride," Mill muttered. "She'll get you boiling on her personality alone."

I rolled my eyes. "Mom, you'll be fine. I've been hanging out with these two for months and they haven't eaten me yet."

Her eyes were wide as she stared at me.

That apparently was not the answer she wanted to hear.

Iona had already walked to her car, and the start of the ignition made Mom jump nearly a foot in the air.

"Mill?" I asked, turning to him. "What about Lockwood? Seeing how we're reaching out to all of our battle-ready friends…"

"Already contacted him," Mill said. "Where should I tell him go to?"

I hadn't really thought about that. All of our houses were going to be off limits. Any place that I had frequented in the last few months was pretty much off limits, and that included places like the school and Xandra's house.

Where could we go that would not only be big enough, but completely off Draven's radar? It would have to be someplace safe for the vampires in the day time…

Then it hit me. A small, wicked sort of smile crept onto my face.

"I know just the place."

Chapter 8

The mansion was just as gorgeous as I remembered it. A modern three-story building and at the end of a road that backed up right to Tampa Bay. Tall windows that overlooked the gorgeous view, balconies everywhere, and a garage big enough to run laps in. The yard was starting to look a little overgrown, but the flowers were thriving in the late spring heat. The magnolia tree was in full bloom.

The salty air from the bay surrounded me like a comforting blanket, but there was nothing here that could overpower the dread hanging over me. A wrought iron gate protected the front driveway, but I knew that it was likely unlocked.

After all. The owner was no longer living. Not that he had been living when I'd known him.

"Are you sure about this?" Mill asked.

I shrugged, hands in the pockets of my sweatshirt. "He only chased me across the city, stalked me, confessed his twisted love for me... and nearly killed me." Another shrug. "I feel like I should get a house out of it."

"How very ex-wife of you," Iona said, and I gave her a scorching glare in reply.

"Are you serious?" Mom asked, lurking back a few steps. "You brought us here? Out of all the places you could have chosen? What, was the Four Seasons overbooked? Why here?"

"Because they'll never see this coming," I said.

Byron's house really was the only place that I could think of

45

that fit all of our needs. Not only had it likely been abandoned since I killed him, but Draven would never think to look here. I wasn't even sure that Draven was aware of him or our... relationship.

I almost threw up in my mouth calling it that. What was a good way to describe the whole "stalker/victim" thing we had going?

Doing a quick look to make sure that none of the neighbors were paying attention, we squeezed in through the gate and wandered up the dark driveway to the front door.

Chills raced up my back, and I did a full-body shudder. The last time I had been here, I had been completely defenseless and weak. Some of that terror was returning now, like the echo of an image on the inside of my eyelids after a photo was taken.

I knew that there were people that did struggle with PTSD from traumatic events in their life. I had never imagined that I would be one of them. Forget counseling, though: *Hi, yes, my name is Cassie and I was chased by a vampire.* Unless there was such thing as a vampire counselor, I probably would just have to learn to deal with these fears on my own.

Hopefully, this was the last time I'd ever have to come back to this house.

I was trying really hard to put on a brave face, but the closer we walked to the house, the more intense the memories became.

It was daylight. My parents were gone. All that I had was a note. I was alone. I had no weapon. I had been reckless.

My memories were melding with reality as I stepped up to the front door. The metal handle was just as cold as I remembered it being. It gave easily, too, revealing the interior, beckoning us inward.

I was the first one inside, and it was just as I left it. There was still a broken vase on the floor of the circular foyer, which must have been from when Byron tumbled from the second floor after I had pushed him over the banister. Some of the crystals had been knocked loose from the golden chandelier overhead and were scattered across the wide planks of the wooden floor like shards of glass. I could still hear the thud in my mind as Byron had slammed against the floor. There were drops of dried blood on the white carpeted stairs that circled up to the second and third floors. The roses that had filled every table and every vase were all dead, wilted and brown, their petals littering the floor. The dozens of pieces of the stake that he had taken from me and broken were there, too, among the crystals and petals.

My stomach lurched, and I had to grab onto Mill to steady myself.

"Someone lived in luxury," Laura said, stepping into the house, unaware of my fast-encroaching panic attack. "Even if it looks like the housekeeper got deported."

"Come on," I said through gritted teeth. "We need to make sure that we're actually alone here. Make sure that no one else has been squatting."

"I assume that if someone was here, they would have come running when we opened the door," Mill said.

Mom and Dad had followed us inside, but it was obvious from the looks on their faces that they would have rather been anywhere else. It must have been just as torturous for them to be here as it was for me. After all, last time they'd been here it had been as kidnap victims.

Iona stared up at the crystal chandelier overhead and frowned. "Figures Byron would be so grossly materialistic."

"Wait until you see the pool," I said. "And the bathroom."

I was the one who was spearheading the search, since I was the only one who had actually been inside. The only one who had ran for their life in there.

It was like the house was trapped in a time loop. Everything was just as it was when Mom, Dad, and I fled from it. Everything. The door to the wine cooler was open, blasting cold air out into the hallway. There was a moldy pot of coffee in the kitchen. I remembered that Byron had put that pot on to welcome me in, put me at ease.

My stomach churned.

Mom and Dad were pale, looking around like Byron was about to pop out from some hidden place at any second.

My heart was beating against my ear drums as I drew closer to the dining room. I swallowed nervously as Mill and I approached it.

Mom, who was already there, hovered near the door, staring inside at what I knew was a complete and utter mess.

"What happened in here?" she asked. "The table is destroyed, broken picture frames… and what is that black…thing…in the middle of the room?"

I didn't even want to look. "That's Byron."

And I just kept walking. I didn't have the strength to look in there.

"Wait, what?" she said. "Why is he like…that?"

"Didn't you see the vampires back at the house?" I asked, still walking, trying to keep my stomach from rebelling inside of me. "I staked him."

I peered into one of the bathrooms. It was deserted. As was the kitchen, and study. I even found some rooms that I hadn't seen the last time I was here.

It was harder than I imagined, being back inside this place. It was eerie. The quiet was putting me on edge, and every small sound made me twitch. I knew Byron was dead. I had killed him myself. But my mind was still reacting as if he were creeping just around the corner, just out of my sight. I could almost hear his low, deep laugh, see the heavy-lidded eyes just over my shoulder in the reflection of the mirrors. He didn't have a reflection, of course, but his animalistic gaze was imprinted on my memory forever, projected onto every mirror I passed like some physical manifestation of unease ripping its way out of my subconscious mind.

Mill must have noticed the tension, because he took my hand in his and tried to remind me constantly that he was there with me.

At one point, I found Laura in one of the bedrooms upstairs. It must have been Byron's, because the scent of his cologne hit me when I walked in. I wrinkled my nose, and the little hairs on the back of my neck stood up. The closet door stood open as if it had been left open, as if its owner in a hurry. A bath towel lay in a wad on the floor just outside the bathroom door.

"Vampires really live the high life, don't they?" Laura said, pushing things around in one of the drawers of the desk beneath the window. "There are just wads of cash in here," she said, lifting out a stack easily two inches thick.

I sighed. "When you live forever, money probably means very little eventually."

Laura looked at me, dropping the money back into the drawer as if it were contaminated. "Being here...it's giving me flashbacks of Roxy and Benjy and all of them..."

"I get it," I said. "I've got this pit in my stomach, looking at everything here."

Laura frowned. "I was really hoping that I was over all of this vampire stuff after Roxy was killed," she said. She wrapped her arms around herself as if she were cold. "I thought I could move past it like it was a bad dream."

"I understand," I said. "That's how I felt when the vamps came after you. 'No way, not again'..." I shook my head. "Ever since Byron showed up in my life...it's just been in upheaval for months now."

Laura gave me a sympathetic smile. "I know exactly what you mean."

"I'm sorry you got dragged into it again," I said. "I don't know what would have happened if you and Gregory hadn't come to help."

She gave me a smile, and I could see why everyone thought she was the prettiest, nicest girl at school. "I couldn't leave you out there all alone, Cassie. That's not what friends do."

Friends. I wasn't aware that we had reached that milestone together. I gave her a small smile. "I appreciated your help. I don't think I've actually thanked you for it."

Laura shrugged. "Don't worry about it."

"You're right, though," I said. "This really does suck."

We both sighed.

"What do we do now?" Laura asked. "Looks clear. I don't think anyone's been here for a while."

"No, they haven't," I said. "I guess we should go find the others. Come up with a game plan."

Laura nodded. She didn't want to stand here in this room, dwelling on the things of the past any more than I did.

Chapter 9

I decided on the dining room for our meeting. I was going to have to face my fear of this place if I had any hope of getting through it. Byron was dead. His house, while filled with reminders of him at every turn, could not hurt me anymore than any other building could. I shoved aside my irrational aversion for the room. The emotions were running high, but I didn't want to dive into them all that deeply. If I did, I might not come back out.

Everyone was sitting, the table flipped back over by Mill and Iona, the chairs all righted by us. There were enough still intact to let us all have a seat, which was good, because to my surprise, I sank right in like all the life had left my legs. Everyone else seemed eager to sit, too, adrenaline finally wearing off after a long night.

Except for Mom, who was still standing near the wall, eyes on the pile of black goo heaped onto the carpet. "So…how did that happen again?" she asked.

I rolled my eyes. "A stake."

"Like a T-bone? Or a ribeye?"

Dad had apparently had enough with Mom and her inability to accept the situation we were in. "We need to get on the same page, dear. Wooden stake. These are vampires."

Mom gave him a quelling look before turning her dangerous gaze on me. "We never should have left New York."

I was sitting with my back to Byron's puddled remains so I didn't have to look at it. One step at a time. I figured that the only way I would really feel contented in this house was if I could be sure where he was, even if he was nothing more than a dried pile of glop on the floor. "Obviously the question that is on all of our minds is what are our next steps?" I asked.

Eyes moved around the table. Nobody said anything. Looks were traded, but I couldn't decipher many of them.

"All of us are out of a home now," I said. "Mom, Dad, and I don't have a house. Mill, you can't go back to your condo. Laura, same for you, and Iona, well…"

She nodded her head. "Yeah, yeah, I'm homeless, too. Thanks for that. Pretty soon I'll be a smelly bum, living on the streets, just like the rest of you. Do I have to pick up a heroin habit now or can I wait a few weeks?"

"Ouch, harsh." Laura said. "And very stereotypical. You know—"

"I don't care, cheerleader," Iona said. "Save your self-righteousness for someone who does."

"Gregory's still in danger, too, isn't he?" Laura asked.

"He is," I said, "But probably not much. Seems unlikely Draven is going to start randomly going after my neighbors, though who knows with him. He says he's fine, I'm not going to fight with him."

Mill's brows turned into one, thick distressed line. "What about your other friend?"

"Xandra?" I asked. "I was just thinking about her. I need to get a warning to her somehow. I don't know her number off the top of my head…" I looked at Laura. "You wouldn't have Xandra's number, would you?"

Laura frowned, and shook her head. "Is that the girl with the emotional support wombat that she brings to school?"

"No, she's the one with the blue hair."

Laura's eyes narrowed as she scratched her chin in concentration. "I don't think I know her."

"She's in our grade," I went on. "I know we have like three hundred kids in our grade, but still. I think she's the only one with blue hair. Let me correct myself. She's the one with blue hair *all the time*, and blue hair that actually looks good on her."

Laura shook her head. "No, sorry. I don't think blue hair looks good on anyone. There's some shades of magenta and pink I can get behind, but blue just doesn't work with most complexions, in my opinion."

I drummed my fingers on the table. "Her mom owns that noodle shop over on—"

"Oh my gosh, *yes*. I know that shop. Yes, okay, I know who she is," Laura said.

"She also helped us save your life," I said, finishing the thought.

Iona was counting on the tips of her fingers.

"What are you doing?" I asked.

She looked at me. "Xandra. That's only six letters."

Laura gave her a questioning look.

"Okay, we still need a plan," I said before Laura could answer back. "I'll worry about Xandra later. Besides, Jacquelyn never had contact with her."

"We've been on the defensive," Mill said, folding his arms and leaning back in his chair. "They've forced us to run, and until we can figure out what's going on, we have to keep out of Draven's sights."

"I agree with the mighty forehead," Iona said. "It isn't like we can fight back. Not against Draven."

"We sort of did tonight," I said.

"Yeah, but could you do that again?" Iona asked.

I looked at Laura. "No, I don't think so. We had the element of surprise. We won't get that chance again."

"Who's this Draven that you keep talking about?" Dad asked.

"Oh, you cannot be serious, Mike," Mom said. "You're buying into all of this?"

Dad craned his neck to look over at her from his seat. "At this point, I'm willing to believe what my lying eyes have seen."

Mom clicked her tongue in disgust. "This is just some...bizarre dream. I have more important things to be dealing with right now. I have clients to call first thing in the morning, I have a court appearance the day after tomorrow that I have to prepare for." She shook her head, her lawyer face on. "I don't have time to be going on some wild adventure, running from fake *vampires*."

"How about real ones?" Iona asked. "Because trust me, I wouldn't waste time running from the fake ones."

"There are fake vampires?" Laura asked.

Iona moved a hand in front of her mouth. "You know, the Halloween kind. With plastic teeth that can't even sink into a neck. I mean, unless you bite really, really hard." I felt a pause as everyone seemed to take a deep breath at that. "What?" Iona asked, looking around. She bared a canine, pointed and sharper than a normal human's tooth. "Look at these babies. These were made for tearing through the skin and into the vein."

Laura cringed and did not follow up on that. Mom just glared in the silence.

"Okay, thank you, Iona, for that...horror," I said, glancing back at my mother. I didn't know what it was going to take to get her to listen. Dad was quiet, but I could see the wheels turning as he looked from her to me. He had been silently observing our conversations up until that point. He was trying to make everything fit.

I understood. It's like trying to shove the square toy in the circle hole. Vampires just didn't make sense.

Dad looked at me again. "Can you answer me about who this Draven is?"

"He's a vampire... With a lot of power," I said.

"He's the vampire Lord of all of western Florida," Mill said.

Thanks, Mill. Ever the blunt one.

"What happened?" Dad asked. "How did you get his attention?"

I fought the urge to glance over my shoulder at Byron's remains, just to make sure that he really wasn't going to wake up. I licked my lips. "Well, I was dealing with Byron. Iona stepped in to help, gave me directions to a vampire party. I was supposed to find out more about him, but instead, I kind of...killed one of his underlings, and he took it as a personal insult."

Dad's jaw hung open.

"Well, you can't really blame the guy," Laura said, holding her hands out, palms upward and shrugged. "You killed someone at his party."

"In his house, no less," Iona said. "If you killed someone in my house—back before this happened, when I had a nice, comfy, cozy home, you know—I would have taken it personally. I would have gone all bitey." She stroked a finger idly over her tooth.

Laura looked at her sideways. "Is there a reason you keep touching your teeth?"

Iona sighed, theatrically, since she had no need to breathe. "Yes. You interrupted me in the middle of making dinner. I'm hungry." She made a show of looking at Laura's neck. "Any chance you'd like to donate some blood?"

"Why did you kill that person, Cassandra?" Dad asked, adjusting his glasses. He was staring at me as if he was just seeing me for the first time.

"He was a vampire," I said to him in as reassuring of a tone as possible. "He was trying to kill me."

"Draven? Or the vampire you killed?" he asked.

"Both," I said. "But the one I killed... His name was Theo."

"Just for the record, I sent you to that party to get information," Iona said. "Not to kill people. Why is it always violence and fire with you, anyway?"

"Why is it always blood with you?" Laura asked.

"I told you, I'm hungry," Iona said, rolling her eyes. "The motive is obvious. Cassie's—less so. Unless she's just psychotic and a pyromaniac. Which I don't rule out."

"Escaping Draven's condo was how I met Mill," I said, ignoring the hell out of Iona's little assertion.

"You met your boyfriend at a party?" Mom asked. "Not at school?"

"I haven't been in school in over a hundred years," Mill said.

"Well, I guess we can just add that lie to the pile," Mom said, eyes blazing.

"I never said we met at school," I bristled, looking at Mom.

"I did," Mill said, unable to meet my eye.

"It's great to see that your boyfriend lies for you," Mom said, her eyes narrowing. "You two are like peas in a pod."

"I used to eat peas," Iona said, a little dreamily. "Back when I was human. Loved the taste of them then. Now they taste like ass. Or ash." She smacked her lips and looked at Laura's neck again.

"Can you blame me?" I asked. "How would I explain it if I

had told you the truth? You never would have believed me, so it wouldn't have mattered anyway."

"Cassandra." It was Dad. He was using his Dad voice, trying to convince me to calm down.

Mom was glaring. She still wasn't ready to see the truth staring her in the face.

"Unfortunately, Cassie is in the most danger," Mill said, getting right back on topic. "The rest of us are too, of course, but she will be their main target."

"And that means that nowhere in Tampa is going to be safe for her," Iona said.

"It seems likely that Draven doesn't know where we are, at least not yet," Mill said.

"If he did, I assume that they would be kicking in the door?" Dad asked.

I nodded. "Yeah. Likely."

A movement near the doorway drew my attention, and I looked up.

Lockwood was standing there, a rucksack tossed over his shoulder. He had returned to his human-like self, with his dark hair and startling green eyes, and was wearing a sharp navy blazer over a white button up and faded jeans. When he caught my eye, he smiled.

"How did you find us?" I asked, standing up.

"Who is this?" Mom said. "Another one of your friends?" Her eyes narrowed. "Your lying friends."

"I cannot lie," Lockwood said, holding out his hand to my dad. "So please take my word that it is a pleasure to make your acquaintance, finally. My name is Lockwood. I count myself one of Cassandra's friends—and very fortunate to be in that number." He inclined his head in such a proper way that I felt like I was in a fae court. I understood Lockwood so much better now, and his body language, always so formal, now held a lot more meaning than it ever had before.

Dad took his hand and shook it, mouth hanging open slightly.

"Long time no see," I said to Lockwood.

"What has it been…" he said with a small smirk. "Three hours? Four?"

"In Faerie time, that's practically an eternity." I smiled. I looked back at Mom and Dad. Might as well keep going with the honesty thing. "He's a Fae," I said.

Laura's eyes were wide with awe again.

Mom just scoffed. "I really don't care about the sexuality of your friends right now, Cassie."

"Fae, not... Never mind," I said, shaking my head. "It doesn't matter either way."

Dad looked skeptical. Faeries might be a bridge too far now.

"Ah, so we are sharing all truths now?" Lockwood asked.

"Yes. I am so over lying after our last adventure," I said. The prospect of being turned into the liar's version of an Avara— a pig-like evolution of greedy humans too long stuck in Faerie—had been the last straw in scaring me straight. No more lies for this girl.

Lockwood gave me a quick wink and moved to shake my mother's hand. She leaned away from him, folding her own. He inclined his head toward, her, ignoring the snub, and turned to stand beside Mill.

"So, do you have some kind of like…Faerie GPS?" I asked. "Did you inject me with a tracker or something?"

"Mill shared his location via his phone," Lockwood said, pulling his cell phone from his pocket. "Not everything is magic, Cassandra." But he gave me a bemused smile.

I looked at Mill. "You should probably turn off your location on your phone in case Draven—"

"Already done," Mill said. "And I brought Lockwood up to speed with... All this."

"Another interesting adventure commences." Lockwood looked across the table at me, green eyes glittering. "Have you ever considered giving yourself a break?"

"I don't want to hear it, Seelie." I said. "Getting my house burned down and having my old bestie turn evil vampire snitch on me wasn't exactly the 'Welcome Home' party I was hoping for after spending a week at war in Faerie."

"Draven will be in his penthouse," Mill said. "It'll be all-hands-on-deck, heavily fortified, he will be defended." He looked at me with great significance.

"Are you thinking I wanted to go at him, like, head on?" I

asked.

"Well... This is *you* we're talking about, Cassie," he said, almost offering a shrug.

"You do tend to have a penchant for direct action in the face of trouble, Cassandra," Lockwood added oh-so-helpfully.

"How come you let him call you Cassandra?" Laura asked. "I thought you hated that."

I pinched the bridge of my nose.

"I wondered that myself," Dad said.

"He just…" I said, and then groaned in exasperation. "I don't know. Listen to the way he talks. He's practically old-world British. It sounds endearing when he does it, okay?"

Mill's lips twitched ever so slightly as if he was trying to smother a laugh.

"Anyway," I said. "I'm not some kind of suicidal idiot looking to get herself killed, all right? I just spent the whole night trying *not* to die."

"I'm just saying that a direct assault is not a smart move," Mill said. "It's too dangerous. We need another option."

"Which is what?" I asked. "This is where we keep hitting a snag. We don't really know what to do." All I got in reply was a bunch of blank faces as I looked around the table.

"We need to rest," Iona said. "Well, at least you humans do. You've been awake through the whole night, right? Not to mention whatever this trip to Faerie cost you. I saw enough beds in this place. We can take shifts until someone has a bright idea about what to do next." She smacked her lips together. "We can send someone out for food. Maybe have them make a quick stop at the blood bank…"

Mill frowned. "Every blood bank in the area is controlled by Draven. Why not just send them into his condo?"

"So, you think that'd be suicide?" Iona asked, utterly casual. "I agree. It'd be a blood bath. Better they just give a little— y'know, straight to us and skip dying. Am I right?" She looked around and got no approval, though Laura gave her another wary look.

I leaned back in my chair and sighed. I didn't like any of these ideas, except for maybe sending somebody out for food (but not to the blood bank). We were just sitting on our hands, hiding like terrified rabbits. How could any of us rest in a situation like this?

"I'm sorry," I said finally.

"For what?" Mill said.

"For everything…" I looked at Dad. "For our house…and the one in New York." I looked at Mill, and then Iona. "I'm sorry that you can't go home, either of you." I looked at Laura. "I'm sorry we dragged you with us."

Laura shrugged. "It's pretty much a good thing, especially if it is going to save my life." She looked at Iona out of the corner of her eye. "Though, admittedly, there are some creepy aspects."

"Still…" I looked at Lockwood. "And I am sorry about dragging you into my messes again."

He shook his head. "You don't have to apologize. You agreed to help me, even without knowing the full extent of my problems, and you saved my life more than once in the process."

Mill gave me a sidelong look. What a lovely date night that was going to be, retelling the story of barely escaping death in Faerie. Magic and glamours and Unseelie…good times. I thought of Orianna and what she was doing for the Winter Queen right then. I wondered if she had forgotten all about me by now.

"I just don't know what to do," I said, head falling into my hand. "I don't want to sit here and wait, but I know we can't leave, either."

"We need to be patient," Mill said. "And hunker down for now."

"I do believe we are safe," Lockwood said. "I did a thorough search of the area before coming inside. There are no signs of surveillance."

"Good to hear," I said. I really was exhausted. I couldn't remember when I had slept last, but I was so wound up being in Byron's house and near what was left of his body that I knew there was zero chance I could actually rest here.

"Let's take a break," Iona said. "I need blood. Really. Volunteers?"

"Can't you just miss a meal?" I asked, my head against the

back of the chair, my eyes on the intricate mural painted on the ceiling. It was cherubs and puffy cotton candy clouds, with gold leaf pressed into the hair and harps of the winged babies. Too much of a happy image for how I was feeling at that moment. I looked away.

"Fine," she muttered under her breath. "Let's see you miss a meal and let the hunger really set in."

"I miss meals all the time," Laura said. "It's fine."

Iona gave her a sideways look. "Of course you do."

That seemed to break up the meeting. Dad went over to Mom, who seemed lost in thought, and helped her out of the room, his arm around her shoulders. He shot me a look, and I knew our conversations weren't over.

"I have a little blood available," Lockwood said to Iona, who went from sullen to pleasant in about half a tick.

"Your own?" she asked.

"I don't know whether Fae blood would be beneficial to you," Lockwood said, leaving with Iona in tow, "but in my trunk I keep a supply on ice for my clientele..."

Laura yawned and stretched. "I might grab a shower. Maybe it will help me settle down." She wandered out through the doors, trudging as though it were the middle of the night. Which it was.

I caught Mill looking at me with concern. We were the only two left in the room.

"I'm fine," I said, looking away. A chill ran down my spine.

It was a lie, of course. And I'd been doing so well.

Chapter 10

"Listen, Cassie…" Mill said. "You don't have to put on a brave face for me."

Now that the room was totally empty, aside from Mill, me, and Byron's puddle of black glop, I realized just how cold the room felt. How eerie.

"Can we…move out of here?" I asked.

"Sure," Mill said, and together we left the dining room, passing through the shattered French doors that clung desperately to the hinges.

Once out in the hall, I was able to breathe a little more easily. Not a whole lot, but at least somewhat.

"Where do you want to go?" Mill asked. He was standing close, speaking in a low voice, but seemed unsure if I wanted any more contact than that.

"Honestly, there isn't anywhere in this house that I want to be," I said. "But it's probably better if we stay close. I guess maybe… The kitchen?"

We walked down the hall to the ultra-sleek modern kitchen, with stainless steel appliances, dark granite counters and warm lighting beneath the cabinets.

It was like something out of a magazine. Why did a vampire need a place like this? I pinched my nose as I inhaled, and then coughed. The coffee pot was definitely molded over, enough that spores were probably filtering into the air.

"Why would Byron have brewed coffee?" I asked, and dumped the pot down the drain, holding my nose closed with my fingers.

"Because, among other quirks, Byron ate food sometimes," Mill said. "Gross."

I glanced at him. "You think it's gross?"

He arched a brow at me. "I do remember what mold is, you know."

I coughed just thinking about it coating my lungs. I turned on the hot water and stuck the glass pot underneath.

"You're just looking for something to distract yourself, aren't you?" Mill asked.

I stared at the water filling up the pot, bubbling and churning inside. It was exactly like my brain at the moment; ceaselessly moving, like a leaf caught in violent river rapids.

"Cassie... Please tell me what you're thinking," he said, deep voice low and gentle.

I looked up at him, seeing his expectant face, his thick eyebrows almost reaching his hairline on his tall forehead. Even if I hadn't really thought so initially, he was handsome. His chiseled jawline, his high cheekbones, his dark blue eyes that were flecked with silver...

"I'm thinking I don't really want coffee tomorrow, because it's probably going to suck," I said, looking away. "But...most of all, I feel guilty about putting everyone in this situation."

"You didn't—"

"I did, though," I said, squeezing some sickly-sweet smelling orange soap into the pot, wrinkling my nose. It was almost worse than the moldy coffee. "If I hadn't killed Theo, Draven never would have found out about me."

"What was the alternative, though?" he asked. "Let yourself be killed?"

In some ways... That would be easier than what I had to deal with right now.

"Cassie..." Mill said in a warning tone, as if he could somehow read my thoughts.

"I'm okay," I said. "I—"

I noticed Mill looking over his shoulder, and when I followed his gaze, I saw Dad in the doorway of the kitchen, trying to look like he wasn't listening to our conversation.

"I'll give you guys some space," Mill said, then slunk out of the kitchen, giving my dad a nod as he passed.

Dad watched him walk down the hall for a minute before stepping into the cavernous kitchen. He gazed up at the copper pots hanging from a rack over the island.

"I didn't mean to interrupt," Dad said, coming to stand by me at the sink.

I rolled up the sleeves of my sweatshirt and pulled a paper towel off the roll to scrub at the inside of the coffee pot. The warm water was almost up to my elbows, and there were little bubbles floating in the air around me, the light from the recessed bulbs overhead making them twinkle. It reminded me of Faerie, and everything pretty that I had seen there, with all the tiny rainbows swirling around the sudsy orbs.

"It wasn't anything important," I said, rinsing the paper towel off with more hot water before scrubbing at the pot again.

Dad leaned against the counter and crossed his arms over his chest.

Time for the Dad talk, huh? I was so tired that I didn't even have it in me to fight back. It felt like life had taken a dive. And not a short dive, either, like into our swimming pool. No, the kind of dive that would get you to the bottom of the Mariana Trench.

"I…want to apologize, Cass," Dad said.

I blinked and looked up at him, pausing my furious scrubbing.

He was watching me steadily, lips pursed. He meant it. He actually wanted to apologize. To *me*. "Why?"

"I think that I'm starting to understand what's been going on here," he said. "All of this…stuff that's been going on with you. You've been under insane pressure, haven't you?"

My stomach flipped, and I looked away. I didn't want him to see the sudden flush in my cheeks. I went back to scourging the pot.

"When did you find out about vampires, Cassie?" he asked.

"So you believe me?" I asked. "Puts you ahead of Mom, I guess."

"Hard to ignore the evidence of my eyes," he said. "Give your mom some time. But seriously…when did you find out about... all this?"

I turned back to the pot, and anger blossomed to life as I pulled out the old memories that I had been working so hard to bury.

"You can probably figure it out if you think back to when everything here started to go wrong," I said, looking around the kitchen as if it might close its jaws down over me and swallow me whole. "It was the night I didn't come home for the first time."

Blood started pumping more quickly through my veins, my heart beating faster as I recalled the sensation of Byron playing cat and mouse with me and Xandra on a quiet street not far from home. "I had no idea Byron was a vampire, but...I was terrified. I was sure that I was going to die that night. That night was when I first broke my promise to give up lying."

"Cassie...why didn't you tell us?" Dad asked. His tone was mingled horror and sorrow. I hadn't ever heard it from him before, and it made the knots in my stomach become even more pretzel-like.

"Because I couldn't really believe it, so why would you?"

"Because I'm your dad," he said, "because I'm the one who's supposed to be in your corner when no one else is, kiddo."

"And you might have been," I said, "if I hadn't been such a damned liar that we had to leave our whole lives behind in New York." I shook my head. "I just couldn't see you guys buying the line, 'So, the reason I didn't come home last night? A vampire. Totally a vampire. For real this time, you guys'!" I rested my hands on the side of the sink for support, covered in bubbles. The water from the faucet still ran endlessly into the basin of the sink.

"So Byron was the one who kidnapped us?" my dad asked. "And that's him, back in the dining room?"

"Yeah," I said, feeling the silent judgment at me killing someone. I still had a hard time wrapping my head around the fact that I had actually killed anything, let alone someone who looked, sounded, and acted human.

"Mom and I assumed you were lying." He sounded shell-shocked. "Or being lazy. We had no idea that...all this was going on."

I had goosebumps, so I submerged my hands underneath the scalding water.

"You had no one to go to, and your entire world had been upended," Dad said. "Mom and I were definitely not on your side, thinking this was nothing more than a continuation of everything that had happened in New York…"

"Yeah…" I said. What else was I supposed to say?

"Cass, I…" he said.

"It's okay," I said. "You don't have to say anything."

"No, I do," Dad said. "Everything that's been going on with you, we didn't know any of it. Byron kidnapping us was just the start of it, wasn't it?"

I thought about all that had happened since then— the Instaphoto vampire gang, my sojourn to New York where I'd fought the Butcher and seen Jacquelyn turned into a vampire, my trip to Faerie where I'd been stuck in the middle of a magical war…

But to my dad, all I said was, "Yes. That was just the start."

"I feel like, just looking in your eyes now, you've been through a whole world of pain that we didn't even know about," he said softly. "Whatever happened... I can see the guilt in you, in the way you won't look at me right now. But you can't blame yourself. These things that have happened, they're not your fault."

"Yes they are," I said, thinking of Jacquelyn, in particular. If not for me, she'd be human, and safe at home in New York. Probably dating Gary Haze. Ugh.

"No, it's not. You're doing whatever you can to set things right. And sometimes, things just don't go the way that we want them to…no matter how hard we try."

My hand tightened around the paper towel in my hands, tearing it in two soapy pieces.

"I feel like I don't know you anymore," Dad said. "I don't even recognize you. You've done things I can't even imagine. Despite the whole world being against you…you persevered."

I tried to swallow passed the giant lump in my throat.

"I'm just—" Dad started. "I am so sorry that we weren't there for you."

All those nights in my room, lying awake, staring at the

ceiling, I had been all alone. They had no idea what I was going through.

The distance between me and my dad felt insurmountable in that moment. Everything that I had done, everything he had learned, it was just... Too much.

It would always be too much, wouldn't it?

I feel like I don't know you anymore.

It was because the person that I had become through these insane circumstances was entirely different from his little girl. She lay across an ocean of lies from where I stood. Of course he wouldn't know me anymore. "Dad?" I said. "I—"

But my words were cut off by a crashing sound from out in the main hall. I dropped the pot in the sink and the glass shattered. My hands were still slippery with soapy water.

"What was that?" Dad asked, twisting around to look through the doorway.

"Someone's coming in!" shouted Mill from down the hall.

My stomach dropped, and the hair on the back of my neck stood up. Someone had just kicked in the front door.

Draven had found us.

Chapter 11

My heart pounded like a thundering drum in my head. I had been so sure that this place was safe. Draven barely knew Byron, if he knew him at all. How could he know where Byron lived? He couldn't know where every vampire in his territory was at all times, could he? And how could he possibly guess we would have come here?

I looked around the kitchen for a weapon, anything that would work as a stake, as shrieking filled the air. Whether from my mother or Laura, I couldn't tell. All I knew was that it was probably not Iona. Probably. Everyone else in the house was becoming aware that we had intruders.

My eyes fell on the knife block, and all of the knives inside had wooden handles. Would that work? I had no idea. If I plunged the knife in far enough, could that kill a vampire? Like a second-hand stake?

Using a steak knife as a stake. The irony was not lost on me.

I had nothing else. At the very least, maybe I could slash some skin if I had to. I pulled out the longest knife I could find, a blade that was probably used to gut fish or other meats. Vampires definitely felt pain, and if I had to cause them some, then that would have to be Plan A.

"Cassie, where are you going?" Dad shouted as I ran out into the hall.

"Stay there, Dad!" I called back.

From the sound of the footsteps behind me, I realized that he hadn't listened to me.

I tore out into the foyer and stumbled to a stop as I saw three people standing just inside the door. All three were wearing long, black trench coats that grazed the floor. They had dark sunglasses covering their eyes and wore black boots with wicked heels on them.

What was this, a *Matrix* cosplay conference?

A flicker of movement caught my eye from above, and I looked up just in time to see Mill leap over the banister on the second floor and land beside me. He straightened, head cocked to the side slightly as he stared at the strangers— two women, one man, all leather clad.

The man had a long, thin black cane in his hand. One of the women pulled at the black ribbon choker around her neck, and as it came into contact with her hand, transformed into a rod of some sort, long and rigid. The third had withdrawn two silvery rods from the inside of her coat, and after ramming them together, end to end, created a single, cylindrical pole that reminded me a lot of a metallic chopstick.

And then, just as quickly, she shot brilliantly colored lights out of the end of it.

After being in Faerie, I didn't even have to think about ducking. Magic was magic, no matter the source. I threw myself to the floor and yanked my dad down with me, dragging him by a handful of his shirt.

"What's going on?" Dad asked, pale face sweating.

I dragged him, unresisting, around the corner to the living room. Mill must have been caught off guard by the magic, as well, because he had scrambled into the living room, too, huddling on the opposite side of the archway.

Flashes of green, blue, and red light, struck the wall over our heads, and I could see the reflection of the magic being shot up into the second floor off the ceiling.

I covered my head as another blue ball of light struck the wall over my head, creating a downpour of plaster around us, like rain in the Fall. My heart was racing, making it hard to think clearly. "I don't know. Magic of some sort."

"How do you know?" Dad asked.

"Because laser guns aren't a real thing." I peered around the corner as I heard Lockwood shout something unintelligible.

Our Fae magician had entered the fight. "Ergo, magic."

There was a flurry of more blues and reds, all bursting from the ends of their little instruments they had in their hands. Were they like wands?

"I don't think so, ladies and gentleman." Lockwood was just on the other side of the large foyer, throwing white hot balls of light in their direction.

"We need to get out of here," Mill shouted from the other side of the doorway.

There was a crackle like a firework, and little sparks fell to the carpet just beside my hand, singeing it. I yanked my hand away. "Who are these guys?"

"A wizard," Mill said. "And witches."

"Great, we've got a leather-bound Gandalf and two-thirds of the biker version of *Hocus Pocus* after us," I said. "What are we going to do against their magic?"

"Overpower it, of course," Mill said, and before I could even try and change his mind, he dashed out into the foyer.

Horrified, I stared around the corner and saw him sneak in behind Lockwood and use him as a shield. Lockwood was standing between our attackers and the living room. There was a great shimmering green shield surrounding the doorway, some sort of magical barrier to protect us.

Mill, it seemed, was able to get through. He ducked around Lockwood and threw himself at the cluster of black-cloaked magicians near the door. His movement hadn't gone unnoticed, though. The woman on the end had been watching. With her long silvery rod, she shot a blast of green magic at him, and it struck him in the arm.

He hit the floor with a loud crash.

"No!" I shouted as I tried to get up to run to him. Dad grabbed my arm and yanked me back behind the wall.

"You can't throw yourself into danger like that," Dad said.

"But they hit Mill—"

"We have to wait," Dad said under his breath.

"For what?" I asked.

"I don't know, but we have to—"

I didn't want to wait. I still had my knife, so I untangled myself from Dad's grasp and scrambled behind the shimmering green barrier. I hesitated as I saw Mill struggle to his feet. The spellcasters apparently didn't notice him, because he used the opportunity to throw himself at the nearest witch, knocking her over. The red spell she had been trying to send at Lockwood ricocheted off the ceiling and hit the floor, shattering marble tiles.

My heart swelled with relief, but in that same second, the other two noticed me, and redirected all of their fire power at me.

Lockwood shouted, "Cassandra, get down!"

But it was too late.

The magic that they were shooting at the barrier were weakening it. It rippled like a pond being struck with a stone, and the shimmering green grew fainter.

"Cassie!" I heard Dad shout. He had gotten to his feet and was just about to reach me when the barrier shattered, and one of the blue spells that the women were shooting at me collided with one of Lockwood's brilliantly white spells.

It kept coming, and all I could do was watch it, mouth hanging open…

… And it struck Dad square in the chest.

He went flying through the air, across the living room, only to slam against the metal shaded windows. He crumpled to the floor, unmoving.

The whole world stopped. Everything.

And then I heard the sound of a panicked scream escaping from my mouth.

Chapter 12

Something about my dad getting struck drew something out of me. Awoke a blood thirst that I never really knew I had. The adrenaline was pumping through my veins, and it was as if Lockwood had given me some sort of magical elixir. My blood ran hot. I felt strong.

I felt heedlessly, recklessly invincible.

And I was going to make them pay with their own blood.

Iona appeared. I wasn't sure from where, or how, but she was on the stairs, obviously taking the opportunity of the missing witch to enter the fight.

Wait. One of the witches was gone, the one Mill had attacked. Where had she gone? She had been laying there on the floor, but was now missing, dead for all I knew.

Mill was on all fours behind Iona, panting, a pained look on his face. His hand was clamped around the spot where the spell had struck him.

Laura appeared, with Mom not far behind, higher up the stairs. The spellcasters near the door hadn't noticed them. Their focus was all on me.

Lockwood scooped me up with one hand, dragging me behind his body. Once again he was shielding me. "Are you all right?" he asked in a strained tone.

"I'm fine," I said. "But my dad—"

Then I heard an unfamiliar voice…and in an unfamiliar language. It was the wizard. Or the witch. No, both.

It was obvious they were distressed. They continued to

shoot spells at Lockwood, who was throwing them right back. I blinked a few times. He actually was doing exactly that. He was somehow able to grab their spells in midair and throw them back as though lobbing thrown softballs.

I glanced over my shoulder at Dad, who was still slumped against the wall.

I adjusted the long knife in my hand, the memories of the Butcher flashing through my mind. If these spellcasters were vampires, then cutting them wouldn't kill them.

But it would hurt. And a dark, angry part of me was relishing the thought of causing them pain. The knife had a wooden hilt, too. If I buried that all the way to the heart, it would turn them right into black goo.

I heard one of them utter the word *Draven*, and my ears perked up. It was buried in the middle of a long string of foreign words, a deeply guttural language.

"They're human, Lockwood," Iona called. "That's German they're speaking."

"Yes, I just realized that as well," he said, straining beneath a volley of their magic as it collided with his shield and he failed to hurl it back. His arm was tight around my waist, and he was holding me off the ground so I couldn't set my feet and pull free. "Of the—" he made a guttural noise of his own, that sounded very much like German, "—school of magic."

"So there really are witches and wizards?" I asked, watching his shield ripple from another hit. Sparks flew brightly across the surface, and I flinched from the light's intensity. "And they're hunting me for Draven? Great. Because I needed more to deal with than the Lord of Tampa and a newly converted vampire best friend." Now I had vampiric spellcasters on my tail.

"Well, you do seem to excel at managing these larger conundrums," Lockwood said, sticking the hand that wasn't wrapped around my waist out toward the enemy. A white glow formed in his palm, then quickly doubled in size and turned a sickly yellow color before he shot it at them.

The wizard in the middle who had taken a fraction of a second to glance at his compatriot took it in the side of the face, and it sent him flying into the frame of the door, which cracked upon impact. His face went slack, and he tumbled to the ground with a thud.

Lockwood sagged; he must have put quite a bit into that spell. I felt the strength of his grip on me fade, and I took the opportunity to wriggle free. I rushed out from behind Lockwood, screaming into the air, at the last witch standing there.

She had pin-straight black hair that fell to her shoulders, and while her sunglasses hid her eyes, they didn't hide her incredibly high cheekbones or her pouting lips.

She brandished her cane, raising it to send a blue ball of light at me, but having trained with a vampire, I'd learned when to expect attacks and respond quickly. I ducked, and the spell flew over my shoulder, grazing the cloth as I came in low.

I rose, and before the witch had another chance to send a spell at me, I plunged the knife into the center of her chest.

It sunk in all the way up to the hilt, and I shoved it in, hard. The wood was in her flesh, the blade buried in her heart, and one more good shove would—

Hot, scarlet blood gushed out over my hand.

I screamed when it touched me, warm and unexpected, not the thick black goo I'd anticipated.

Human blood. It was *human* blood.

The witch stumbled backwards, grasping at the knife.

She muttered something in German, her teeth gritted tightly, and yanked the knife out, staring at it. She flicked her gaze up at me, whispered something—

In the next second, she had disappeared with nothing more than a rush of wind.

Her companion in the doorway struggled to his feet. I met his gaze, looked right into the black sunglasses, and then he, too, was gone.

"Laura!"

I whirled around and saw Mom and Iona hovering over Laura, who was sprawled on the stairs, her perfect hair splayed out around her head like a golden crown.

"She got hit with one of those blue lights," Mom said, cradling her head gently.

My heart hammered, and the room swayed.

"Still breathing, though…" Iona said, checking her pulse.

"That spell was meant to hit me," I said.

Lockwood turned around, his face sweating, his breathing heavy. He didn't sugarcoat it. "Yes, it was," he said.

"Then…" I licked my lips, "… If Laura is still breathing and caught the full brunt of it…they weren't trying to kill me?"

"I don't think so," Lockwood said.

"They were trying to take me alive," I muttered.

"I don't imagine they thought they were going to run into such a defense," Lockwood said. "To have two vampires and a Faerie in your arsenal is… Unusual, to say the least. For a human."

Mill dragged himself to a wall and leaned against it, face even paler than usual. There was a nasty green spot on his arm, and all the veins were starkly contrasted against his skin.

"I will attend to Mill," Lockwood said. "You should go to your father."

My heart leapt into my throat, but I didn't hesitate. Mill nodded; he'd be in good hands with Lockwood. And at least he was still conscious.

Laura might not have been, but at least she was breathing. Iona and Mom were watching her. I wasn't sure that Mom knew about Dad yet. Better take it one step at a time.

I walked across the cracked marble tiles of the foyer and back into the living room, feeling as if I were walking through some sort of twisted nightmare.

Dad lay at a weird angle, head lolling to the side.

No kid should ever have to see their parents this way.

Was he…?

I crept closer, seeking signs of life. The movement of his chest. A stir. Something.

Anything.

He couldn't be…

No.

He couldn't.

Chapter 13

If the house was a mess when we arrived, it was a hundred times worse after the fight with the witches and the wizard. There was bright red blood splattered all over the floor, and Lockwood was tending to a wound on his arm, his own silvery blood drenching his dress shirt.

I reached Dad in a sort of fog, numb from the fear that was threatening to engulf me. He had a nasty burn on his arm. That was where the spell had hit him.

"Dad…?" I asked, kneeling down beside him. My voice was trembling. "Dad, are you all right?"

He didn't stir.

I reached over and touched his hand. His skin felt cold beneath my sweating, shaking fingers. I hesitated but felt his wrist for a pulse. I fumbled, not sure where it was supposed to be—was it down by the hand, up on the forearm? I'd only ever seen this done on television, and the wrist was like its own territory. I clutched at it with clumsy fingers, feeling like an idiot child trying to play at adult things.

There.

It was there, faint and fluttering, but it was there, just on the side of his wrist beneath the tendons running down its middle. I sighed with relief.

"He's alive," I shouted out into the foyer. I sank back on my heels and almost laughed. "He's got a pulse."

It wasn't long before Mom came to join me. She was teary-eyed as she stared at Dad, brushing her hands over his face. I felt like I was intruding as Mom checked him over. It was very rare for me to see her so unhinged, her eyes blinking furiously, hands moving to his cheeks, drawing quick breaths. She was usually so composed, so cool... To see her flustered like this—

Well, I hadn't ever seen her quite like this. Then again, we'd never been attacked by vampires and witches... ever... before.

Lockwood appeared as I moved away from her. She'd settled slightly, holding my dad's cheeks between her hands, her forehead pressed to his, whispering something to him. Lockwood sidled up, pausing for a moment, indecision rattling across his features. "Mill is not doing well," he said after a moment.

My heart clenched. "What? Why?"

"He was hit with a nasty spell," Lockwood said. "A curse of some variety I'm not familiar with."

"Can you do anything about it?" I asked.

"Perhaps," he said. "I'll need to study it a bit more. But I wanted to see how your father was first." With a curt nod, he brushed past me and knelt down next to my dad. My mom moved out of the way, relinquishing her grip on him with a brief kiss to the forehead, letting Lockwood in closer. He forced a smile and then turned his attention to the spell-burn, touching it ever so gently. "I think he'll be all right," Lockwood said after a moment's consideration.

A breath I hadn't realized I was holding rushed out in relief, and I suddenly felt like all the blood had left my head, it felt so light.

"There is some damage here," Lockwood said, looking at the spell-burn again. "I will need to work on some sort of salve for him, and that may take some... consideration."

"Isn't this just...magic?" I asked. "Can't you just use a spell or something to fix it?"

"Faerie magic is not the same as human magic," Lockwood said. "They come from different worlds, and they do not mix well. Faerie magic is often a poor counter to this world's variety. They collide, and it creates unknown effects, as you saw. This will require some study so I can dress it accordingly."

"But you'll be able to help him?" I asked.

"Yes," Lockwood said. "I know what my spell was composed of, what sort of intentions I had." He opened Dad's eyelids and looked into his eyes. Give him a stethoscope and a white lab coat and he could have passed as a doctor. "I think I can manage to conjure up something that will help, but it will take some time."

"This is all madness," my mother said under her breath, brushing her hand over Dad's forehead. "Madness."

"Mom..." I said.

She gave me a hard look. "Look at what happened to your father. Are you happy now?"

Happy our house had burned down? That my friend had betrayed me? That I'd been dragged through the ringer in Faerie only to return to this knot of horror that had now resulted in a battle with spellcasters and the injury of my father? "That's not the word I'd pick for how I feel right now," I said, trying not to lash at her with all these feelings that were threatening to overwhelm my tiredness. "Could you check on Laura for me? Please."

She stared at me for a moment, her gaze hard, but slowly turned and made her way out of the living room without saying a word.

"Is she going to be all right?" Lockwood asked once she was out of earshot.

It was like a rope was tied around my heart, squeezing it. "I hope so. I've never seen her this... twisted up."

"She's been through quite a lot this evening," Lockwood said. "Between action and revelation. Do you mind if I go check on Mill?"

"No, that's fine," I said. All of the strength had left me, and I wasn't sure if I'd even be able to stand and follow after. At least Mill was conscious, which put him on a better footing than Laura or my dad. "You know what you're doing. And..." He looked at me as he rose to his feet. "Thank you, Lockwood."

He nodded, and a brief smile lit his face. "We will make it through the night, Cassandra. Stay strong, and all will be right before you know it."

"I'm beginning to think you're a bit more of an optimist about these things than I am, Lockwood," I said as he made his way across the living room. Mill was waiting, leaning against the archway, watching us both.

"I have faith in your ceaseless ability to navigate us through these troubles," Lockwood said, turning to smile at me once more.

"I wish I shared that belief," I said under my breath. He heard me, but hopefully no one else did. The last thing anyone else needed was to hear me doubt myself right now, after all.

"I'm fine," Mill said through gritted teeth as Lockwood approached.

My stomach did a somersault. He was leaning pretty heavily against the wall, a tight grimace formed on his lips. "Let me take a look," Lockwood said.

"How's Cassie?" he asked. I could hear him plainly. Even when he was in as much pain as he was, he still wondered about me.

"Uninjured," Lockwood said, giving me a sympathetic look as he started out of the room. "Which is more than I can say for you."

"Next time I'll duck," Mill said.

It felt like someone had thrown a smoke grenade inside my mind, a cloudy murk between my ears slowing my thoughts. There was danger, great danger, but it was distant and muted, out of sight. I just couldn't process it, not with my mind chunking along at quarter speed.

I grabbed a pillow from the couch and rested it underneath Dad's head, so that he didn't have a nasty kink in his neck when he woke up, though that would probably be the least of his problems. His face was pale, and I leaned over and took his glasses off. He wouldn't be happy if they got bent. I laid them down beside him and sighed, resting against the wall beside him.

"Please be all right," I whispered, watching him for some sign of movement. His chest moved up and down in a regular pattern. If he was in really bad shape, his breathing would be more unsteady, wouldn't it?

Magic. I wouldn't have the first clue if something was really, terribly wrong, would I? Even Dad, a doctor by trade, wouldn't necessarily know how to treat himself in this scenario. I rested my chin on my chest and folded my arms in front of me, staring dully at the living room floor.

Black boots clicked into my field of vision, jarring me to look up. Iona was looking around at the scorch marks from the spells on the previously pristine white walls, her thin arms wrapped around her. She had a thick furrow of concern across her brow. "Wow, they did more damage than I thought…" she said.

I sighed. "I know. I'm totally going to have call an interior decorator to fix this atrocity. But, y'know, tomorrow."

"You okay?" she asked, putting her back against the wall and sliding down beside me.

I noticed for the first time since seeing her that she had a little braid in her hair, so tiny that it was lost in the rest of the silvery blonde strands as she brushed it over her shoulders.

Was that because of me? "I'm fine," I said, but we both knew it wasn't the truth. I tried again. "My dad's been hurt, Laura and Mill were both hit…Draven's people found us and escaped, which means they know where we are." I frowned. "They were speaking German?"

Iona nodded. "I couldn't understand what they were saying, but I recognized a few words here and there. Definitely *Deutsche*."

Lockwood reappeared, face grim. His lips were pressed tightly together.

"What now?" I asked. My heart couldn't take much more of this.

He exhaled heavily through his nose. "I'm afraid Mill is taking a turn for the worse."

"I'm fine," Mill said from the archway to the foyer. His voice was tight, as though he were holding back pain.

"He is most certainly not fine," Lockwood said. "He is growing progressively paler."

"He's a vampire. We don't tan. How is getting paler even possible?" Iona asked.

Lockwood gave her a look, arching an eyebrow. "It's not just that. The spot where he was struck is not healing. Which for a vampire is...not good. Nor is it normal."

"It's fine," Mill said again. "It's magic, it'll just take a little longer to heal, that's all." I looked past Lockwood and Mill was...paler, somehow. His face looked like a full moon, almost aglow with whiteness.

"Those people were German sorcerer mercenaries," Lockwood said.

"'Sorcerer mercenaries' is a thing?" I asked. "There is still so much about this paranormal crap that I just *do not know*."

"If it makes you feel any better, you know more about Faerie than Mill and I combined now," Iona said.

"That's not nothing, I guess." I let out a quiet sigh. "So, mercenaries? German sorcerers for hire. Sounds kinda unwieldy. Do they have an official title or something?"

"Not that I know of," Lockwood said. "They are likely a coven that was hired for gold or a trinket in order to find you."

"What would sorcerers find valuable enough to work with Draven?" I asked.

"Anything that could enhance their magical abilities," Lockwood said. "Crystals, rare type of wood for their staffs, endangered frog spleen…things that would not be easy to come across for a person with little connection to the world."

I stuck my tongue out at the last one, wrinkling my nose. "'Endangered frog spleen'? Wouldn't that put them afoul of the U.S. Fish and Wildlife service?"

"I'm sure they're very worried about that," Iona said. "As they shoot magic everywhere."

"I don't understand how they found us," I said. "We picked a place that seemed completely improbable, and they found us in a night."

"They must have gotten a hold of your hair somehow," Iona said.

"What? How?" I looked up at Lockwood, my eyebrows wrinkled. "I thought hair magic was a Faerie thing."

"It is a magic thing," he said. "In general."

"Did your house burn down all the way?" Iona asked, staring into the distance as if thinking.

"No," I said. "A lot of it did, but it was still standing when we left."

"Then it's abandoned now?" she asked.

There was that familiar pit in my stomach. When everything sucked, something always had to come along and just make it worse. So much worse. "You're telling me that they went into my house, and what…found a hair on my pillow or something?"

Iona nodded. "Probably, yeah. That's how simple it is when it comes to magic." She made a face. "I hate wizards. Witches. Wiz-witches. Witchards?"

"So basically I need to start shaving my head?" I said.

"I wouldn't suggest that," Iona said. "It'd throw off the symmetry of your face. Like bangs. You really need to avoid bangs—there's a sweet spot for you, and it's without bangs, but with hair." She held her hands up in horizontal lines at my chin and the top of my forehead. "This…perfect. Any higher or lower…ugh."

"Gee, thanks," I said.

"I'm just trying to help," she said. "I wouldn't want you to make a bad hair decision. You're in high school, these things are still very important."

"I might be able to fool these magicians with a spell," Lockwood said, very clearly avoiding commenting on Iona's hair criticism. "But it is a very complicated incantation. Unfortunately, it will not do us any good until we leave this place, because they already know where we are now."

"I agree," Iona said. "It's best if we move quickly." She sniffed. "Someone was brewing terrible, terrible coffee here, and I can't get it out of my nose."

"How long do we have?" I asked, my heart starting to beat more quickly.

Lockwood hesitated. "As long as it takes for them to get back to Draven, wrangle up some help, and get back here. They will not be able to bring that assistance via magic, so… However long it takes to drive here."

I looked over at my dad. He was still unconscious. "How do we move them?" I asked.

"Carefully," Lockwood said, moving toward Mill. Iona rose beside me, crouching over my dad. She lifted him easily, cradling his head and taking up the slack as she lifted it off the pillow. I followed after her as she carried him through the archway as Lockwood took up Mill's weight with an arm slung under my boyfriend's chest.

"Laura," I said as I passed through the archway into the foyer. She was stirring, my mother leaning over her. I started up the steps. "Are you all right?"

Laura was holding her head, and one of her eyes was squeezed shut, her nose wrinkling. "Yeah…" she murmured.

"I'm really sorry," I said before I could even think. "It's my fault. You shouldn't have had to—"

"It's all right, Cassie," she said with a weak smile. "Really. I'm okay."

It didn't make me feel any better.

"Cassie…" Mill said, with Lockwood's arm wrapped around him. They looked like bros helping each other walk after a night of drinking, and I felt a twinge of guilt.

Could they all just not be like this for a second? Could I not have a second to try and wrap my mind around everything that was going on?

"What?" I asked as I helped Laura to her feet. Mom waited at her other arm, but Laura took up her own weight easily, if a little gingerly, leaning on the banister. She gave me a nod, and I started down ahead of her, my mom giving her a hand as she took her time.

Lockwood held tight to Mill, pivoting him around. His sleeve had been cut away from his arm, exposing a sickly coppery spot just above his elbow. Veins stood out on his waxy biceps, fluorescent green traces moving under the skin.

I stared. "What... What the hell is that?"

Lockwood's face was frozen, strained. He glanced at the wound, but only once; he already knew what he was seeing, there was no need to study it further.

Mill's face was beyond white as a sheet, waxy and taut. He was almost transparent. His eyes were glassy as he looked up at me, head lolling gently. "I think we have another problem…" he mumbled.

And then he, too, slumped over, Lockwood catching him as he went limp in the driver's arms.

Chapter 14

What were we going to do? There was no obvious way out. I felt like a rat trapped in a maze, looking for the cheese. Except the scientists controlling the whole experiment never bothered to put any in for me, and so I was going to spend eternity running in circles, never finding what I was looking for.

It was a dark prospect, and at a time when all I wanted to do was curl into a ball and never move again.

Dad was unconscious in Iona's arms. Mill was conked out in Lockwood's. Laura had just regained consciousness, but she was almost as pale as Mill, and was holding her head between her hands as if trying to ward off a migraine. She probably was.

"What happened to him?" I asked Lockwood.

"It is difficult to say," he started, and then shook his head. "It looks as if he has been poisoned, yet—"

"I think this is what a witch's nightshade spell looks like when it takes effect," Iona said, cradling my father like a baby and peering down at Mill's arm where he hung limp against Lockwood. "Harmless to anything but vampires, but when it hits them, well…" She glanced up from the wound. "It looks like this."

"Is he going to be okay?" I asked. I was desperate for someone, anyone, to give me an answer.

Lockwood gave Mill a few gentle pats to the face. "Come on, wake up." His tone was quiet. The strain in his voice made me that much more nervous.

Mill's eyes tightened, and when they opened, he blinked a few times.

I sank to my knees. "Oh, thank God."

"Can you hear me?" Lockwood asked, his eyes scanning Mill's face.

"Yeah…" he said. "But based on how you asked... I'm guessing I look as bad as I feel."

"You always look bad to me, forehead," Iona said. "You're currently still in the range of ugly to my eyes, so you're probably fine."

"Thank you... So much," Mill said, barely able to focus on her.

I crossed over to him, and he winced as he tried to push himself back up into a sitting position. With Lockwood's help, we got him upright again.

"Don't scare me like that," I said, putting my forehead against his.

"It's going to take more than that to keep me away from you," he said, just barely above a whisper.

I was glad that Mom was up the stairs and didn't hear. My cheeks burned, but I smiled at him. "You're delirious."

"Yeah, and really bad at quoting songs," Iona said. "Africa? Really? Out of all the ones you could have picked?" Mill chuckled, and it turned into a fit of coughing.

"We have to get out of here before the witches get back," I said. "We can't take them again, not with three of us down."

"Especially one of our best fighters," Iona said. "Yes, forehead, I'm talking about you. I can occasionally say nice things. When I feel like it." Mill just shook his head.

"We need to move." I looked at Lockwood. "Can you conjure us up a magic carpet or something? Because if they're coming in cars, we need some way to evade."

"I can't really do that, no," Lockwood said.

"The longer we stay here, the more likely we are to be discovered by the police, and I need time to make a compelling argument for—" Mom said.

"I am concerned about this spell," Lockwood said. "I don't know how to cure it. As I said, the magic that witch was using is very different to faerie magic—"

"Lana is going to need time to recover from her stunning—" Iona started.

"It's *Laura*," Laura said. "Is it really that hard to remember?"

"Laura, yes, whatever," Iona said. "The blonde girl, okay? She's injured."

"Obviously," I said. "And my dad needs attention too, at some point."

"I can only do so many things at once," Lockwood said. He was dabbing some sort of purple goop onto Mill's wound. Presumably a faerie healing ointment. Or maybe repurposed hair gel for all I knew.

I felt like there was a clock ticking in my head. Every second we wasted in this house meant it was going to be that much harder to get away undetected.

"I don't care what we need to do," I said. "We just have to move. Now."

"Where are we going?" Iona asked. "Everyone here has been driven out of their homes except Lockwood."

"I am very likely in that camp now, too," he said, screwing the lid on the jar of purple goop. It disappeared in his fingers as though he were performing a magician's trick. "The sorcerers will have told Lord Draven I'm involved. I'm afraid we can't go to my house, either."

"So where to?" Iona asked.

I was frozen in place, my hand on Mill's cool, room-temperature skin. I stroked his forearm with one finger while I thought. There had to be something. A piece of the puzzle we hadn't seen yet.

Fear was threatening to overwhelm me. I didn't let myself look sad. I didn't let myself look down at Mill. I just sat there. I had to keep my mind working. Mill, Iona, and Lockwood spoke in low breaths, and I ignored them as I tried to think.

There had to be somewhere else we could go. Someone else we knew that could help us.

Gregory's house was off limits. They'd probably be watching the ruins of my place. The same with Laura's.

Mill's condo, Iona's place, Lockwood's... they were all off limits.

Byron's house was now no longer safe.

Who did I know that could still help?

I snapped my fingers, almost ready to kick myself for not thinking of it earlier. Duh. Everyone looked at me, attention drawn by the sudden snap. "I know where to go," I said. And I smiled.

Chapter 15

"Um…what the hell is this? You threw a crazy party and didn't invite me?"

Xandra was staring out onto the front porch of her house, blue hair up in a messy bun on top of her head, exposing the purple she had recently added just above the nape of her neck. She was wearing a baggy, oversized blue sweatshirt with the Florida Gators logo on it, and a pair of track shorts. Her eyes were puffy, and there were creases on her cheeks from her pillowcase.

I sort of grinned at her, doing my best to support Laura, Mom holding up her other side.

Xandra blinked at me. "Cassie, it's…" she rubbed her hands over her face. "It's two in the morning."

"I know," I said, just above a whisper. No reason to wake the neighbors, after all.

The street was quiet aside from the occasional car driving by and the buzzing of the tall power lines over the road. The houses on either side of Xandra's were dark, their occupants likely asleep.

We must have looked crazy, the seven of us crowded on the narrow porch of Xandra's little bungalow. I was covered in blood from my fight with the witch, and Dad was still unconscious. Lockwood was supporting Mill and muttering under his breath. Iona was carrying Dad, because she'd thrown a fit before we left Byron's about how she didn't want to carry Mill, complaining he was too heavy thanks to the weight of his extra-sized forehead.

Xandra stepped out onto the porch in her bare feet and closed the door behind herself.

"Okay, so what's going on here?" She stared at us all. "Is that Laura?"

Laura lifted her head and smiled weakly at Xandra. "Hey."

Xandra shook her head. "What happened to you people?"

"The usual," I said, struggling under Laura's weight. She wasn't really heavy, but I was tired. Really tired. "I'll tell you everything, but we need to get inside first. Xandra, please. We literally have nowhere else to go."

"Why aren't you at your own house?"

I sighed, trying to keep my temper in check. It had been a really long night already. "It got burned."

"What?" she asked. Her eyes widened. "I saw fire trucks go by, cop cars and everything, all heading in your direction…"

"Yeah, that was for us," I said.

"Holy crap…" she said. "I had no idea."

"Yeah, well, can we please come in?" I asked, a bite to my words.

The door opened behind Xandra, and her dad was standing there. He was a tall man with broad shoulders, a balding head and glasses. His blue eyes widened as he took us all in with a glance. "I thought I heard voices. What's going on here?" He caught sight of me, and I smiled feebly up at him. "Cassie? What are you doing here in the middle of the night? Is that blood on your shirt?"

"A little bit," I said.

"Come inside," he said, standing aside and throwing the door wide. "Looks like you guys have been through the ringer."

We stepped over the threshold into Xandra's home. The table by the door was littered with bills and keys. Coats and sweatshirts, way too many for Floridians in this mild climate, hung on the row of hooks just inside the door. Cardboard boxes littered one wall of the living room, a partially finished television stand stood in one corner.

"Sorry about the mess," her had said.

Iona pulled Dad through the entryway, tracing a path over

to set him in Mr. Stewart's recliner. One good grunt and she lifted him like a child, laying him back with a hearty shove to push the seat back.

"This fellow is mighty pale," Mr. Stewart said, following Lockwood as he placed Mill on the sofa. Mr. Steward threw a red and black plaid Christmas blanket over him. "What happened to these two?"

"It's a long story," I said.

Mom stepped out of the crowd and over to Xandra's Dad. "Hi, I'm Mrs. Howell, Cassandra's mother." She held out her hand to him.

"Paul Stewart," he said, taking it. "Guess we haven't met formally, have we?"

"No," Mom said. Her lawyer face was back. "Thank you for allowing us to come into your home. Ours was set on fire by some... crazy person," she gave me a significant look, "earlier this evening."

"That's terrible," he said. "Are these two suffering from smoke inhalation? Should we get them to a hospital?"

"No hospital," Iona said. "There's not a doctor in the world that can fix what ails him." She nodded at Mill. "Maybe a plastic surgeon. Have they figured out how to do a—"

"Will you just lay off making fun of my forehead?" Mill asked, letting out the cranky. "It's not like I have control over it. It's an immutable characteristic. Like the size of that stick up your ass."

Mr. Stewart looked back and forth between the two of them, apparently unsure what to make of them. "Sorry... you said a crazy person burned your house down?"

"Why don't we go in the kitchen?" Xandra whispered into my ear. She was standing at my shoulder, the one that I wasn't using to steady Laura.

"Good thinking," I said, sparing a glance behind me as Mom eased closer to Mr. Stewart to talk.

"Were all of these people staying with you?" I heard him ask her.

"Yes," Mom said. "They're visiting from out of state."

I glanced at her over my shoulder as I left the room, arching an eyebrow. Did she just? Yeah, she did. She lied right to Mr.

Stewart's face. She spared me a brief glance, but all I saw was a flicker of embarrassment before she turned her attention back to him.

I helped Laura into a chair in the quiet kitchen. Xandra sunk down into the chair opposite her. Iona slipped into the room behind us, graceful as a ballerina, taking her own seat.

"Where's Lockwood?" I asked, taking the last seat at the circular table.

Iona pointed through the opening to the living room. I could just barely see the left side of Lockwood. He was standing in the corner, facing the wall, head bowed, and it looked like he was…chanting or something.

He'd been doing it the whole way here in Laura's car while I drove, Iona following behind me. I figured he was doing something to help protect us, but I wasn't sure. He didn't answer when I asked him. He just kept muttering.

"Okay so…what the hell?" Xandra asked.

"I'll keep it simple," I said. "Draven found out about me and burned down my house."

"It was him?" she said. "Like, actually him?"

"Not exactly. He sent in a group of vamps to do it, one of them being that former bestie of mine from New York that was turned into a vampire because of my trip up there a few weeks ago." I puckered my lips. "So… Y'know… You don't have a high bar to clear in the best-ever best friend department anymore."

Xandra pinched the bridge of her nose. "That's good to know. I like to think I can live up to modest expectations. Now… What was all that?"

"So," I said, "they came to the house, set it on fire, then we ran to Byron's to hide—"

"'Byron's?' she asked. "As in *the* Byron? He of the stalker fame?"

"Yeah, that guy. Anyway, some sorcerers showed up—"

"Sorcerers?" she asked. "There are sorcerers now?"

"Is this a bad time to tell that you Faeries are real?" I asked. "And that Lockwood is one?"

Xandra's mouth fell open.

"The sorcerers were sent after me by Draven," I said. "We

needed a place to lay low. We chose you… Because you're the only one left they don't know about."

"Are we safe here?" Xandra asked.

It was a good question, and I looked at Iona for the answer.

"As long as Lockwood keeps up whatever he's doing," she said.

"Wow…" Xandra said. "So, it's full Godfather, all the scores are being settled, huh?"

"Something like that," I said with a heavy sigh.

"What about Mill? And your dad?" Xandra asked.

"The sorcerers hit them," I said, rubbing my eyes. "With spells."

"Are they okay?" Xandra asked.

"Dad is, according to Lockwood," I said. "Mill was poisoned somehow."

"And her?" Xandra said, jutting her chin in Laura's direction. I knew that Xandra really didn't care for Laura, being pretty much the most popular girl in our year. But still.

"I'm all right," Laura said, rubbing her neck. She seemed better. She still looked exhausted, though. It was the first time since I'd known her that she looked at all disheveled.

"So we're on a time limit," Xandra said. "Between the poisoning and this Draven coming after you."

"Xandra… I don't want you to get involved," I said. "We just need a place to lay low."

"You got me involved when you showed up on my doorstep," she said.

"Draven is not going to stop," Iona said, folding her arms across her chest. "He is relentless, and he has a grudge to settle, an axe to grind. And he's going to grind it on Cassie's face. Jacquelyn, too. She doesn't seem the forgiving type."

Xandra gave me a look.

"Former holder of the 'bestie' office," I said. "Fighting Draven and the sorcerers doesn't seem like a great idea. What about running? Maybe leaving the country?"

Iona shook her head.

"Come on, there has to be something, like a vampire witness protection program, right?" I asked.

She kept shaking her head.

"Well, I don't hear you giving me any suggestions," I said, glaring daggers at her.

"No," Iona said. "You could never run far enough to escape them."

"What do you mean?" I asked. "He's the vampire Lord of Tampa. We go to Miami, it's a different Lord's territory. Why can't we just run outside his reach?"

"Because vampire Lords watch their territories jealously, always looking for trouble coming," she said, her gaze darkening. "It's not like you did something small, Cassie. You're a human, and you've been slaying vampires. Whether or not you believe it, you've drawn a lot of attention, and made yourself a threat to every vampire Lord the world over. When vampires have a common enemy, they help each other out. The safety of the vampire community is more important than petty differences when it comes to situations like this."

The skin on my arms popped out in goosebumps. I shifted uncomfortably in my seat.

"They have eyes and ears in every corner of the world," Iona said. "They are not above using governments or technology like facial recognition in order to find you. And they will find you."

"Seriously?" I asked.

"Seriously."

"So even if we were to run to Canada—" I said.

"Draven has you on the vampire equivalent of a *Most Wanted* list right now, Cassie. Any area you venture to, the vampire Lord there will be looking for you. You know how easy it is to miss a vampire as you pass them on the street. But they won't miss you, the vampire slayer who's been making waves. Word will get back to their masters, and Draven will be made aware of you so quickly that you won't be able to do a thing to respond."

"Even in the middle of nowhere, like, New Zealand?" I asked, desperate for any kind of hope.

"There are definitely vampires in New Zealand," Xandra said. "Didn't you see *What We Do In The Shadows?*"

"You make them sound like the boogeyman." I sighed and laid my head on the dining room table. The wood was cool

91

beneath my forehead, and I took a deep, steadying breath. "We can't run, and we can't fight. We can't just hide here forever. So what do we do?" I was asking anyone who would listen, but I was almost hoping that the table would give me some sort of magical inspiration.

I sat up. Magic.

"Faerie," I said. "We can cross over to Faerie. It's—"

"No."

I turned at the sound of Lockwood's voice. He was still staring at the wall. But he had a hand in the air, waving it around to get my attention while still trying to concentrate on what he was doing.

"O…kay," I said. "I guess that option's out."

"Faerie is not very friendly to vampires," Iona said.

"I guess," I said. "I vaguely recall Lockwood saying something about that. Plus, I guess a decent portion of Faerie is mad at me right now, so..." I sighed. "If Lockwood says it's not an option, it's not an option." Lockwood gave me a thumbs up when I glanced at him.

"Wait, Faerie?" Xandra asked. "Like… A world of faeries?"

I looked at Xandra, desperate now. "What?" she asked.

"I'm exhausted," I said, all my vitality sapped. "We all are. We need a fresh brain."

"You're a zombie now?" Xandra asked. "Kidding, but... I have no idea what to do. This whole world of magic and vampires and faeries? It's so weird to me. I don't have a clue what to do."

Iona was scratching her chin, staring at a knot in the wooden table.

"What are you thinking?" I asked her.

Her eyes narrowed in concentration. "I might… I don't know."

"What?" I said. "Iona... we are at the end of the road, okay? We can't run, we can't fight with who we have available now. Mill's injured, Lockwood is going to be chanting into perpetuity to keep these sorcerers off of us, which means if we have trouble, you and I are going to be fighting off Draven's minions all by our lonesome. The only thing we've got going for us is that they don't know where to look, and eventually Lockwood is going to have to stop chanting and go to sleep. We need something. Help. A chance. So if you have any ideas...any at all...please." I set my chin. "Now's the time."

She looked up at me, her sad eyes pensive. "Even if it's a crazy idea? So crazy that it barely makes sense to contemplate it?"

I sagged. "I think crazy might be all we have left."

She nodded slowly. "Well...if we're down to crazy... I might know someone—just a little crazy—who could help us."

Chapter 16

Iona and I left just before dawn, the air filled with cool night moisture. We drove along in her car, following the coast, heading south along the interstate, roads empty save for the truckers that took advantage of the lack of crowding at four in the morning.

Leaving had been tough, if quiet, appropriate to the hour. I had hated leaving Mill, but he had insisted that I go. Dad had seemed to be regaining color, and Laura had passed out on the table in the kitchen, sleeping peacefully, hair pooled around her and her shoulders covered with a blanket Mr. Stewart had put on her as he passed through. I'd told Xandra to keep an eye on her. Lockwood had kept up his steady chanting in the corner, only nodding when I asked if I would be okay if I left.

The steady thrum of the engine threatened to put me to sleep as the miles passed. It felt like we had been going for hours, my sleep-addled brain dragging with every minute that I stayed awake. I would look at the clock, then have to look again seconds later, unable to remember the time even though I'd just stared at it hard enough to commit it to memory.

We pulled off the highway at the exit for one of the gulf coast beaches, our smooth highway cruise at an end. Iona dialed back the speed accordingly, and suddenly we got stuck at nearly every red light, which was roughly every quarter mile. Iona screeched to a stop at every single one, riding the brakes rather than tearing through a yellow light at top speed the way my mom would.

"You know, I never had you pegged for a Volkswagen Beetle kind of girl," I said. "Or for being a grandma driver."

"Well, I am old enough to be your grandmother." Iona gave me a sidelong look with the slightest hint of a smirk.

"Where are we going?" I asked her for the tenth time. "Why are we in Sarasota?"

She kept silent as we turned right at the next stop light, onto another three-lane road.

Sarasota County was what I always imagined Florida to be like. Beautiful palm trees in every yard, perfectly manicured landscapes at every business and in every median, every one of which looked brand new. Even in the dark, this place looked like it was made of money.

"There are people here that I think might be the only ones who would even consider getting involved in our… issue," Iona said. "You have to understand. Vampire Lords are dangerous. No one wants to be within ten feet of someone who has a target painted on their back. The potential to get hit by splash damage is high."

"That didn't stop you or Mill," I said.

She chewed on her lip. "Look, I chose to help you with Byron. And because of my decision to help, you got mixed up with Draven, so… You can almost say that this whole thing is my fault."

I stared at her. "You think this is your fault?" I barked a laugh. "Iona, you weren't the one who told me to shove a stake into Theo's chest."

"Yes, but I was the one who gave you the stake in the first place, wasn't I?" Her eyes were so sad, morose to a level she didn't typically inhabit.

"If you hadn't, I'd be dead," I said.

"And that would have been my fault, too," she said.

I shifted in the seat to look at her more closely. "Iona, I don't blame you for what's happening to me."

"Yeah, well…" she said, her brow furrowing, and she tossed her silvery blonde hair over her shoulder. I caught sight of the tiny braid again. "I do. So does Mill, for that matter."

My cheeks burned. "I don't think Mill believes that."

"He's not stupid, Cassie," Iona said. "He can draw the line

between me sending you to that party and all the consequences that have come out of it. If I hadn't put you into that situation, none of this would have happened."

"But I wouldn't have met him," I said. "And I'd probably have been eaten by Byron. I might even be part of Draven's little community at this point, if Byron had turned me."

She seemed to think about that for a moment, then shook her head slowly. "I don't believe you would have. I think you would have found another way out. You're resourceful that way."

I stared ahead, the bright red of the tail lights in front of us making the inside of the car glow crimson as we slowed to a stop. There were more cars on the road now, people heading to their early shifts at factories or hospitals. A horn honked in the distance, and the dull, growing thrum of the engine picked up as Iona accelerated when the light turned green.

"I don't know about that," I said.

Iona didn't reply. She flipped on her turn signal, and suddenly we had rolled into a totally different neighborhood.

All of the houses were... different. And yet, familiar at the same time. Like little cottages, they all looked the same as the one sitting beside it. White siding, little brick chimneys poking out of the roof. The street was darker than the rest of Sarasota had been...almost as if they didn't use electricity—

"Is this an Amish community?" I asked.

Iona, who was leaning forward in her seat, straining to peer out of the windshield into the darkness, gave me a quick look. "Yes," she said.

"What are we doing in an Amish community?" I asked.

"It's hard to explain," she said.

We turned into a small, narrow driveway halfway down the street. There was light inside the house, a warm yellow that flickered against closed blinds. I glanced at the clock on the dashboard. It wasn't even five a.m. yet.

Iona brought us to a stop and killed the engine, then opened the door, sliding out of the car as gracefully as if she were dancing.

A slight pang of jealousy welled in me as I scrambled out after her, bumping my head as I got up. I rubbed my head as

I followed her up the small flagstone path that led around the back of the house. The air was warm, even for the early morning. I'd been told that Florida weather was like that, especially the closer we got to summer. Thankfully it was still bearable, despite the sweat beading on my back.

There were three bikes parked next to the small covered front porch, but I had never seen bikes quite like these before. They all had three wheels, like a grown-up tricycle, and there was a small metal basket soldered between the two back wheels. As I glanced up and down the street, I saw them parked in front of every house. What, had they replaced their horse and buggy with those?

I also hadn't ever seen the Amish living so closely together. Where I was from, there were acres and acres of land in between the houses in Amish communities, even if they all did live in the same general area. There were no barns here that I could see, nothing to suggest any farming was going on.

So...what were they doing here?

"Iona," I hissed into the darkness, hoping to not trip on the darkened path. "Where are you going?"

She didn't answer. I watched her silvery blonde hair flow in the breeze as she stepped around the corner of the house. I groaned and hurried to keep up with her.

The backyard was small. There was a tiny porch out back, with a few of those Adirondack chairs that seemed to be all the rage. There was a clothesline in the yard next door, white, black, and blue clothing drifting in the wind. A small pink dress dancing gently in the breeze provided the only color contrast.

There were no fences separating the yards. In the middle of the one we were crossing was a small shed with a wire-mesh screen on the front. A chicken coop, I realized, as I heard some of the hens clucking, their wings fluttering as we approached. A small battery powered lantern hung on the porch, light filtering out into the lawn. Standing there in the back yard, silhouetted against its light, three people were staring at us.

One was a tall, broad shouldered man who looked like he worked hard every day of his life. His large belly overhung his belt, and rounded biceps bigger than my head spurred to mind what a lumberjack's arms would probably look like. He wore a black brimmed hat, and I could see red tufts of hair leaking out from beneath the hat that matched his long, coppery beard. No mustache, though. As was the Amish way.

Two women were huddled at the chicken coop, both with wicker baskets in their hands. One wore a pale blue dress and a white bonnet, the other a dress of cobalt blue. They were staring at us with wide eyes.

That was it. Iona had finally lost her mind. Or I was hallucinating from the exhaustion. One of the two.

The coppery haired man was giving Iona a wary look, but he didn't say anything. Did they know each other? Why wouldn't they be freaking out about two strange girls showing up at their house at four in the morning?

What had happened to my life? Here I was, standing in some sort of Amish backyard, with a vampire no less, looking for someone to help us deal with some crazy sorcerers determined to kill everyone I cared about. Oh, and my house had burned down last night, the second one to do so in the last couple months.

Was I losing my mind? None of this made sense, and none of it was normal.

And yet somehow it all made perfect sense. Someone could have written a screenplay about my life and it would have come off as the schizophrenic rantings of a madwoman. It would be a blockbuster—if anyone could follow the crazy turn of events from compulsive lying to vampires to Faerie to an Amish neighborhood in Sarasota, Florida.

What was happening to my life?

The women stood up straight, looking to the man for some sort of signal. The back door to the house opened, and a boy no older than me stepped out. "Father, I was wondering. Did we—"

He faltered as he followed his father's gaze.

The boy was a chip off the old block. He had ginger hair as well, but his lack of a beard told me he was not of marriageable age yet. His time probably wasn't far off. He staggered to a halt beside his dad, only a half a head shorter than the big man.

They even folded their arms the same way as they stared at us.

"What do you want?" The man's voice had some sort of northern accent. I had heard it before. Pennsylvania Dutch. My mom had loved going down to Southern Pennsylvania to all the Amish communities there. Her favorite things were the quilts. She'd buy them and give them away as Christmas gifts every year.

Iona took a step closer, and while none of the Amish moved, the hesitance was clear in their expressions. I was impressed, though, that none of them stepped away. They were standing their ground.

"Greetings, Elder Obadiah," Iona said, more formally than I had expected. "I know it's been a while since you've seen me."

"Not long enough," he said. His voice was deep, gruff, almost a growl. Did he know what she was? Like, really was?

Iona gave him a toothy smile. She really was pretty when she tried. Not for the first time, I could see why Byron had picked her. I was a little less clear on why he'd picked me.

"Who is this?" Elder Obadiah asked, nodding his head in my direction.

Iona's eyes flashed as she looked at me. "Her name is Cassie. She's my friend, and the reason why I'm here. Cassie, this is Elder Obadiah. An old friend."

He grunted, his eyes narrowing further. *Friend* was obviously not a term he would have chosen.

"Father, who is this?" the boy beside Elder Neckbeard asked.

Obadiah rolled his shoulders menacingly, muscles rippling, as he looked down at his son. "Her name is Iona. And if you can't smell it already, son, Lord help you, but she's a vampire."

I blanched. Um...'smell it'? Vampirism had a smell? I sniffed, but couldn't catch a scent of anything but the chicken coop.

The boy's eyes widened, leaning away, then turned his gaze on me. He stuck his nose in the air, sniffing.

"She's not a vampire," Iona said.

"I knew that," Obadiah said in a gravelly voice.

"This is your son?" Iona asked. "Didn't know you had any

children."

Obadiah looked down at his son, whose blue eyes grew wide. "This here is Jedediah," he said. His face hardened. "Let me ask you again, Nightwalker. What brings you here to our door?"

Iona's shoes scraped in the gravel as she took a step back to stand beside me. "There have been some interesting things going on that I thought might be of concern to you."

Obadiah's face remained blank. "Such as?"

Iona's eyes flashed. "Did you know that there are German sorcerers operating out of Tampa?"

A hush fell over the yard. Even the clucking hens fell silent. There was a splatter as one of the eggs fell out of the hand of one of the women standing at the coop.

Obadiah suddenly reminded me of a bull ready to charge. His eyes flashed dangerously as he stared down at us. His mouth became a hard line, and his eyebrows knit together. Like a boiling teapot, he was ready to burst.

"That is a true shame," he said. "An affront to our Lord, certainly...but I don't believe this is my problem."

The women standing near the coop stared up at Obadiah with large eyes, faces pale in the lamp light. Even Jedediah seemed shocked, his brow one thick line as he watched his father for direction. Obadiah, for his part, was like a wall, unmoving. He showed no more reaction, nor a hint of offering more commentary than he'd already given.

Iona slid her hands into the pockets of her jacket and shrugged. "Oh, well. Sorry to bother you, then. I thought that affronts to God were your business. My apologies. We'll leave you be."

She turned away and gently grabbed my elbow, turning me around too, and she started leading me back toward the flagstone path around the house.

"Just like that, we're leaving?" I whispered.

She shushed me.

"Oh, for the love of Abraham..." Obadiah said.

Iona stopped, the grass crunching beneath our feet.

And there he was, suddenly in front of us. He moved almost as quickly as Mill or Iona.

Iona allowed him to stop us, and when I looked over at her, I saw the ghost of a smug grin on her face. She'd wanted this to happen. She had banked on his reaction.

"I am not pleased at being perceived as some sort of disposer of your problems, Nightwalker," he said, his tone dark.

"Hey, if you don't think that German sorcerer mercenaries in the Bay area is your problem, then whatever." She shrugged airily. "We can leave."

"I want to know everything," he said. "And don't toy with words. I'll know if you are lying."

Iona grinned, showing her fangs, but she obliged. She told him pretty much everything, from my encounter with Byron which led to Draven, and then all of the events of the night that led us to their backyard.

Obadiah listened throughout. It was obvious by his glower that he did not like any part of the conversation. But he stood there patiently for nearly a quarter of an hour as Iona spoke right to the heart of things.

"I won't sugar coat it," Iona said. "This would definitely be helping me. And Cassie here. I know that magic being used in your territory is the sort of thing that you won't stand for. I'm not trying to pull the wool over your eyes. I'm genuinely just asking for your help. Think of it as us working together, helping one another, not just you taking care of my problems." She laughed. "Besides. You're still listening, even though my very existence is an affront to God."

Obadiah glared. "You are protected under our peace with Draven."

'Peace with Draven'? What was I missing? What were these Amish, and how were they related to the vampires of Tampa?

Obadiah let out a sigh, and turned to look at his son, who was still at the back door. He was listening to everything that was being said, his eyes wide with curiosity.

"Jed? Go with these two. Find out where this is all happening, and then call the store and leave a message when you're done." He turned back to Iona. "We can get a few people out there in case these sorcerers come back before dawn."

This was all just so weird. Iona talking about God, this big burly Amish man sending his son with us, talking about sending more of them?

Who were these people?

Young Jedediah's face lit up and he dashed back into the house, moving just as eerily fast as his dad.

Obadiah turned back to us. "I'll help you and your friend. Our interests seem to line up here, and yes, it is my responsibility to deal with matters of the occult."

"Even though it is really wounding your pride, isn't it?" Iona dug the knife in. "Stooping so low as to help a vampire like me?" Her grin widened.

"I would much rather avoid you lot all together," he said.

So not a vampire. Then…

Jed reappeared with his wide grin firmly in place, a pack thrown over his shoulder.

"You've got a change of clothes?" Elder Neckbeard asked him. Jed nodded. "Good lad. Keep calm. Don't make a fool of yourself."

"I won't," Jed said, his smile growing.

"And you," he said to Iona. "I swear to you that I will rip your unholy accursedness to shreds if you let anything happen to my boy." He was serious. Those words were awfully menacing coming from a pacifist. He must not have regarded vampires as people.

"I'd rather you not use those claws, either," Iona said.

Claws?

"Wait a second…" I said.

"What?" Iona gave me a small smirk, arching a brow. "Did I forget to tell you that they're werewolves?"

Werewolves.

I blinked at her a few times.

Amish werewolves.

Because of course they were.

"Let's hit the road," Iona said, still smiling as Jedediah jumped off the porch to join us. "We've got a ways to go before daylight.

Chapter 17

The ride back to Xandra's felt twice as long as the way down, which was saying something, because the trip to werewolf Amish country had seemed to take forever to my sleep-fogged brain.

Werewolves. I kept repeating the word over in over in my mind. All I could think of were the stories I'd heard as a kid, about the twisted men whose souls were beast-like, filled with torment and uncontrollable. I'd always imagined angst, fury, howling at the moon madness and moodiness.

Never in a million years would I have imagined the scrawny teenage Amish boy with messy red hair who was grinning at the two of us through the rearview mirror.

"I've never met a vampire before. Is it true that you'll burn in the sunlight?" Jedediah asked, not even waiting for an answer before launching another question. "Is it true that you can only drink the blood of humans to survive? How old are you? Did you become a vampire by choice?"

The look on Iona's face told me she was clearly starting to regret her decision to ask for the werewolves help, or at least Elder Neckbeard's decision to send his son along with us. "This is his revenge for me asking for his help," she muttered. "I should have known he'd never let me get the better of him without reprisal."

"Aren't the Amish supposed to be Godly and forgiving and turn-the-other-cheek?" I asked, also keeping my voice low as Jedediah bombarded her with an unending barrage of questions from behind us.

"Those rules only apply to humans," Iona said. "I'm a devil to them, and clearly he has no problem inflicting vengeance on me."

"So, is it true that werewolves can only transform at the full moon?" I asked, trying to spare Iona and turn the tables. She shot me a look of sweet gratitude as Jed shut up for a second and turned his attention to me.

He shook his head, nearly sending his black hat flying. He readjusted it quickly. "No, not at all. We can turn whenever we want, but it's devilishly uncomfortable." He twitched slightly, and I realized that he reminded me of a happy puppy. If he had a tail under those Amish pants, it would surely be wagging, and his tongue would be lolling out of his mouth if it were long enough.

"How long do you stay a werewolf? After you change?" I asked.

He shrugged. "As long as I want."

"And you are fully aware the whole time?"

"Oh, yeah," he said, a musical lilt to his words. "Definitely. That's the best part, honestly. I love when I get to turn into a wolf. At least when it's not the full moon. That time of month we all go completely mad."

"There's a catch to everything, huh?" I said. I sank back against the seat, shaking my head. "Man. First fae, then witches and wizards, now werewolves. What kind of crazy night is this?"

"It's not over yet," Iona said in a low voice, gripping the steering wheel.

We made it back into town about half past five. The city was starting to wake up. More cars streamed by us, and the lights were busier once we got off the interstate.

"I've never been to Tampa before," Jed said, staring out at the window in wonder. "It's bigger than I expected."

I shared a look with Iona. He really was like a puppy. I kinda wanted to keep him.

Xandra's house was quiet when we pulled into the driveway. The lights were on inside, but even as we came in the front door, I could sense a sort of exhaustion hanging over the place. Xandra appeared from the living room, a wan and weary look on her face.

"You're back," she said with a smile. "Good. I—" she hesitated, her eyes falling on Jed. "Uh. Who's the Amish kid?"

"Werewolf," I said, strangely satisfied to see the confusion register on her face just like had for me.

She blinked a couple times. "An Amish werewolf? Where'd you find him? An Amish animal shelter?"

"Haha," I said.

Xandra didn't stop. "Like you've seen one too many of those SPCA commercials and couldn't help yourself?" Xandra said. "Did you hear the stirrings of Sarah McLachlan's "Angel" playing as you stared into his sad eyes?"

"I do not have sad eyes," Jed said, a little honked off.

"Listen, we don't have a lot of options," Iona said, closing the door behind her. "Or time."

"Anything happen while I was gone?" I asked, walking farther inside.

"Nothing as noteworthy as your pet adoption," she said. "Mom left a little while ago. She always goes in really early so she can make her noodles from scratch, and also give them time to rest. Dad's getting ready for work."

"Yes, definitely tell me about the two people who were in the least bad shape first," I said. "What about my parents? And everyone else?"

She nodded toward the living room, and I made my way past her without a word.

Mom was passed out on the couch, as close to Dad as she could be. Dad's color had returned, and his breathing was easy. He looked almost back to normal.

"Don't wake them," Xandra whispered. "Your mom just fell asleep a little while ago. Popped a Xanax, I think. Said something about dealing with the regret later. She decided she needed to after your dad woke up."

"He did?" I asked. "Why didn't you say so sooner?"

"You sort of surprised me with the Amish werewolf, but yeah, your dad seems to be okay. Complained about a headache. He was awake long enough for your mom to get some hot bone broth in him before he needed to sleep again.

I guess getting hit by magic is exhausting," Xandra said.

"I know it's exhausting me," I said. But there was a rush of relief that seemed to pipe through my veins knowing that he was okay, and that he had woken up.

I just wished that I had been able to be here when it happened.

Lockwood was still in the corner, face toward the wall, speaking gibberish in a low tone. I could see the tension in his shoulders, see how he clenched his hands together. His head was bowed, and I could see a bead of sweat at his chin, threatening to drip onto the carpet. I wanted to ask him to stop, but we weren't ready for that yet.

"Just a little longer, Lockwood," I murmured. He didn't seem to acknowledge it, but I didn't see how he could miss it unless he was in a deep, sleepless fog. Which was a strong possibility, given how our last twenty-four hours had gone. From Faerie to here, and not much time to draw breath between.

"Where's Laura?" I asked.

"Sleeping in my room," Xandra said. "Peacefully, last I checked on her."

I took a deep breath. Only one more to check on, and I quietly made my way over to him.

Mill was stretched out on the other side of the couch, and he was awake, his eyes on the ceiling. He couldn't focus as he stared up, past me. It was like he was looking at something over my shoulder that I couldn't see.

"You're...back," he said with so much effort it frightened me.

"Yeah, I'm here," I said, taking his hand in mine. "And I brought help."

He tried to lick his dry, greying lips, and when he blinked, I wasn't sure he was going to have the strength to open his eyes again.

My heart clenched, then raced like a hamster in its wheel.

"Good," was all he said. His head sagged against the back of the couch as he lost consciousness again.

"He's not doing any better," Xandra said from behind me.

I looked up to find her staring at me, brow puckered in

concern. "After you left, he woke up, shouting for you. But I think his little fit used the last of his strength."

He was...crying out for me? I brushed some of his sandy hair away from his face. There was no sweat, since he was a vampire, but the sallowness of his skin was making me twitchy.

"He's as weak as a puppy," Xandra murmured. "But not quite as cute...That forehead. Thanks to Iona, it's all I can see now."

I smirked mirthlessly. "You thought he was so cute when you first met him in that coffee shop."

She shrugged. "My tastes are complex and change with the wind."

I stared at him, my stomach clenching like I had swallowed a whole bucket of ice. "I noticed it first, too." I ran fingers through his hair. "But it doesn't bother me anymore for some reason."

"It's because you're *soul mates*," Xandra said.

I jabbed her in the knee with my elbow, though my heart ache eased a little at the thought of her words.

He was important to me. Which was why I had to fix this. It was my fault he was poisoned.

Iona appeared, kneeling beside me. She turned his arm over, and the orangey spot had changed to a dark green. It was shiny now, almost like it was coated in fresh paint. "This is just getting worse," she said. I saw Lockwood nodding his head out of the corner of my eye.

I looked around the room. It was a little like that field hospital in Faerie. Except here, all of the people who were hurt...were all my responsibility.

I couldn't attack these sorcerers on my own, and two of my three heavy fighters were down for the count, one poisoned, the other doing everything in his power to keep me hidden from my enemies.

I was the center of all of this. And if I wanted to save everyone, I had to end this madness as quickly as I could. We couldn't handle another battle like the last. Iona was my last piece on the board that wasn't a pawn, near helpless against the vampires and sorcerers arrayed against me. If I lost her... I was done, as sure as if I was the king and I lost all of my knights.

But they were after me, trying to checkmate me. If we could somehow use that to our advantage, turn the tables against them by just using the fact that they wanted me...

I could be bait.

Bait meant a trap.

A trap meant...maybe we could finally get an advantage.

"Jed?" I asked.

Jed, who had been standing just inside the door, uncertain, his head hanging, perked up at once when I called his name. "Yes?"

"Your dad mentioned sending help, right?"

"He did, yes."

The sorcerers would know Mill was out. Maybe they'd be overconfident.

Maybe. I didn't like to hinge my plans on 'maybe'. We needed something else.

We needed a battlefield.

And I knew just the place.

Chapter 18

I walked out onto the dry, dead grass of the Florida State Fairgrounds. It was still dark, though the first grey light of dawn was showing up on the eastern side of the city. I could hear cars driving by on the interstate, which was close enough that I could see it, but not so close that anyone driving by would be able to clearly see us standing there in the middle of the grounds, bathed in the shadows.

It was humid. The salt from the ocean was heavy on the air as a breeze rustled some of my loose curls from my face. A heavy backpack weighed on my shoulders, moving with every step I took as momentum transferred through the items in it and they seemed to take on a life of their own, moving left as I moved right, then the opposite. It was very disconcerting, but I reconciled myself to it.

There I was, standing with Jed, Iona, and Lockwood, who was chanting under his breath still. Iona and I had led him from the car so he didn't trip on any of the gaping holes in the ground, one of which I nearly rolled my ankle in.

I was aware of each beat of my heart, here in the still of the morn. It resounded in my head, a dull throbbing at the base of my skull. My skin prickled with fear, so much so that every nerve burned as if it were on fire. Even though my hands were shoved in the front pockets of my sweatshirt, I was trembling.

Running would probably help me burn off some of my anxiousness, but I needed to conserve my strength. The adrenaline would only last so long, and then who knew what would happen?

"Do we still have the bags?" I asked.

Iona hoisted a tattered red backpack of Xandra's before letting it sag back to the ground with a thump.

"Okay, good," I said. But it really didn't make me feel any better.

I touched the messy bun on top of my head for the hundredth time, making sure that the stakes that Lockwood had procured for me were still securely stuck in there. I was glad to have some stakes back. It felt like it had been weeks, even though it had been less than a day I'd been back on Earth.

My throat was tight, my eyes darting at the first sign of any movement.

As long as Lockwood kept up his spell, we would be safe. We had been safe up until this point. By now his face was papery pale, his eyelids sagging with exhaustion, his lips dry and cracking from his ceaseless muttering.

I looked at Iona and Jed. "Okay, let's go over it one more time."

Iona rolled her eyes as she snapped on a pair of leather gloves, her silvery hair flowing behind her as she shook her head. "Again?"

Okay, maybe I was stalling a little bit. I had to wrap it up before dawn, before Iona would burn off like a Roman candle in the sunlight.

"Our biggest issue right now is the sorcerers," I said. "Without them, the vampires can't track us, right?"

Iona nodded, clearly not wanting to play along right now. She was ready to fight, too, one eye on the eastern horizon and the lightening sky. The talking was not only meaningless to her but could potentially get her killed if we dragged it out too long.

"Without the ability to track us, we can hide again until we can figure out our next move," I said, scanning the field again. Still not a soul out here but us.

Jed flexed his arms, rolling his shoulders just like I had seen his dad do.

"On top of that, whatever happened to Mill was because their spell hit him. Since we have no idea how to cure it, we need to take one of them alive. Incapacitate them somehow."

"Yes, we know," Iona said. "Can we get on with this? Night is fading, and there's not enough sunscreen in this state to protect me from a fatal sunburn if this drags on until daylight."

"They should make an SPF 10,000 for vamps," I said, and looked back at Lockwood. He stuttered his next chant, then blinked himself back awake. He was ready to be done.

But I was afraid. I didn't know if I was ready for this or not. The idea of facing the sorcerers down again…the image of Dad's body flying across the room came to me, followed by the thought of Mill getting struck and taken out of the fight, of Laura taking the shot on the stairs that had been intended for me…

I hated vampires. And they frightened me.

But witches had magic. And after being in Faerie, I realized just how scary magic was, especially magic that Lockwood couldn't easily protect us against.

I took a shuddering breath. "Lockwood?" I said, hearing the crack in my own voice. "…Drop the spell."

With my words, Lockwood ceased his, and he gasped for air behind me, coughing and sputtering. We had brought some water for him, which he took from Iona and began chugging. The plastic bottle crinkled loudly in his strong grip, making me wince as I stared around into the darkness.

It was quiet for about three heartbeats, before—

"Here they come," Iona said, turning, falling into a defensive stance.

I heard growling and turned to see Jed with his teeth bared, staring out into the darkness. It was still strange to see an Amish kid with us, let alone knowing he was a mythical werewolf. For now, though, he remained human, though the noises he was making suggested otherwise.

It took a second before I saw it. Swirling green sparkles filled the air about thirty feet away, like a cyclone of glowing glitter and light.

"Jed? Are you ready?" I asked, not even turning to look at him. Lockwood's breathing was still heavy behind me.

"Ready as I'll ever be," he said, a lot more eager than I was. This was a man who'd never actually battled vampires or sorcerers, I knew, one who'd never felt the touch of danger hitting the people he loved.

But I knew those feelings.

And yet...

I was ready.

"Let's do this."

Chapter 19

The spells were flying before I even knew what was happening. Greens and reds and blues, all darting from the two witches that had appeared on the field in front of us.

Two. My brain was only registering two magic users as I ducked and weaved around, attempting to avoid the spells flying toward us. Where was the wizard?

Lockwood had cast a shield spell, much like the one he had made back at Byron's house. All of the spells that the witches were throwing at us were sparking off of it and disappearing into the night.

"I can't hold this for very long," Lockwood said through gritted teeth.

"No need," Jed said with a wild grin on his face. "The cavalry is coming."

And with that, I watched as Jed transformed. He sprouted fur so fast it was as if he were being drenched in a wave. His nose elongated, his limbs stretched and bent like a wolf's. He stood on all fours, and even still, he was nearly as tall as I was. He turned and looked at me, shaking out coppery fur that was the same color as his hair. His eyes, weirdly, were the same shade of blue, and I could see the intelligence in them.

He growled, low and deep in his chest before unleashing a howl into the night.

And I jumped as twenty or thirty howls came back in answer.

Then Jed was off, bounding across the field toward the witches, his large paws beating against the ground with each leap.

The other wolves appeared like a herd of Wargs from some *Lord of the Rings* movie, bursting onto the field from out of the darkness behind us. They were grey and black and gold and brown, like a torrent of precious metals. They steered around Lockwood's barrier and charged straight at the witches.

The first few wolves were almost upon the witches before they could turn their spells from us to the new threat. Almost. But it didn't take them long before they were turning their spells onto the werewolves, and I watched in horror as a purple blast struck a wolf and it flew nose over tail and came to a rest, utterly still.

"No…" I said. "Wait, no—"

No one was supposed to die for me. That wasn't part of the deal. The witches were ruthless, clearly, but they only wanted me, not the wolves.

I hadn't considered them killing anyone who stood in their way.

But I should have. Draven certainly would.

All my dreams of a bloodless battle that ended in our resounding victory and the sorcerers' utter destruction seemed to evaporate with that first hit. But the battle didn't stop there by any means, and the spells continued to fly and the mewling of wounded dogs filled the air with heartbreaking swiftness.

Swirls of green filled the air above the witches, and I winced as one of them released a shockwave of magic, pushing it outward from all around her like a Jedi Force push. The shock of the spell sent the werewolves, who had been trying to surround her, flying backward. They came down in a hard rain, slamming against the ground some thirty feet away.

Iona was suddenly in the fray, too. She was clambering over werewolves, trying to get close. She moved with blurry speed, but the witches seemed to anticipate her. Spells were flying in her direction and she was diving, rolling. It kept her off balance, didn't give her a chance to strike.

How could two witches defend themselves so easily against so many oncoming attacks? They were cackling as they did it, too. The werewolves were howling in pain, a sound like the most frightening nightmare of an animal shelter I could have ever imagined.

A body flew through the air wearing Amish clothes. It landed in a roll and remained motionless as it came to a rest. Flashes of gold and white lit up the predawn hours like fireworks over the fairgrounds.

I couldn't stand this another moment, watching this battle unfold while I was on the sidelines. People were dying around me, dying—

For me. They were dying for me.

I started forward, reaching for a stake in my hair, unsure what I would even do with it against the witches. But I had to do something. I had to—

A firm hand on my shoulder stopped me before I even got moving. When I looked back, I saw Lockwood staring down at me, face pale and glistening with sweat. "I know your heart yearns to get involved, but please, Cassandra... Think. This is not a fight you can engage in on equal footing."

"But I can't just stand here," I said. "People are dying because of me."

"There will come a time to fight," he said. "This is not it. You are defenseless against these foes, and they clamor for nothing but your blood. Should they get it, Mill will most certainly die." His bright green eyes, so rimmed with concern, riveted me in place. "I know this is difficult to endure. But if you value his life, you must stay the course and allow the werewolves to follow their own heart's calling."

He knew exactly what I needed to hear to keep my feet rooted to the spot. But that didn't mean I liked it. I would have rather been in the fight than standing here away from it, watching as werewolves were getting their asses handed to them.

And watching as another one changed back to human, head lolling, eyes slack and staring at the sky...

That was hardest of all.

"Lockwood, we aren't going to win this," I said, snugging my backpack strap tighter against my right shoulder. The contents moved again after I'd stopped, making me feel like there was something alive in there even though there wasn't.

The werewolves were swarming, fighting back against the

occasional burst of magic that seemed to bat them away every time they'd get close. I saw one get struck, then drag himself back up. A few seconds later, he launched back at the witches again. Another got a good bite in, causing one of the witches to howl and shoot a spell that blasted out from her body a few feet, knocking the wolf clear. It blazed bright and yellow, and shot skyward like a spotlight. The wolf rolled and came back to his feet, snarling, teeth bloody.

Man, these guys hated witches.

Iona screamed in triumph as she grabbed one of the witches, and I saw a spurt of blood geyser, pale blond hair flashing behind a shadowed form. Growls followed as wolves poured onto the witch and Iona staggered back, lips bloody as a tide of angry Amish werewolves dragged one of our enemies to the ground.

My heart soared with hope.

One down.

I grimaced. That was a human being, and I was pleased for her death. This was not an improvement over my days of being a horrible compulsive liar.

The pack of wolves turned from the now limp body of one of the witches and darted toward the other, a flood of furred pups growling and yapping as they turned on her. She was staggering back, spells glowing from her weapon, panic rising on her face even beneath her black sunglasses.

"Wait," I shouted, and before Lockwood could stop me, I darted off toward the last standing witch. "Wait, don't kill her, we need her alive—Iona!"

I saw a flicker of pale blonde hair behind the writhing ocean of fur that was the enraged werewolf pack. They seemed to take no notice of me as I pushed my way through the wolves, making little headway against the massive creatures.

From where I stood in the middle of the raging wolves, I saw Iona standing over the witch, her hands knotted in the witch's filthy, stringy hair, yanking it backwards to exposing her neck. A dozen wolves bayed in front of her, each seeming to vie for the privilege of leaping to tear out her throat.

Iona's steady hand rested a silver blade against the witch's throat. "Tell me how to break it," she said, her bright eyes flaming with anger. She brought a large canine down on the witch's neck, poking the woman as if for emphasis.

The witch laughed, her dark sunglasses askew. Blood ran out of the corner of her mouth.

"You've lost, little one," she said in her thick German accent, turning her to me. "Do what you will to me. The spell will not break unless the one who commanded it is killed." She laughed again. "You have no hope. Not against *him*." Blood dripped down her chin, red and fresh.

Iona just stared at her for a moment, then pulled the blade back from the witch's throat, throwing a glance my way. "You hear that?" I nodded. "You believe her?"

I nodded again.

"Me too," Iona said, "but just in case, you heard her. Do what you will."

And she shoved the witch to the wolves.

It was a feeding frenzy turned loose as the witch disappeared under the wall of fur that had been positioned in front of her. The ones around me seemed to go nuts with the sudden action at the front, too, and I almost got knocked over by the grey-haired wolf nearest me.

Blood splattered through the air like a summer rain, and I tried not to vomit on the ground right there.

"Cassandra!" Lockwood's voice lacked calm, cracking through the early morning fairground and over the snarling, feeding wolves.

I turned in time to see another cyclone of glowing green forming a dozen paces away.

The sound of squealing tires and roaring engines overwhelmed the crackling magic and furious wolves as five or six cars skidded to a halt a hundred feet away. There were no headlights blazing into the darkness; they'd come with them off, able to see through the darkness as though they lived in it all the time.

Because they did.

Vampires.

Doors opened, thrown wide by the strength of their occupants. They showed their speed as they appeared as if by magic, just behind the wizard as his spell evaporated and he waited at the head of them, watching my little army as they unfolded their own into a battle line.

And there... At the head, sneaking out from behind a vampire in a suit, shorter than any of the rest and wearing a dress that would have been radically out of place on her until so very recently...

Was Jacquelyn.

Chapter 20

A wizard. A horde of bad vampires. My former best friend, now a vampire.

A Paladin of Faerie. One good vampire. A pack of Amish werewolves.

Oh, and one reformed liar turned vampire slayer.

The Florida State Fairgrounds.

How the hell did I end up here? Other than by driving, which was the obvious and literal answer.

Right. Lies. Lots of lies that destroyed my old life, drove me out of New York, and pushed me into the path of a stalker, the meteor that caused my innocence to go extinct and finally annihilated any hope that I could have anything resembling a normal life.

"So," I said, calling out to Jacquelyn in the distance between her army and my pack of wolves, "I've expanded into the pet care business since last we met. Felt like I needed a new hobby, sorta like how you've embraced arson and bloodsucking as a career path. I don't want to say I was spurred by jealousy, but... You know how competitive I get."

Jacquelyn gave me a pitying look. "It was always like this with you. You could never let me have a moment in the sun."

"You can have all the time in the sun you want now. I have no problem with that." I raised an eyebrow at her. "Interesting choice of words, though."

"You know what I meant," she said, souring quickly.

The wolves howled around me but made no moves to attack

the vamps. We'd known this was a possibility, but I wasn't sure they wanted to cross Draven since they had some sort of peace. We seemed to be at a standoff, which was... Interesting.

"I think so?" I pretended to wonder. "But if you wouldn't mind waiting a few minutes, I'm happy to serve that moment in the sun up for you." I looked to the horizon. It was lightening even still, purple filling the eastern sky.

"Sorry, Cassie," she said, not remotely apologetic. "But you don't have minutes." And she jerked her hand, pointing at me.

"Crap," I said as the wizard let loose a blast and the vampires broke into a charge.

"Cassandra," Lockwood said, pushing me down as a spell blast passed through where my head had been a moment earlier. "We need to move. The wolves will not break the peace, and they will not be able to protect you against—"

"An army of bloodthirsty vampires?" I asked, and broke into a run, backpack sloshing against my back. I slung it under my arm as I went, opening the top zipper. Water balloons moved around inside. It looked like most of them had survived my bouncing around inside the werewolf scrum. "What about the wizard?" I threw a balloon over my shoulder at the nearest vamp blurring toward me and watched him veer out of the way. It hit a vampire behind him and the scream was bloodcurdling. I saw blood and pale skin wash away like the end scene of that really old movie where they opened the Ark of the Covenant and faces melted off.

"Let's worry about your safety first," Lockwood said.

"What do you think I'm worrying about?" I asked, sprinting, tossing another balloon over my shoulder. It landed in a thick knot of vamps, splashing five of them. Two fell down, screaming as they nursed wounds. The other three seemed to slow, smoke rising where the holy water had hit them. "World peace?"

"That seems a little out of the question at the moment," Iona said, appearing at my elbow and yanking me along. "I mean, even if you solved the Middle East issue, I think these vampires are still going to want to murder you."

"I'm more worried about the wizard," I said, and chucked another holy water bomb into the path of the fastest moving vamp after a quick feint. "We can't let him leave this place alive."

As soon as I realized which way the vampire frontrunner was going to dodge, and he'd committed to it, I adjusted my aim and landed it right in front of him. It caught him squarely in the groin, and I cringed. "Oof. Looks like somebody peed his pants." The vampire collapsed screaming, his shirt turning black as his guts seeped out underneath his clothing.

"We need to get you out of here," Lockwood said. "They will stop at nothing to get you."

"Well, I don't really want to be gotten," I said, looking for Jacquelyn. She was pretty far behind, letting the brave idiots charge after the girl with the holy water balloons. I readied my next shot, my hand wet from so many repetitive throws.

A vampire with shockingly blond hair was leading the field. I pretended to throw, and she dodged, exceptionally well. She looked a little like a pixie-cut version of Iona, and I feinted again. She dodged, cutting closer to us, now only about ten paces back and moving with blurry speed.

"Hey," I said as she closed the last distance between us, "you're really fast. Good for you. You win the race." I held my hand out, ready to toss the balloon.

She snapped a claw-like vise grip around my hand, halting my throw. A loud snarl left her lips. "No more."

I squeezed the balloon and it popped, raining water down on her hand, arm, body and face, and she screamed as she fell over, Iona dragging me forward, my feet not even touching the ground. "Pro tip, guys," I said, shaking out my wrist from her grip. "Like horseshoes, hand grenades, and nuclear warfare, close does count with holy water balloons."

"Here," Lockwood said, and Iona let me go. I fumbled, caught my balance, and found myself standing up on the last row of seats in the fairground amphitheater.

I looked around. We'd covered a lot of ground with Iona dragging me while I was busy chucking water balloons into vampires.

Lockwood dropped, taking a knee, breath rushing out in great gasps. The werewolves were somehow behind us, rushing into the amphitheater now, bursting past like a herd,

ROBERT J. CRANE with LAUREN HARPER

barking and snarling as they went and flooding down the main row toward the stage. What they were after, I didn't know, but they seemed focused on something.

I blinked a few times. Sparkling lights dotted the corners of my vision, and not the kind that came from failure to breathe. The vampires were quite a distance behind us, and it took me a moment to realize something magical had happened.

I turned on Lockwood, who was looking quite pained. "What did you do?" I asked.

"He leaped us forward," Iona said. "Short-cutted us through Faerie."

So that was what had happened. And it had taken some fight out of him, by the looks of it, tapping into magics when Lockwood was already running low on sleep and stamina. "You shouldn't have done it, Lockwood," I said.

He smiled faintly. "It was either that or be run down."

"I guess being run down would be worse," I said, glancing around. So we hadn't just appeared at the amphitheater while I was distracted hurling holy water balloons. I looked up at the white seashell roof that overhung the building, then down at the rows and rows of blue seats set into a manmade hill. It sat higher than the rest of the fairgrounds, and I could see everything from here—the highway, the parking lot, the swarming army of vampires following in our wake.

The air was growing warmer, stickier. Dawn was not far off.

"Get ready," Iona said, looking at the vamps. "They're coming."

I checked to make sure the stakes were still my hair. That was the last resort, and I reached down to fill my hands with water balloons as the main course. But if the vampires got that close, well…then we'd be in a world of trouble, wouldn't we? I'd have to seriously consider just swinging my bag and hoping the splash damage would do enough to keep them at bay.

The werewolves were snarling, like rabid dogs tearing apart a helpless rabbit. Did that mean they got to the wizard already?

It was hard for me to say. It had seemed sure that I'd killed that one back at Byron's when I plunged the knife in, yet there she'd been, on the field of battle not five minutes ago, until a few hungry werewolves had finished the job I'd started.

"Will they help us?" I said, glancing at the roaming pack, swirling around near the stage, clearly enraged about something.

"Who, the werewolves?" Iona said. "Doubtful. The vamps and wolves do their best to avoid one another, keeping an uneasy peace. Their fight is with the witches and wizard." She looked down at the stage. "And unless I miss my guess, they've got a sniff of one of them now, down there."

I swallowed nervously as the first flickering shadows indicating the arrival of the other vampires crossed my vision. I looked at the horizon. Dawn was definitely coming soon.

"Here, take one of these," I said, thrusting a water balloon at Iona.

She raised a perfect blond eyebrow. "Those have holy water on them from when you filled them. Unless you want to hear me scream as the skin melts off my hand, keep them away from me."

"Oh," I said, "right," and chucked one at the top of the stairs. It hit the ground and splashed, sending a vampire scrambling to dodge at the last second. He ended up in the last row of seats, where he caught a spell from Lockwood, howling in pain as it struck.

"I feel like I should have taken up softball given how good I am at this," I said, launching another one after a solid feint. It landed right in the center of a vamp's chest and he squealed, keeling over and melting right there. "Do you think the Tampa Bay Buccaneers could use a quarterback?"

"I think you have to be able to throw it farther than thirty feet," Iona said as I splashed another one at a vampire's feet, sending him tumbling into the vamps behind him, making a pile. I launched another one and it hit him on the side of the leg, splashing him and the two vampires he'd knocked over with him, prompting a cacophony of howling that set off the werewolves behind us. Hopefully no one would hear it and call the cops thinking it was a dying animal.

"It's working," I said, lobbing another and sending vampires scrambling out of the way. Not one of them had been brave enough to push through the balloons to get to us.

My heartbeat was loud in my ears as I tossed another one. It fell short, but the water splattered high into the air, sending them back even farther in retreat. Smoking, melted black piles of ick filled the aisle at the top where the vamps I'd doused had melted like the Wicked Witch of the West.

"Cassie," came Jacquelyn's voice, "we're leaving."

"Awww, but you haven't even participated in the water balloon fight," I called back. "Come on, Jacquelyn. Remember your eighth birthday party? The one with the Slip N' Slide, where you broke your arm getting a little too aggressive with the slipping and sliding? This could be like that, but with you ending up as a puddle of black goo."

I couldn't see her face, but I could hear her burning in the tone of her answer. "See you again soon, Cassie."

I turned to look at the stage. The werewolves were gone, and there was a bloody mess in the middle of the stage, with drag marks leading off. I wondered if that was the end of at least one of them...?

"Where'd the werewolves get off to?" I asked, tentatively hiking up the amphitheater steps, avoiding the thick puddles of vampire tar.

"They exited, stage left, once they finished with the sorcerer down there," Iona said, pushing past me to stand at the top of the steps. "They tore him to pieces and...well, just be glad you were busy taking care of the vampires."

I blinked. "It was that bad?"

She shrugged. "No, it wasn't bad. Kinda made me hungry."

I could just make out the car doors slamming, and the roar of engines in the distance. I caught the last flight of the vampires as I crested the top of the steps, peeling out as they left the fairgrounds.

"They gave up awfully easily," I said. Two cars remained, abandoned. Must have belonged to the puddles of goo down the steps.

"They already watched you vanish once," Lockwood said, finally reaching the top with us. "I suspect your friend concluded that attempting to storm this particular castle would result in unacceptable casualties, with no victory at the end."

"Yeah, if you killed almost all of them and then vanished

before they got you, that probably wouldn't raise Jacquelyn's stock in Draven's eyes," Iona said. "More like sink it. Better she retreat now and tell him she lost a few than lead her people into a catastrophe and explain losing all of them."

"Yeah," I said. "But we don't know how to fix Mill."

Iona shook her head. "Cassie...the witch. She told you, remember?"

My heart felt like it was splintering, like someone was squeezing it to breakage. "You think she was telling the truth?" Her laughter filled my mind, and I had to shake my head to clear it, goosebumps popping up on my arms.

"Oh, she was telling the truth," Iona said. "Why choose her last moments to lie? What good would it do?"

"What good did it do for her to say what she did say? What did she gain?" I said. "I don't know—driving in the spite a little deeper. Depriving us of hope as the wolves deprived her of her life."

Iona shook her head. "That wasn't spite you saw from her." Her face fell. "It was triumph. Come on, we should head back to the house. We need to check on Mill."

I thought I might be sick. Since when did she call him "Mill" and not "Forehead"? Had Iona just given away her own worry for him? "Yeah. We should go," I said, desperate to see him and terrified all at once.

"It will be all right, Lady Cassandra," Lockwood said. He looked about as poor as I felt, but he walked tall beside me as we headed for the car. "We are with you."

Those were the sorts of things you said to a person who just lost someone. Mill was still alive. And I quickened my pace, resolving to do everything in my power to keep him that way.

Chapter 21

The first light of dawn was starting to show up on the horizon as we drove, that bright, burning ball of yellow hanging in the eastern sky. I'd forgotten my sunglasses and Iona had none (for obvious reasons) so I squinted as I drove, torn between my own thoughts and the occasional shouted suggestion from the back seat.

"If you get one scratch on this car, I will kill you myself," Iona said through the fleecy material of the blanket that covered her. She carried a bag in the trunk with clothing and blankets for emergency sunlight survival, and now she was speaking to me from beneath several layers of heavy cloth. She made herself clear over the material between us, though, so much so that it was driving me slowly nuts.

"Touchy much?" I asked.

"It's late and this might be the only possession I still have at the end of all this," she said. "If you ruin this last thing like you have the rest of my afterlife, I'm going to find some way to get my revenge, and it's not going to be as gentle as a frat joke, either. We're talking a full-on assault of vengeance, from itching powder in your laundry to hiring a barbershop quartet to sing you embarrassing songs in the school cafeteria at lunch. I will investigate your class and find the worst possible crush you could have and send you flowers in the middle of class and have the delivery guy say they're from him."

I glared at the lumpy blanket that was her in the back seat but held my silence. She had a right to be angry.

"And don't glare at me," she said.

"What, now vampires have X-ray vision?"

We made it back to the house before she had too much more opportunity to be grouchy with me. Not that she didn't have good reason. Lockwood and I led her inside, making sure that every inch of her was covered. The sunlight was not quite in Xandra's yard yet, but even still. The last thing I needed was for her to give me hell about burns.

"We're back," I said as we stepped inside the front door.

Iona cast off her layers of clothing, looking around through messy hair that covered her face until her eyes came to rest on Xandra, who had come to meet us at the entry. "Do you have a bathroom?"

"Um…yeah?" Xandra blinked a couple times, probably at being greeted with this question from a vamp.

"Without windows?" Iona asked.

Xandra's look got more confused. "Yeah? Why?"

Iona turned to me. "Mill and I are probably going to need to camp out in there. The sunlight—"

"No need," Xandra said, hopping over one of the arm chairs in the living room and landing beside the window. She reached up and pulled one of the drapes down, smothering the morning sunlight. "Blackout curtains," she said with a grin. "Dad works weird hours sometimes, so we had these installed to help him keep his sleep schedule. He has sleep apnea, so—"

"You have mistaken me for someone who cares," Iona said. "All right, this will work. For now."

"Cassie?"

I looked up to see Mom sitting on the couch beside Dad, who looked pale, but was at least awake and sitting up.

"Where did you go? When we woke up and you weren't here—" Mom asked

"I'm sorry, guys. I had to go take care of…" I said.

What was I thinking? I'd almost lied, purely out of habit. But they knew the truth now. There was no sense in trying to lie or be vague about it. As I looked around, everyone who was there was watching me expectantly, waiting for the latest news.

Mill was still lying on the couch, the only person in the room not watching me. If I hadn't seen the violently green and coppery colored wound on his arm, looking just a little larger than when I'd left, I might have thought he was just sleeping.

"So…what happened?" It was Laura, standing in the archway to the living room, arms crossed over herself as if cold. Her eyes were wide, and she was staring at me hopefully.

Why did that hurt so much? Was it because I wasn't bringing good tidings?

I looked over at Iona, who gave me a flat look, shrugging her shoulders, as if to say *you do it*.

I tried to swallow my nerves, and looked from person to person, waiting for something, anything, about what was going on.

"The witches and wizard are dead," I said.

Laura made a gasp of excitement, clapping her hands. I caught a hopeful look from Xandra, too, but I held up my hands to stop her from getting too worked up. "But overall…we failed."

Laura's brow creased, all that excitement fleeing. "How's them dying a failure? That's what we wanted, right? So they couldn't track us anymore?"

"What about the Amish kid?" Xandra asked.

"They took off after the fight," Iona said. "Didn't even leave a note saying goodbye, thanks for the good times, anything. I swear, those Amish need some work on their manners. Maybe they didn't have a quill handy, I don't know."

"Amish?" Dad asked. "How do the Amish fit into this?"

"Because I went to a barn raising this morning," I said.

His frown deepened.

With more than a little frustration, I retold what happened at the fairgrounds, including the bits about Amish werewolves, covering the death of the German sorcerers, and then getting into Jacquelyn's appearance with her vampire pals.

"We killed a few vampires," I said. "But not enough. They retreated, and now I'm assuming they're just going to bide their time. I doubt Jacquelyn is going to come rushing into a confrontation again anytime soon, but I'm sure she'll be looking for us." I took a deep breath. "But that's not all."

I wanted nothing more than to curl up in a ball on the floor right there. Maybe take a little nap. Or die. I wished Lockwood or Iona would take over for this part. I didn't know if I was going to be strong enough to do it.

"Why do I get the feeling you're about to drop a bomb on us?" Xandra said from the floor, her arms wrapped around her knees. She brushed a couple of stray blue strands of hair out of her eyes.

"The only thing we found out about was the spell that hit Mill," I said, trying really hard not to look over at him. "Apparently, the effects will last until the person who commanded its use in the first place dies."

It was harder to say out loud than I thought it would be.

"So...that would be the big shot, right?" Xandra asked. "Lord Draven?" I nodded.

Laura's face fell. "Oh. That is bad."

"Yes. It's bad," Lockwood said. He was standing over Mill, checking the site of the spell once more. "And only getting worse."

"So the only way to reverse it is to kill Draven?" Xandra asked.

I nodded again.

She shook her head. "That's a total bummer, dude."

I could feel my eyes stinging, so I ducked my head. "Excuse me for a second…"

I turned and made my way out of the living room and toward the kitchen. I collapsed into one of the chairs and laid my head down on the cool table.

How long had I been without sleep now? For a few minutes, I just listened to the sound of my breathing. I forced myself to draw breath in, hold it for a few seconds, and let the breath out. It was a technique I had read about for panic attacks. With my life as full of insanity as it was, I had a feeling it might come in handy eventually. I wasn't wrong.

"Mind if I join you?"

I lifted my head and saw Mom standing there next to the table, looking down at me, concern rimming her eyes.

I put my head back down. I was in no mood for a lecture. If I ignored her, maybe she'd go away.

"So…" she said, taking the seat opposite me. "I just wanted to say…that I'm sorry. About Mill."

I looked up but didn't say anything.

"I just wanted you to know that Dad and I are here for you…all right? Whatever happens."

'Whatever happens'. That stung, opening up possibilities I was trying to ignore. "Thanks, Mom…" I said.

She patted me gently on the arm and disappeared through the archway.

Whatever happens.

I had to face the reality that Mill might not make it through this. No matter how hard I fought, no matter how brave I was…

It was possible that Mill could die.

I couldn't imagine it. Mill was one of the strongest people I knew and had overcome so much.

But what was he supposed to do against magic? Against some curse running through his blood?

Sitting there and wallowing wasn't helping anyone. If anything, it was only making me more and more disgusted with myself.

I dragged myself from the table back into the living room. No one was in there, and I vaguely recalled hearing movement, a door in the distance, quiet talk about sunlight. I put it all together and decided they must have gone outside.

No sunlight in here, though, the blackout curtains darkening the room.

Iona had curled up in a corner with a book. She spared me only a glance until she realized what I was doing and returned to her book.

I picked my way over and sat down on the floor beside the couch, resting my head on the shoulder of Mill's undamaged arm. I wished I could take comfort from him breathing, but he didn't breathe, so that was out. And his skin was as cold as stone.

I lay there for a while, wishing I could get him to open his eyes and look at me again. Why did I keep feeling like this was going to be the last time that I ever looked at him? Why couldn't I shake the feeling that no matter what I did, it wouldn't be enough?

Because it wouldn't be. Either Mill would die, or Draven

would. And Draven wasn't exactly easy pickings.

I closed my eyes. I didn't want to leave him. Not now. Not when it was possible that these were the last days, hours, moments, we had together. Who even knew, now that the sorcerers who had done this were dead?

It wasn't fair. None of it was. I'd only had a few short weeks with him. And now he was about to be ripped away from me. None of it made any sense.

What I wanted…what I needed… none of it mattered.

All that mattered now was that I stayed with him so that he wasn't alone.

And honestly? I didn't want to be alone, either. So I settled in against him and fell asleep on his shoulder.

Chapter 22

"Cassandra?"

I heard the voice, but it was distant, far away.

It was dark. I was warm, comfortable. Something soft was wrapped around me.

"Cassandra…?"

I smiled as I snuggled down more. Come on, Mom. Just five more minutes. I took a shower last night before bed so I could sleep in this morning. It's fine, I'll have plenty of time to get ready.

"Cassandra!"

My eyes snapped open, and I blinked furiously, darkness surrounding me even awake.

There was a hand on my shoulder, which I quickly realized was Lockwood's, as was the voice.

My head was throbbing. I had fallen asleep with a lumpy couch pillow under my head, and someone had wrapped a frilly, thin blanket around me. I brushed it away, sitting up. "What's going on?" I asked.

I looked around and my heart sank.

Mill was on the couch behind me, looking more like a corpse than a vampire.

The heaviness that I had been carrying with me returned full force. I had been so blissfully unaware for the seconds before my brain caught up with me, reminding me with roaring sirens and pumping adrenaline that everything was wrong, nothing was good, and *Mill was going to die*.

"How long…was I asleep?" I asked, rubbing my bleary eyes.

"About twelve hours," he said. "We barely slept in Faerie, and then you came home to this particularly long night..." He leaned in a little more closely. "I may have cast a spell to help you to sleep a bit more soundly."

I frowned, but I wasn't ungrateful. I knew I was going to need my strength for whatever was coming next. "So I slept through the whole day?"

He nodded.

A strong scent of ginger and garlic wafting in from the kitchen. "Oh man, Xandra's parents—" I said, trying to get to my feet.

Lockwood shushed me and eased me back down to my makeshift bed on the floor. "Easy. They're fine. Events have been…explained…to them. After a fashion."

"I take it you took a wide pass on the true details of the vampires and Faerie stuff?"

"Naturally," he said with a gentle smile. He sat down beside me on the floor and took a deep breath. "But I did wake you with purpose, Cassandra. We need to talk."

I didn't care for those words. Especially not now, when everything was already as bad as it was. Images flashed across my mind of hordes of vampires and werewolves. They towered over me, their teeth snapping shut like a mousetrap. The vampires, their eyes gleaming red, teeth drenched in blood. The witches with their cackling, the sound of their limbs being ripped from their bodies…

I tried to swallow the bile rising in my throat. "What is it?"

"Mill is…out," he said in a gentle tone. "I have not been able to stir him for some time. His veins are green and they run all over his body. He has been moaning in his sleep…"

In other words, he was getting worse.

"This is a very dark magic," he said. "Very dark indeed."

I turned and looked at Mill. I could see what Lockwood was talking about. His veins were like emerald spiderwebs across his skin. Every ten seconds or so, the veins pulsed with a dull green light.

"Your father made a brief examination, and… well, if he was holding out any doubts about your tales, I think he truly believes you, if that helps anything."

I couldn't imagine that was very pleasant for Dr. Howell. Looking for a heartbeat, finding none. Checking temperature, finding he was as cold as a cadaver.

"I… I really didn't want to tell you this, but…" Lockwood said.

"What?" I asked. "Just tell me, please."

Lockwood focused his green eyes on me, so bright. "He has two days, Cassandra. Perhaps less."

It was like he had taken a hammer and struck me right in the forehead with it. Why couldn't I get good news for once? At least when I didn't know how much time he had, there was some weird hope that maybe he could last long enough that we could find an alternative cure somewhere, somehow. Maybe the spell would just… Wear off.

But it was all wishful thinking, and I had known, deep down in my soul, that this was happening, for real. It wasn't some illusory lie that would vanish given enough time. I just didn't want to admit it.

Two days.

I'd been a fortunate kid. I hadn't lost many family members in my life. My grandparents on my dad's side had both passed away when I was young, and I barely remembered them. My mom's dad died when she was a little girl, and her mom lived with her brother back in New York still. There was some distance there, and I hadn't seen her in years.

The only time that I had really been faced with death was when my aunt had been killed by a drunk driver. It had hit us out of nowhere. The phone ringing in the middle of the night is the scariest thing to wake up to; those phone calls are never good.

I still remembered the next few days very clearly. Sitting around the living room with my cousins and aunt and uncle, Mom and Dad, listening to the funeral director talk to us about the service, the arrangements. Watching as Mom and her sister picked out an outfit for her to wear in the casket. I had to help choose the earrings she wore.

I couldn't do it. I ran to the bathroom to vomit instead.

I always knew that eventually, I would have to face the death of someone close to me, but…

I was seventeen years old. I was too young to deal with this kind of crap.

Especially since it was my boyfriend.

Then again… I was far from a normal seventeen-year-old, wasn't I? I'd gotten myself mixed up with vampires and werewolves and witches...oh my.

All I could do was stare at Lockwood, helpless and hopeless.

"Well…what can we do?" I asked. "There's got to be something, right?" I could almost taste the desperation, I knew it. Stupidly so. I could hear it in my words. And it didn't matter how much I wanted things to change. Desire alone would do nothing.

Lockwood frowned, a crease appearing in his brow. "I suggest we make him as comfortable as possible...and prepare for the inevitable."

"Just keep stacking on the pain, Lockwood," I said, tact out the window. "You're doing great so far. Why don't you rip my heart out of my chest while you're at it?"

He flinched, green eyes fluttering, losing some of their brightness. He said nothing, though.

"That's it?" I asked. "Nothing else?" I reached out, seizing his lapel. "There has to be another way."

"I understand the spell," Lockwood said, staring past me at Mill's arm, which was draped over his body on the couch. "I can see plainly how they did it. Now knowing the origin, it makes sense to me. However…" He sighed, shaking his head. "I cannot reverse it. It is not my branch of magic. This is Earth magic, and while I understand the concept, it as familiar to me as a fish is with the sky."

I sighed, leaning back against the couch. I could feel Mill's shoulder behind me, leeching some of my heat, the cool of his flesh clammy through the sleeve of his T-shirt.

"Then…who could we talk to whose forte it is?" I asked.

Lockwood shook his head. "I do not know," he said. "If I did, I would have suggested it already."

"Not all witches and wizards can be bad, right?" I asked. "What about that one from Oz? She was a good witch."

"She's fictional," Iona's voice came from the far door. She

was standing there, almost motionless, not even breathing—obviously.

"How long have you been there?" I asked.

"Long enough," she said, arms folded across her chest. "I might know someone."

I stared at her. "You're the most antisocial person I've ever met, Iona. How is it that you're suddenly the one who knows everyone?"

"I'm only antisocial with people I don't want to socialize with. To those I do, why, I'm practically effusive. Giddy, even." She shrugged her shoulders, flicking her long, silvery hair over her shoulders. "Anyway, I know someone. But…" and here she blinked, sliding across the room toward me, "it will not be easy. So you need to decide how far you're willing to go for even the slightest sliver of a chance—"

"As far as I need to," I said. "You tell me we're going to the moon, I'm on my way to Cape Canaveral in minutes." I got to my feet, looking her in her shining eyes. "I will go as far as I have to for him, Iona, so you tell me—how far do I have to go? The ends of the earth? Beyond? Back to Faerie? Say where, and I'll go."

"Cassandra…" Lockwood said, "you have more left to lose than you can see right now."

"No, I don't," I said, looking him right in the eye. He looked away, unable to meet my glare.

"It's not quite to the moon," Iona said, unblinking. "At least not in terms of distance. But maybe farther." She was almost whispering now. "In terms of what you'll give up."

"I'm about to lose everything anyway," I said, brushing Mill's cold skin with my fingertips as I turned to face her again. "What's a sacrifice of a little more of me?"

Chapter 23

"Okay, so is this person that you know a witch?" I asked, pulling my sweatshirt over my head. Being a northern girl and having not experienced a Florida summer yet, it just felt hot all the time to me now. We were getting out of spring now, and the heat at night was what surprised me the most. T-shirt and shorts for me, thanks. I'd probably never need a sweatshirt ever again.

It was dark outside, just after seven thirty. The last few streaks of pink were hanging on the horizon like fingers, as if they wanted to pull the sun back out. I waited on the front steps, watching the light recede in the heavy, moist air.

Please, no, sun…don't leave us. The darkness is where the scary things lurk.

"No, not a witch," Iona said. "But she knows magic."

Laura was doing the opposite of me, pulling her pale pink Victoria's Secret Pink sweatshirt over her head. "Is it a vampire?" she asked.

"Vampires don't use magic," Iona said, scrolling through her cell phone, not even looking at her.

Xandra made it out the door last of all, wearing a black beret and denim overalls. Apparently we'd not only attracted a follower, but a fashionable one. "What?" she asked. "The nineties are back, and I'm so loving it."

I rolled my eyes.

Lockwood was already at the car. Laura and Xandra had both followed us out, and nothing I said seemed likely to change their minds. In spite of my epic nap, I didn't have much energy for argument anyway.

Mom and Dad were sleeping in Xandra's guest room. Her parents had taken pity on us, Lockwood had told me, insisting that we stay until our house was repaired. They seemed happy to have all of the commotion and seemed to think that Lockwood worked at Mom's law office, and that Iona was one of our friends from school. No one had apparently said anything to the contrary.

They assumed that Mill was just some teenage boy who was really sleepy all the time, and that the sickly streaks on his skin were just strange tattoos. Again, no one had corrected them. I wasn't entirely sure Lockwood hadn't done something to bewitch them, but I was afraid to ask.

"Do you girls want some tea for the road?" Xandra's mom appeared in the doorway. She was wearing her dark hair in a tight bun, and had a pale, yellow apron tied around her waist.

"That'd be great, Mom. Do we have any more of the matcha from Whole Foods?" Xandra walked back up to the front steps. Whether that was to distract her mom or not, I wasn't sure.

"Are you sure you want to come?" I asked Laura again.

"Definitely," she said. "I've been in this house all day. I need some fresh air."

"But it's dangerous," I said. Maybe if I knew how dangerous, I could spell it out for her and scare her off. Unfortunately, Iona had once again clammed up without telling me a damned thing, so I was stuck waiting to find out where this mysterious trip was going to lead us.

"It's dangerous here, too," she said, adjusting the shoestring ties of her sweatshirt. "Why does that matter?"

"Iona," I said, looking at her, "tell them they shouldn't come."

Iona pursed her lips and shrugged. "Yeah, I don't care. They can come if they want."

I narrowed my eyes. "They…what?"

"Whatever. It doesn't matter to me," she said.

That was…odd. Iona was usually the one who was staunchly against anyone going anywhere with her. Why the sudden change of heart? I briefly pondered whether she was having them come along because it was going to be dangerous and she wanted them to die so she could be rid of them.

She wouldn't do that, would she?

Xandra reappeared with several mismatched plastic tumblers with straws. "Homemade matcha Frappuccino's," she said, passing them to us one by one. "Sorry, Iona. Didn't think you'd need caffeine. Or milk. Or ice. Or anything." She looked at Laura. "And I figured you'd like this most of all, Ugg boots."

Laura hesitated before taking the drink. "Did you just call me Ugg boots?"

Xandra shrugged. "If the boot fits."

Laura opened her mouth to protest, but I really wasn't in the mood for petty squabbling. "Thanks, Xandra. That was really nice of your mom."

"Okay, so are we ready?" Iona asked, shoving her hands into the pocket of her black leather jacket. "Did everyone pee? Because I'm not stopping and getting your blood in my upholstery is not going to bother me at all."

Laura just stared at her. "I thought you said pee...then you went to blood."

"You pee on my upholstery, I bleed you," Iona said. "Covering the smell of pee with something yummy."

Laura wisely shut her mouth at that point, and white-knuckled the tea tumbler.

"I think you guys should stay here…" I said once more.

"Why?" Xandra asked, brushing passed me, straw already clenched between her teeth. "It's not like we're going to visit those dangerous Amish, those angry, angry puppers." She paused halfway down the steps. "Wait, does this trip involve the Amish again? Because I feel like my life could be complete if I get to pet an Amish werewolf."

"No," Iona said, walking past us when we got out onto the porch. "And you're not wrong about that completing your life. By which I mean it would end, probably in the grip of angry Amish werewolf teeth."

"So, how far we going?" Xandra asked, ignoring Iona's crack at her. "Gainesville? Orlando? Jacksonville?"

"About six miles, actually," Iona said, tossing her hair over her shoulder as she walked around to the front of the car.

"Cool. Local is always better, right?" Xandra grinned at me. "Who knew all of these mystical creatures lived in my backyard? It's crazy, right? Like discovering your Kombucha brewer is the best, ever."

Xandra was enjoying this a little too much.

Lockwood was standing beside Iona's car. "Shotgun," he said, in his soft, formal, Lockwood way.

"Whoa," I said, "even in Faerie, the sacred rite of calling 'shotgun' is recognized."

Laura looked at him, then at the rest of us. Five was going to be a crowd for Iona's little VW. "Should we take mine, too?" she asked.

"No," Iona said, opening the driver door and lowering herself inside. How did she make that look so graceful? If I wasn't worried about catching my foot in the door by accident, I worried that I'd hit my head on the way. "I'm not waiting up for some Valley Girl cheerleader to follow me." She cast an irritated look through the open door. "I can just imagine you sitting there, driving two miles an hour over the speed limit bopping your head to Ace of Base—"

"Ace of what?" Laura asked.

"—or whatever you kids listen to these days," Iona said. "I will leave you in the dust, princess of the brats. You and your little Prius with the mango-chutney-pineapple air freshener."

"Okay, I hear your angry rant and surrender on driving myself," Laura said. "But I am so not sitting in the middle. I get car sick."

"Annnnnd now I don't want to sit right next to her," Xandra said, making obnoxious sounds with her straw.

"Fine," I said. "I'll sit in the middle."

We all climbed in, and somehow, it felt roomy enough.

Lockwood took his place in the front seat beside Iona and turned around and gave me a wink. Now that I knew about his magic, I realized that I could see it almost everywhere. I made a mental note to thank him later. Extra space in the back seat was always nice.

"Where are we going, Iona?" I asked as she pulled out of the driveway. "You're being tight lipped. Which is, I suppose, kind of usual for you, except when you're delivering an insult or quip."

"Well, I'm fresh out of those at the moment," she said. "I'm too busy holding back my absolute terror."

I frowned. "Why do you say that?"

"It's not dangerous, is it?" Laura asked.

Iona laughed, but it was more like a bark of disbelief. "Of course this is dangerous. Absurdly so."

Laura's eyes widened, and Xandra snorted.

"It's not like we could die, or whatever, right?" Xandra said. "We have a vampire and a faerie with us. What could possibly go wrong?"

"Famous last words," I said, staring at Iona's face. There was something about the smirk on her face, the glint in her eye…

"Wait, we could actually die?" Laura asked, sitting up in her seat, leaning toward Iona.

"Oh, yeah. It's almost certain that one of you will," Iona said. "Which is why I was so glad we had many volunteers. Reduces the danger to me when the blood starts to really fly."

Silence fell over the car; an unpleasant, prickly sort of tension that made my skin crawl.

"Wait, so…why did you let us come with you?" Xandra asked. "That really doesn't make any sense. We're just squishy humans after all."

"I don't really like any of you," Iona said, giving Laura and Xandra brief glances in the rearview mirror. Then she looked at me. "When we get there, Cassie, you should stay close to me so you aren't the one who gets mangled."

"If you knew that it was dangerous—" Laura said.

"I get that you aren't a human anymore, but seriously—" Xandra said.

"I don't suppose there's anything that you could tell us to prepare us for what is coming?" Lockwood asked. "I, too, am rather curious about what to expect."

Iona's grip tightened on the wheel. "Just shut up, all of you. You're making it more difficult for me to manage my terror. And I can't afford to go to pieces right now." She shifted in her seat. "I only have one more infraction left on my license before it gets revoked."

Xandra collapsed back against the seat with a huff, crossing her arms over her chest. Laura deflated and started to pick at the chipping blue fingernail polish on her thumb, one eye on Iona, as though waiting for her to declare everything she'd just said was an elaborate joke.

I glared at the back of Iona's head. She was often bullheaded for no reason, but I could see that she was uneasy about this. Her posture was hard, her muscles tight.

We were driving farther into the city, where the highways all began to snake in and around one another, overhead and underneath. The skyscrapers were like giant fingers reaching into the sky, their brilliantly colored signs and patches of lit windows scaling their tall, metal sides. The city was alive, but completely unaware of us and the war that we were fighting.

Lockwood was staring out of the window. Xandra was scrolling through her Instaphoto feed. Laura was leaning back against the seat, her head on the head rest, staring at the ceiling.

It was quiet. Like the calm before a hurricane.

I had a bad feeling about all of this. Was it because I was worried about where Iona was taking us? Or because I worried that whoever this person was, they wouldn't be able to help Mill?

Mill.

It physically hurt to think about him, like someone driving a frozen knife in through my heart, robbing me of any warmth or happiness. I couldn't really remember the last time that I had really felt at peace with anything in my life. And within the last…what…forty-eight hours or so? My life had completely been turned upside down… Again.

My parents knew about vampires. And faeries and werewolves and witches.

I closed my eyes and tried to focus on my breathing again. I hated feeling like the walls were closing in on me. My heart was racing. My head was swimming.

Panic attacks were a thing, right? And with everything I was dealing with, it only made sense that I would be the one to deal with one…

Because yeah…that's about where I was right now.

Closing my eyes, I settled back, trying to put my thoughts at ease as we rolled down the freeway into the coming night, and I tried not to think about what terrible evils might wait ahead at our destination.

Chapter 24

Ikea.

We went to Ikea.

"I'm sorry, but I feel like I really missed something…" I said, staring out into the dark parking lot. Even an hour from closing, the giant blue and yellow store's parking lot was still pretty busy.

Iona was scrolling through some old messages on her phone, and despite how I shifted in my seat, I couldn't read them.

"How is this magical…at all?" Laura asked, peering out of her window.

"I can kinda see it," Xandra said. "I do find something spellbinding about discount Swedish furniture."

Laura gave her a scathing look.

Xandra ignored it. "I mean, who doesn't want an Ektorp to take home?"

"How did you know that off the top of your head?" Laura asked with a glare.

"Like I said, who doesn't want to take one home?" Xandra asked.

"What is an Ektorp?" Laura asked, folding her arms.

Xandra rolled her eyes. "If I have to explain it, then it's not a joke anymore, is it?"

"I have to agree with the girls," Lockwood said. "This place doesn't look like—"

"You of all people should know that these things are never how they appear," Iona said, still reading through her messages. Whether she was looking for information or killing time, I didn't know.

"So, it's not actually a Swedish furniture store?" Xandra asked. "Does that mean the meatballs aren't real? Or caloric, maybe?"

Iona made a noise of disgust and threw open her door, stepping out into the humid night. She slammed it shut behind her.

Xandra followed suit. "Wait, so is this not actually an Ikea? Is it secretly a demon hideout?"

I scrambled out of the car after Xandra, and found Iona glaring at Xandra over the roof of the car.

"Of course it's an Ikea!" she said. She rolled her eyes in disgust. "Just…let's go. And try to contain your stupid thoughts within your stupid self." She started toward the entrance.

Laura fell into step beside me, Xandra on my other side, Lockwood trailing behind.

A vampire, a fae, and three teenage girls. What a sight we must have been.

We wandered inside, the bright lights on every surface contrasting with the dark, industrial ceiling, making the place surprisingly cozy.

"Oh man, I wonder if they're still serving food," Xandra said as we stared around the entrance. An escalator led upwards, with signs above it indicating different areas; living, dining, kitchen, bedroom. "Their Swedish meatballs are the bomb dot com."

"Nobody says bomb dot com anymore," Iona said with utter disgust.

"I'm bringing it back," Xandra said.

Iona made a noise like a gagging sound deep in her throat. "You would, you anime-loving hipster."

"I just can't believe an Ikea could be dangerous," Laura said, shoving her hands in the pocket of her pink sweatshirt.

"It's very dangerous to your wallet," Lockwood said. "I challenge you to come in here and not walk out with something."

"I've actually never been here before," I said, looking

ROBERT J. CRANE with LAUREN HARPER

around. "It's actually pretty cool."

Laura's face lit up like a Christmas tree. "Wait until you see the apartment displays. I designed my bedroom around one. The hanging lights? So gorgeous."

Lockwood nodded his head. "My point is made."

"I don't really think that any of us are of the home organizing age yet," I said. "Or at least I'm not, being somewhat more concerned about vampires at present. Besides. My wallet was back at the house...probably lost in the fire, with all five dollars it contained." RIP Mr. Lincoln. How keenly I will miss you the next time I want a chicken sandwich.

"Come on, there's no time to dawdle," Iona said, motioning for us to follow her up the escalators.

It was like a totally different world at the top of the escalator. Mini room displays were set up with vibrantly colored couches, chunky coffee tables with glass tops, and dark espresso pieces along the faux walls set up around them.

Laura flounced over to one of the couches, touching the mustard yellow fabric, her eyes wide with excitement. Xandra had turned and started toward the elevators, and I noticed the sign for food hanging from the ceiling in that direction.

There were quite a few people here, all absorbed in their own dreams for their homes, totally oblivious to us. One couple was totally entranced by one of the couches, the husband marking it down while the wife plopped down happily, over and over.

"I always thought that Ikea was really cheap stuff," I said, touching one of the green paisley armchairs. "But I'm actually kinda impressed now that I see it."

Iona loomed beside me and nodded, just once. "I have some pieces in my place from here." Her look soured. "Or I did...before I had to abandon my home to wild dogs and street gangs and whatever other unwashed horrors might wander in now that I'm gone. Street mimes, probably."

"Sorry," I said. "About your place." I paused, thinking about it. "Also, about any possible street mime infestations you have to deal with once this is over with. Those things are impossible to get rid of."

She shook her head. "Come on."

"Oh, I like that white one," Laura said as we moved into the couches, "but I really like that blue one, too. Do you think it would show cat hair? I wonder how much it costs? Maybe Mom will let me get that for my dorm in a few years."

"Let me guess, you want to go to FSU, right?" Xandra asked. "Like every other person around here?"

Laura's eyes narrowed. "No. I want to go to a school down in Fort Myers, thank you very much."

"Wow, I'm impressed," Xandra said. "You're so cookie cutter in every other way, I was sure you'd be an FSU loser."

"We need to split up," Iona said, hanging back.

"What, do we look too suspicious like this?" Xandra asked.

"No, I just really don't want to be seen with you," Iona said. "And I don't want to have to listen to you. I'm also very hungry, because *somebody* interrupted my dinner last night." She gave me a pointed look.

"Okay, now she's scary," Xandra said.

"What exactly are we looking for?" I asked, moving along the path, following the arrows. We had made it into the kitchen section, which from the map hanging from the ceiling suggested we were at the back of the store. Plates and glasses sat in the sleek cupboards. Vases with flowers lingered on the tablets and counters. Homey touches like that filled every surface. They really made you feel like you lived there.

"Are we looking for a magic lamp, by chance?" I asked as we passed by a really cool green glass lamp. I made a note to ask Mom to come here with me. I was going to need a whole new room, right? And the prices weren't all that bad...

"No," Iona said.

"How am I supposed to know when you won't tell me anything?" I asked.

Iona didn't reply, just kept walking through the kitchen displays.

"Oh come on, he follows you around like a little puppy," I heard Xandra say.

"He does not," Laura said.

"He so does," Xandra said. "He's your neighbor. Isn't that awkward?"

"Gregory is a really nice guy," Laura said.

"Friend-zoned him already, huh?" Xandra asked. "Smart move."

"He doesn't like me like that," Laura said, her words as cool as ice.

I held in a snort. Gregory totally did. She was just in denial. But that was probably easy for her, since almost the whole male population of our school was in love with her.

"Okay, we're here," Iona said, and she stepped off the path and into one of the displays.

It was a combo kitchen and laundry room, with a small walkway between them. It gave shoppers the chance to wander around among the pieces, touch them, get a feel for them. Open the fridge, see if you like the height of the cooking surfaces.

Iona looked up and down the path, making sure that we were alone, then ducked through into one of the next displays. Another kitchen, but it also had a small pantry tucked away in the back, out of the eye of anyone on the main path between displays.

"What's in here?" I asked, following her. It wasn't very big inside, and when Lockwood, Xandra, and Laura were all squeezed in there with us, we were all standing shoulder to shoulder.

Iona, who was near the shelves, was eyeing the back wall.

"So…a pantry." Xandra said, nodding. "Super magical. Why, it's practically out of *Harry Potter*, it's so magical."

I watched as Iona pressed the tips of her fingers together, closed her eyes, and started murmuring something under her breath.

"Um…Iona?" I asked, my heart starting to race.

Lockwood had gone pale. "I can feel it."

Xandra snorted. "You can feel what? The savings?"

"No," he said, "the power."

I thought it was just the close proximity to all of them, but I realized I could sense a shift of some sort too. Like running my hand over a balloon, feeling the static electricity.

"What's going on?" I asked.

But before he could answer, against the back wall, where the shelves had once been, a huge, swirling, glowing doorway appeared, crackling and humming. Wind rushed past us, creating a tunnel effect. Light poured out of it, like a great cyclone of blue and white. It smelled like ozone, like water evaporating off hot pavement.

"Holy crap," Xandra said, throwing her arms around Laura, who was as pale as white cake batter.

Lockwood looked even more terrified than Laura, and that made my heart slam against my ribs. If Lockwood was afraid…

Iona ducked her head as she stepped through the portal, treating it like nothing more than a low doorway.

"Iona, wait—" I said.

She disappeared from view, the swirling blue tide pool of light swallowing her up. Her hand appeared back through it, beckoning us forward.

A magic portal. In the middle of Ikea.

She was joking, right?

"What do we do?" Xandra asked.

The humming was so loud that my bones seemed to vibrate.

I swallowed my nerves. I had to rescue Mill. And if that meant that I had to go through some creepy, unknown portal to a place that Iona had completely left me in the dark about, then I would do it.

For him. I was going to find a way to save him.

I stepped into the light and left Ikea behind.

Chapter 25

"You have got to be kidding me…"

Xandra's words struck me as being just about right.

We followed Iona through the portal, winds battering me as I stepped through, my hair twisting and twirling around my face, flapping my T-shirt, pulling at my shoes.

As quickly as the tempest had begun, it ended, and I found myself in an entirely different place.

We stood on a cliff overlooking a giant chasm, waterfalls tumbling down into its dark depths. The falls were of differing heights, stretching along the wall of the cliff and sending spray into the air. Cool spritzes flecked my face, making me squint away out of instinct. In the distance, over the higher cliffs, I could see huge, craggy mountains, grey against the bright blue sky overhead.

But the most impressive aspect of the valley where we found ourselves was the immense temple in the distance, surrounded by waterfalls.

A red bird appeared in the sky overhead, as big as a dragon, wings shimmering in the bright sunlight. As it flapped its wings, they seemed to change color, the long feathers like glass, with light piercing through.

The waterfalls made a dull roar, like background noise. Growing up in New York, I was no stranger to waterfalls, but these were even bigger than Niagara Falls by at least double, if not triple. The bottom of the chasm was blackness. Who knew if there actually was a bottom? It could have gone on forever, and I never would have known, the depths disappearing into endless dark.

Something felt off with this place. There was nowhere like this on Earth, but it was similar. The sun was warm, we could breathe the air…but I couldn't put my finger on what was—

I blanched as I saw Iona standing in direct sunlight.

"Iona—" I said, reaching for her, "What are you doing?"

She yanked her arm out of mine the moment I touched her. "It's fine. This isn't Earth's sun. It's not even a real sun."

I blinked and stared around. Laura was hanging back near the portal, and Xandra was slowly making her way to the cliff's edge beside Iona.

"What is this place?" Xandra asked, staring around. "It's like something out of a dream."

"It's dangerous, is what it is," Lockwood said, standing straight, angrily shooting daggers at the back of Iona's head with the heat of his stare. "Why did you bring us here?" he asked in a more threatening tone than I had ever heard him use. "This is suicide, Iona. If we do one thing, *one thing* wrong, then we—"

"We won't be doing anything wrong, okay?" Iona said. But I could see that even she was a little shaken. "Or at least I won't. Can't speak for the blue-haired hipster or the zombie queen of the cheer squad."

Lockwood fumed, but said nothing, and I knew it wasn't because of Iona's clever nicknames.

"What's going on?" I asked him.

He shook his head. "I care about Mill, too, Cassandra," he said, never taking his eyes off Iona. "But he would not approve of us going to these depths to help him."

"You're just mad she can do what you can't," Iona said. "Now come on. We have to get to that temple."

Of course we did.

The cliff faces spanned the outside of the chasm. Every few hundred feet, another waterfall tumbled down onto the eaves, then continued flowing down into the darkness below. Bridges spanned the short rivers that fed the waterfalls ahead, giving us a path to the temple, some several miles distant.

The temple itself was a dark blue, three stories tall, like three boxes all stacked atop one another from biggest to smallest. There was ornate detail on the rooftops, almost as if it were a Japanese temple, trimmed in gold and silver, with a tall, pointed spire at the very top.

A massive set of stairs led up to the entrance. And there were no windows visible from where we were.

We followed Iona, none of us speaking. Words wouldn't really do this place any justice. What could we say? *Wow, cool, this place is awesome. Look, there are strange birds and waterfalls with green rainbows! How amazing.*

Even in my head it didn't feel like enough, like children trying to describe the Grand Canyon. *It's so huge! It's hugenormous! Can I have some mac and cheese now?*

My stomach rumbled. Actually, mac and cheese sounded pretty good about now.

I felt safer walking closer to the wall of the cliff, my hand trailing the rough rock wall on my left. Laura and Xandra were doing the same, Laura spared a look over the cliff into the chasm, then turned green. I made a mental note not to look down.

We came to one of the bridges spanning a pool before the churning waterfall's edge, which tumbled over the cliff to my right. It was made of smooth black wood, simple, and completely dry.

The roar was deafening this close to the waterfall, but it stole the breath out of my lungs as I stared down the cliff face at the falling cataract.

"Look!" Laura pointed at something yellow in the churn of the pool. I had seen it too. There were long, bright yellow fish swimming around up to the waterfall's edge as if it were as still as a pond. They wriggled their little tails and swam along, unaffected by the volume of water pulling off the cliff.

"Like some sort of super salmon," Xandra said, staring over the ebon bridge rail.

Lockwood appeared beside Xandra, his face still hard. "Do not let this magic seduce you," he said, his tone stern. "It will morph and adapt to what you want from it. The longer we are here, the more dangerous it is. Especially for you three."

"Yeah, no stopping to gawk," Iona said from the other side

of the bridge, already back on the rough rock of the cliff's path. "Or at least not you, Cassie. The other two I could do without, but I've invested a lot of time in our friendship and I don't want to start over with having to find a new person to hang out with. Especially now that Byron's dead, finding people with a common frame of reference would be so beyond time consuming."

It was hard to pull us away from the fish. I shook off the magical effects as I stepped off the bridge. "Is this a part of Faerie?" I asked as we continued along the cliff path.

Lockwood shook his head. "No, it isn't. And I must be honest… I can feel myself growing weaker the longer we are here."

Cold rushed through my veins. "What? Why?"

"Because," he said, "this is not Faerie magic. This is Earth magic."

"But we definitely aren't on Earth anymore," I said, staring around.

"In fact, we are," Lockwood said. "This is all just an illusion."

"Wait, are we still at Ikea?" Xandra asked. "Because I never did get those meatballs."

"Yes," Lockwood said. "Our bodies are still there, standing there in that tiny pantry."

"That's going to seem super rude if anyone comes over to talk to us," Laura said. "Will we just ignore them?"

"Your consciousness is here," Lockwood said. "All higher brain functions are on hold while we are in this place."

"So yes, you'll probably still answer them," Iona said, "since you don't use your higher brain function... Well, ever. Especially when speaking."

I shook my head. "This is as confusing as Faerie…"

"But far more dangerous…" Lockwood said. "Come on."

I hung back a second as he pressed on, assessing the respective moods of Laura and Xandra. I saw a lot of worry on their faces, though Laura looked less rattled for some reason. "You guys okay?" I asked.

"I just can't even with what my eyes are seeing you know?" Xandra shook her head. "It's more amazing than I could ever think up on my own."

"It's like a painting," Laura said. "So beautiful that you could just stop and stare." As she said it, her pace slowed and she stared out into the distance.

"Come on," I said, grabbing her hand and dragging her along. "We really don't want to linger here. Lockwood's right. Magic is not something you want to mess with."

"Yeah, you know all about magic now, don't you?" Xandra asked.

"Hardly," I said. Iona and Lockwood were crossing another bridge a short ways ahead, this one a little broader, as the pool they crossed was much wider. Lockwood's words were haunting me, making me very uneasy.

But...I had to do this for Mill.

The temple was ahead, over one final bridge. Now that we were closer, I could see that it was surrounded by waterfalls on all sides. I had thought it was sitting on a cliff, but it was actually just floating over the chasm, linked to the nearest cliff's edge by another of the black wooden bridges. I followed after Iona as she crossed it without a second thought.

The temple was like smoke, shifting its shape but hiding anything that lay beyond. Iona hesitated for a second before plunging her hand into the substance. She winced, but when she pulled her hand out, it was unscathed. "It's fine," she said. "Probably just a cleansing spell of some sort."

"Or she means to track us," Lockwood said, his eyes narrowing.

Iona shrugged and stepped through the thick fog. Lockwood shook his head.

"You don't have to do this," I said.

"Yes, I do," he said. "I have to protect you three. Because within...we may find much more than we bargained for." And then he followed Iona through the thick, dense doors of fog.

I stared after him. There was no sound aside from the tumbling waterfalls.

"Great," I muttered, Laura and Xandra bunching up behind me, neither eager to take the lead. "Stepping through more magic. How could this possibly go wrong?"

But step I did, right into the smoky partition.

It felt like a cold, misty day as the smoky black brushed my skin. The air was icy, like the middle of winter. I was sure my eyelashes had frozen. Another step, and warmth washed over me.

I opened my eyes and gasped.

I found myself in a large room with a black tile floor, black walls, and a (big surprise) black, vaulted ceiling far overhead. Golden bowls of fire burned in all four corners of the cavernous space, as well as beside the large, gilded throne at the far end of the room. It sat on a tall, ebony dais, with a set of golden stairs leading up to it.

Lockwood and Iona were already at the foot of the stairs, looking up into the face of the woman who was draped across the throne as if it were a loveseat. She slumped, utterly casual, as if she were home alone, bingeing on the latest season of her favorite show on Netflix.

"I wondered how long it would take you three," the woman said in a voice I can only describe as sultry. She smiled puckishly as her eyes met mine across the wide temple space. "I've so been looking forward to meeting you."

Chapter 26

Cold prickles ran across my skin, remnant of the smoky doors that had brought us into this strange black and gold temple. I stared at the woman lounging on the throne as if it were an armchair. She was tall, slender, her hair as blue as cotton candy, with pink highlights. It was tied up on top of her head in the most perfect messy bun, a style that any girl, even myself admittedly, would kill to be able to do.

"Oh. Em. Gee." Xandra said, looking up at our host. "Move over, Cassie. I've found my new best friend." I could see why Xandra was excited. She had a very similar look to this lady, whose eyebrows matched her hair, her long eyelashes violently pink. Her lilac eyes were so pale they were almost white, making her pupils stand out.

But then I realized that her pupils weren't black. They were dark blue. Even in the flickering light of the fires, I could see the difference. She flashed us a smile from between her pink lips that matched her lashes, stretched her legs, and rose to her feet.

"Why the glum faces?" she asked, looking around at all of us. "Other than Xandra, you people look like you're ready for a funeral. You reached me, and in good time, too." She smirked. "I was sure that some of my little tricks would snare you, too."

Lockwood crossed his arms.

"Oh, lighten up, faerie boy," the woman said, waving her hand in Lockwood's direction. "It's just harmless, shiny magic.

Why would I hurt those I call to come unto me?"

"'Call'?" Xandra asked. She looked at Iona. "She called us?"

"What?" Iona blinked furiously. "I didn't get any calls, other than from those damned telemarketers. No, I don't need a new roof, I don't even have a house at the moment—"

"Easy, don't get your braid in a knot," the woman said. "What made you think of coming to see me in the first place, hmm?"

Iona furrowed her brow. "I don't know. I overheard Lockwood and Cassie talking about who to call and…"

"Yeah," the woman said, clapping her hands together, the sound echoing around the room, causing us all to jump. "Inspiration strikes. It's kind of a signature of mine." She grinned, planting her fists on her hips. "Now… For those of you who might not know...I am the Oracle."

I looked at Xandra, then Laura. Blank faces all around.

"Of course you don't know who I am…" she said, shaking her head. "Humans. You're so magilliterate. That's a word, by the way. I just made it up to describe how little you know about magic. It'll be in the dictionary by next year, just laying down a marker right here. When you see it, remember this moment and remember me. Boom. That's the power of the Oracle."

"Oracle," Iona said, "we've come—"

The Oracle waved dismissively. "Yes, yes, I know why you're here. I'm not magilliterate, after all."

"Wait, you already know?" I asked.

The Oracle's gaze fell on me. "Of course. I know everything that's going on here."

"Oh yeah?" Xandra said, jutting her chin out. "Then who am I?"

"Alexandra, but you prefer 'Xandra' because 'Alex' is sooooo overused these days. Seventeen. Only child. Parents both living, you get along with them—rare for your age bracket— and you have decent taste in music, if we could just wean you off your experimental forays into Maroon 5. Don't do it, darling. Adam Levine will only make you feel cheap and then break your heart."

Xandra flushed. "I do not listen to Maroon 5." Her eyes

flitted around, furtively. "Most of the time."

"Make it 'all of the time' and you'll be a lot better off," the Oracle said, turning her attention to Laura. "And here we have Laura. Captain of the cheerleading squad, secret book worm, and lover of all things pineapple. It's okay, my darling, pineapple is perfectly fine on a pizza, don't listen to those heretics saying otherwise."

Laura's eyes nearly bulged out of her head. "How…how did you know all that...?"

"That's nothing," the Oracle said. "What else, hmm? How about the fact you have a really big crush on—"

"No one," Laura said, cheeks flame red. "I have a crush on absolutely no one."

The Oracle chuckled. "Oof, you humans. So afraid of what other people think. By the way, he likes you too. So get on it, girl."

Laura looked down at the floor, saying nothing to that.

Then the Oracle turned her eyes on me. "And then we have Cassandra. Or Cassie, as she prefers everyone but Lockwood to call her. She doesn't mind her Faerie friend using her full name, but she doesn't let her boyfriend use it. Weird, isn't it?" She smiled. "It's because he's different, right? That Paladin formality, some sort of courtly air he brings to it? It'd sound strange if the word 'Cassie' passed his lips. Like Dame Judi Dench swearing up a storm, or a politician telling the honest truth, there's just something unnatural about it."

My blood went cold, and my fingers went numb as I stared up at her. I could see now why Lockwood was so frightened of her. Her power was unlike anything else I had ever known. Her easy knowledge alone was unsettling.

"Your magic lets you see all of this about us?" I asked. "I mean, you could have found out some of this stuff on our social media, by spying on us."

"Oh, I have been spying on you, yes," the Oracle said, nodding her head. "Definitely been spying on you. Your little group has grabbed my attention."

"What do you mean, 'my little group?'" I asked.

"Oh, come on. I find you absolutely fascinating. The girl who keeps winning, who keeps overcoming all these paranormal oddities. Who doesn't love an underdog story, rooting for the little engine that could? Especially since in our world, you're a nobody. Nobody important's daughter, nobody important's cousin. That makes it all the more interesting."

I stared up at her as she studied me, leaning forward, towering over me from her pedestal.

"So…" the Oracle said, starting to pace back and forth on the dais. "You killed the witches and enlisted the help of the werewolves. Who does that? No one, that's who. With Iona's help, sure, but she helps no one. So points for that. Very clever."

Iona remained passive, but if she'd been human, I bet she would have been blushing.

"That was a battle worthy of tabletop RPG. High defense, top tier weapons, good location. Not to mention the stats of your team involved. Outnumbered, sure—but you still had the advantage. I hate to use the cliché, since everyone says this now, but truly: Well played."

I was waiting for her point. If she really knew as much as she claimed—

"But that isn't why you are here," she said. "You want to deal with the vampires, yes…but your first concern is for Mill. Which is touching." She put a hand between her collarbones. "See? I'm touching myself."

"Yes," I said. "You're right. We need help." I swallowed heavily. "*I* need help."

"Damned right you do," she said. "But what makes you think that I can help you?" She tipped her head to the side, resting a thoughtful finger on her chin. "I mean, they say knowledge is power, but that's dumb. You can know everything, but if you don't do anything with it, it's about as powerful as an encyclopedia sitting on the shelf. You need to pick that bad boy up and plant it upside someone's head for it to be any good in your current fight. Meow." She a made a clawing motion with her fingers. "That seems like something you'd do, am I right?"

"Iona said you understand the magic poisoning Mill?" I asked. My heart was starting to race again, but I was hopeful.

159

The Oracle knew things. Maybe here was the help I'd been so desperate for.

The Oracle nodded. "I know that magic well. Those sorts of spells have gone out of style. I mean, who has the energy for a spite-curse like that anymore? So tiring. You really got under Draven's skin."

"I noticed," I said. "Please. I need help. Lockwood says that Mill only has two days."

"Less," the Oracle said. "That was a potent spell. The only good news was that it hit his arm and not his chest or head. If that had happened, game over, K.O., death number two for the man with the legendary forehead."

It was like my nerves were alive and on fire.

"You have to understand, little Seelie," the Oracle said with a wink, "the spell Draven ordered is a very personal thing. Less a 'To Whom It May Concern' and more of a 'To Hell With You and All Your Kin and the Horse You Rode in On and the Dog That Followed Behind You', signed in one's own blood. That sort of magic, *emotional magic*, is deep stuff. Personal. Powerful."

"So the spell was meant for me?" I asked.

"No," the Oracle shook her head, "definitely meant for Mill. Because hurting him hurts you more. Draven knows that you put yourself in danger to help out those you care about," she gestured to Laura, "example A."

"This is all my fault, then," I said.

"Bingo," the Oracle said. "And you get that—but not in the teenage girl, martyr-complex-y way. You feel it, but it doesn't drive into a deep and forever hole. You understand that if Byron had only passed you over…" Her eyes flashed.

The old, familiar anger bubbled up within me. It burned in my belly like acid.

"But that isn't the hand you've been dealt, and like our dear friend Link, you have to overcome this trial all on your own. It's dangerous to go alone, and all that. You're the chosen one. You and Harry Potter could form a club where your whole life goes to crap and you then have to struggle through somehow with nothing but grit and a plucky attitude and maybe a few close friends. Just be careful. Because sometimes those friends end up dead because of your choices." She gasped, putting both hands up on her cheeks. "Spoilers!"

"What do you mean?" I asked. "Can you not help me?"

The Oracle started down the stairs toward us, her tall, pencil thin heels clacking against the golden stairs as she descended. "Oh, I could definitely help you."

Relief, like an injection to my system, washed over me. "Thank you. I don't know what—"

"Upupup—" she said, holding up a thin finger, silencing me. "I said I *could*. Not that I was going to."

"What?" I said, feeling like the floor had been dropped from beneath me, plunging me back into the icy pond of grief.

"But…" she said, arching an eyebrow as she looked at me. "I will tell you how *you* can help him." The Oracle stepped over to me. This close, she wasn't all that much taller than me, even in her heels. A strong earthy scent wafted off of her clothes, like pine in the winter, or freshly cut grass. "The only way that you can save Mill is to subject yourself to your greatest fear."

I blinked. After being straightforward about everything else, she was choosing to be cryptic now?

"I don't understand," I said. "If you have all of this power, and you can help me...why won't you?"

"I might be interested in your life, Cassie," the Oracle said, "but that doesn't mean I'm jonesing to step into your teenage drama on a whim so I can fix everything. I'm not your fairy godmother. I'm the Oracle. I know things. And I drink. Mostly Mountain Dew, unlike Tyrion Lannister. Pretty crucial difference, but still—I don't fix."

"Is this some kind of game to you?" I asked, the awe and fear of her dissolving as my anger took hold.

"Duh," the Oracle said, rolling her eyes. "Yes. But it's more than that. Because this really is something that only you can do."

"By subjecting myself to my greatest fear?" I asked, glowering at her.

"So basically she has to go into Starbucks and unironically order a double shot sugar free chai latte with coconut milk?" Xandra asked.

"Those are delicious," Laura said.

"Go live in a yurt, already, you trendy, pineapple-pizza eating freak," Xandra said. "Your judgment is incredibly suspect."

"Whatever, Maroon 5. Why don't you go listen to 'Sugar' on repeat until you lose your mind? Oops, too late," Laura said.

The Oracle held up her hands for silence. Xandra and Laura stopped, and I wasn't convinced that she hadn't used magic to do it.

"This is all on you, Cassie. I'm not the bad guy," the Oracle said. "I didn't get you into this mess, and I can't get you out of it."

I glared at her.

"Don't you get it? All your choices have led to this," she said. "Every lie you ever told...has brought you here."

There was no denying that. It was all of my choices.

Not Lockwood's. Not Iona's. Not my friends.

We had come to this scary, dangerous place to meet with this Oracle because of *me,* and *my* boyfriend, because *my* enemy, who I made all by *myself* had ordered a hunt for *me* and did whatever he could to hurt *me* in the process.

"I can see the wheels turning," the Oracle said, eyes flashing. "You get it. It's all on you."

I frowned. She didn't have to make it any harder than it already was.

"Don't get angry with me," she said, brow contracting. "You need to face this. Own it. It's the only way you're going to win. You are the only one who can get yourself out of this mess."

"How?" I asked. "I don't understand."

"All of your lies brought this before you. All of your choices brought you to the end."

She was still speaking cryptically.

"You will try everything, hope for everything, wish for something to come in and spare you your consequences. But that's not how this works, this funny life thing you people are going through." She winked at me. "I know it sounds stupid, but—responsibility. It's more than just an adult buzzword they sling out when they punish you. *Own this.* It's yours. Your failure. Your choices. And you...will have to surrender yourself to your greatest fear…and only then will you get what you want."

She gave me a sympathetic sort of tilt of her head. There was pity in her pale lilac eyes, and she sighed, shaking her head.

"I know. I lost you at 'responsibility'. It's a parent-lecture-mental-turn-off word. But you'll figure it out," she said. "I've seen you overcome the impossible. Don't disappoint me." And then she reached out, touched me on the forehead, and then *zap*.

We were standing in the little pantry in Ikea.

I blinked a few times, my eyes adjusting to the dim light. I looked around, saw the others doing the same, safely returned from our shared vision.

Nobody said anything.

I don't think anyone had any words left after all that.

Chapter 27

I pondered the words that the Oracle had left me with in silence as we left Ikea, no one daring to speak until we were several miles down the road, the VW rattling in time with my own thoughts. It had a been a bumpy road I'd been on lately, and I couldn't shake the feeling that the Oracle had nailed it, holding my failures up for all to see, driving home points of guilt I'd been chewing on for months.

"Of all of the vile, preposterous, disturbing ideas that you have ever had, Iona, this one might top them all," Lockwood exploded, rather suddenly, and drawing every eye in the car as he lit off. "If I had any idea what you were thinking, I would have put a stop to it immediately."

"How?" Iona asked. "Jinxed my car? Put up a forcefield around Ikea? Because, really, that would just be hateful, separating people from their Swedish furniture options and forcing them to go to those rip-off high-end stores."

"All this, and what did it come to, hmm?" Lockwood asked. "We still have no answers."

"I thought she was cool," Xandra said, shrugging, her face bathed in shadow and light like a strobe at a rave as we drove beneath the streetlights.

"You wouldn't think that she was so 'cool' if she was eating your heart right out of your chest," Lockwood said, turning around to peer at her between the headrest and the window. It wasn't like him to get so worked up.

"She probably would think that *was* cool," Laura said. "This is a Maroon 5 fan we're talking about here."

"Listen, Cheerleader, just because we don't all dress in trendy Ugg boots or contour our makeup—"

"Now see here, Iona," Lockwood said, speaking over the two of them, "I understand that you want to help Cassandra. But the Oracle is a soul-skinning, power hungry, blood sucking—"

"Shut up unless you have a better idea," Iona said. "Because I don't see you firing off any great ideas, Mr. Wings."

Lockwood fell silent, staring at the side of Iona's face with a dark look that I had only recently seen him give the man who had betrayed us in Faerie: Roseus.

The car rattled on, the engine humming as it decelerated to turn off the highway and onto the roads that would take us back to Xandra's house.

"I—" Lockwood said. The tightness in his eyes told me that he really didn't want to say what he was about to say. But he couldn't lie, either. "I suppose…"

"Put up or shut up," Iona said.

"I..." Lockwood licked his lips. "I suppose I might...'know someone', as you are so lately fond of saying."

Great. This was the day of meeting new people and humiliating myself in front of them all with my tale of woe and misery.

"You're just saying that because I popularized it first," Iona said.

"I should emphasize that I never would have considered this person under normal circumstances," Lockwood said. "Never, not ever." He shifted in his seat to turn around and look at me. "I fear that I am leading you horribly astray by placing this option before you. But…" He took a deep breath and looked me square in the eye. "How far are you willing to go with this?"

It was a startling question, like a spear filed to a point, piercing right to the heart of the issue. If I was honest, part of me just wanted to…give up. To go back home, pretend like none of this ever happened. It was too hard to deal with, especially if it was going to end in Mill's death no matter what I did. And I was starting to suspect it would, because...

Because Mill's death was my greatest fear.

I shook my head. I didn't want to face any of this anymore. It was getting too painful.

I wouldn't say I loved him. Not yet, at least. But that didn't mean I didn't care about him or want him around. But I was the one responsible for all this mess, and I was the one who cared the most out of anyone about him.

"I don't know, Lockwood," I said. "I want to help, but…"

"How much do you want to help him?" Lockwood asked, his gaze hardening.

Everyone's eyes shifted to mine, and I froze to my seat.

Is this what peer pressure was like?

The Oracle's words just kept circling around in my head as if they were stuck on repeat:

It's all on you.

"I can't let him die, Lockwood," I said. "I'll meet this…friend of yours."

"Very well, then," Lockwood said. "I should suggest that we do drop off the girls, first, though." And he turned his head, his profile in shadow. "Because unlike Iona, I do care about what happens, and this…this place we go…" He bowed his head. "…it is not safe. No. Not remotely. Though," and he lowered his voice to a gentle timbre, "I suppose nowhere really is, anymore."

Chapter 28

We pulled up to Xandra's house, and nobody moved, silence pervading the car. Laura and Xandra seemed to have no intention of getting out of the car, and I for one was not getting out again. Not when I was turning right around and leaving again. Why would I? So I could do a round of "hi and goodbye" with my parents? Or with Mill? I shuddered. I needed to go, to get this done. Time was wasting.

"I am not saying this to be mean," Lockwood said, turning around. "But you two have to get out."

"This is really that dangerous?" Xandra asked.

"No, I simply cannot stomach any more bickering from the two of you," Lockwood said. "And also, Maroon 5 are a terrible, terrible band, and pineapple on pizza is an unholy evil that I place only slightly lower than Draven. Now...get out."

"Go!" Iona shouted, making both of them jump in their seats.

"Maroon 5 are awesome, I don't care what any of you say," Xandra muttered, throwing open her door. "What do you even know, Lockwood? Adam Levine's voice is magical."

"I know quite a bit about magic and nothing about that man is magic," Lockwood said.

Xandra wheeled around and peered back inside the car.

"Can I talk to you for a second?" she asked me. She sounded pretty serious, so I shot Lockwood a questioning look.

"Is it about Maroon 5?" I asked. "Because I really don't have time for them...well, ever, actually."

"Harsh. But no, it's not about them."

"You have two minutes," Lockwood said when I glanced at him. "If we are going to do this mad, mad thing...I would really would rather get it over with."

He was doing such a good job of filling me with confidence.

I crawled out of the car, and Xandra shut it behind me before I was barely outside. "What's going on?" I asked. "Are you okay?"

Xandra sighed heavily. "Cassie, I have to ask… how far are you willing to go to save your vampire boyfriend? Because I don't know about you, but Lockwood seems really nervous about whatever is about to happen to you. And he doesn't strike me as the person to really…react that way."

"Well, gee, Xandra, you're right." I poured on the withering sarcasm. "That is pretty scary. Because I definitely haven't had my life on the line since the night Byron chased us."

She didn't flinch away from my bristling comment. "Come on, you've been dating this guy for all of what…like, six weeks now? I know that your life has been beyond crazy and I can't even imagine what it's been like for you…" She was being completely serious. She was worried. Her usual sarcasm and wit was set aside, and her big blue eyes were staring intently at me, her whole focus on me.

She wanted me to hear what she was saying. It was coming right from the heart.

"This is your *life,* Cassie. I get that you care about him and all, but…he's kinda already dead."

"Undead, but..." My heart sank. "You're right." I stared down at my dirty tennis shoes. "This is my life. Vampire stalkers. Instaphoto vampire gangs. Road trips halfway across the country to keep my family from getting murdered by vampires. Trips to Faerie to stop wars between the two major faerie courts. And now a vampire Lord is coming after literally everything I care about."

Xandra stared at me, and my mouth went sort of dry. I'd had no intention of just dumping that all on her. I hadn't even realized that all of that had been weighing on me as much as it had been.

"It's just insane, you know?" I said. "I never intended for

any of this to happen. And somehow, all of you got roped into it. And I'm sorry for that."

"Cass, you don't need to apologize," Xandra said. "You know, you can back out at any time. Mill wouldn't want you to suffer because of him. You don't owe him anything—"

"But I do, Xandra," I said. "I owe him so much. He has saved me more times than I can count, all the way up to at Byron's place last night. He's protected me and carried me, bleeding, out of harm's way. He's never complained, not even once, about any of it."

Xandra's face fell, and she looked sheepish.

"And it's not just about him," I said. "It may be the driving force right now, but you're just as much at risk, long-term. So is Laura. My parents. Your parents, for housing us. There is so much I'm worrying about right now that I feel like my head might explode."

To demonstrate it, I pressed my palms against both sides of my head, hoping that maybe somehow, miraculously, it would help in some small way.

"I'm dealing with a lot right now," I said. I exhaled heavily, running my fingers through my hair. "This is my life. A crazy, screwed up mess that I literally can't see a way out of. It's just black. No light at the end of the tunnel for me."

"There's always a way out," Xandra said. "It may be a firefly, or maybe even just a reflection, but that light will show up."

"Yeah, well, I appreciate your optimism," I said. "Knowing my luck, it'll be a train coming straight at me."

Xandra stared up at the moon over our heads, only a few nights away from being full. "You feel stuck."

"Yeah, that's about right," I said.

"I'm sorry, Cassie," Xandra said. "I can't even begin to understand. But I hope you know...I wish I had the power to help. This whole time I've felt pretty useless. I'm not a vampire or a faerie. Werewolves are cool, but I'm definitely not one of those either." Her face split into a grin. "Now the Oracle...her, I'd like to be." She gave me a gentle nudge with her elbow, and I smiled in spite of the icky sick feelings the anxiety was giving me.

"I appreciate you telling me all this," Xandra said.

"Honesty is kind of hard for me," I said. I swallowed hard and laughed hollowly. "The sharing part...it'd be a lot easier to lie about how I'm feeling. It's funny...of all the lies I told in New York, the ones that made basically the whole town turn on me, and made my parents pick up and move across the country...I never could have imagined the life I live now is more unbelievable than any lie I could've ever come up with then." I shook my head. "There's some deep irony there."

"Life's like that," she said. "It feeds you irony until you're stuffed, then serves irony-laden desserts."

"I've had my fill of that." I smiled. "But...at least I met you because of all this. And you've been a better friend to me than pretty much anyone else in my life ever has been. You have definitely vaulted past Jacquelyn in the best friend Olympics."

The familiar sarcastic smile of hers returned, and she gave me a shove in the arm. Then she surprised me by throwing her arms around my neck and giving me a tight hug. "Wow, I'm so awesome, beating out the vampire that burned down your house and helped poison your boyfriend."

I closed my eyes for a second, allowing her affection and support to wash over me. It gave me a boost of strength, bringing warmth to my weary bones. "You are awesome, Xandra."

She went quiet on me. "What are you going to do now?"

"The only thing I can think of is to make different choices now," I said.

She gave me a quizzical look. "What...?"

"All my choices that got us into this mess, right?" I waited for that spark of understanding in her eyes. "So I'm going to have to make different choices to get us out."

"What, like do the opposite of what you'd usually do?" she asked. "Instead of going left, go right? Instead of ordering the crispy chicken sandwich, you go with the grilled instead?"

"Something like that," I said. "Whatever choice I would have made originally, I need to go against my first gut reaction and really think about it from here on out."

"That sounds good, but will it work?"

I shrugged my shoulders. "Your guess is as good as mine."

The car window rolled down and Lockwood peered out at

us. "Come along, Lady Cassandra."

"All right, I'm coming," I said, turning to reach for the door.

"Look, Cassie," Xandra said, moving to stand back in front of my view, holding the door closed. "I just want you to know that I support whatever you do, but I don't want to see you actively throw your life away for some vampire boyfriend that you've only had for a few weeks."

"Well, that's not exactly plan A," I said. "And besides, there's more on the line than just Mill. Though I'd be lying if I said that he wasn't the primary reason I'm sort of in freak out mode."

I glanced passed Xandra at the house and saw my dad standing in the window of the living room, peering out at me.

We made eye contact, and he waved at me. I waved back.

We needed to go. I could explain everything to them after we got back. Hopefully it wouldn't be too late. And we wouldn't die. Because that would be really tough to explain. At least it wouldn't be my problem anymore, strictly speaking.

"Be safe, okay?" Xandra said as she withdrew her hand, letting me open the car door.

"Thanks. See you guys in a bit." And I ducked into the car, letting her close it behind me.

She gave me a hesitant wave as we backed up in silence and drove away into the deepening night.

Chapter 29

"You know, guys, I'm getting kind of tired of running all over the city trying to find someone who can help us," I said, staring at the back of Lockwood's head. "Iona knows a guy. Lockwood knows a guy who might be able to help. Well, I once met a random hobo beneath a bridge overpass that said he had cosmic powers." I sagged against the seat. "I hope the actual help shows up soon, because I'm kinda drowning here, people. Also, when did Tampa become the home for every mythical creature in the universe, huh?"

"Someone's tired," Lockwood said in a way that told me that he was annoyed that I had opened my mouth in the first place.

"Someone's boyfriend is dying, and therefore, she's taking it out on those closest to her," Iona said.

"You don't have to say it so starkly," I said, trying to ignore the swelling fear inside me. "And why are all these mythical, paranormal people and creatures clustered up around Tampa? I went my whole life without seeing any vampires or werewolves or witches and boom—now in the space of months, more than I can shake a stick at. Or a stake at."

"Tampa's not that unusual as cities go," Iona said. "There's not an abnormal amount of paranormal activity here over other cities of similar size."

"So there are people like the Oracle everywhere?" I asked.

"She's…a bit different," Lockwood said.

"She doesn't actually live in Tampa," Iona said, glancing at me in the mirror. "There are other portals to access her in different parts of the state, or the planet. There's actually one in a bathroom at Disney World. You just go in the stall and leave your body behind until you come back. Makes it a little awkward if you do it around closing time. You might wake up in jail, or a hospital."

"Okay, but why Ikea?" I said.

"It's kind of a two-way portal," Iona said, "and she likes the meatballs, I guess."

We made our way out of the city heading north. There was a lot less development up here. The city and all its lights were behind us, and now we were surrounded by farms, sprawling cookie cutter developments, and a lot more open sky.

"So, Lockwood..." Iona said. "Who's this person you're taking us to go see?"

Lockwood suppressed a shiver. "He's a faerie."

"Wow, way to sound excited about that," I said. "You're talking about him like you did about Orianna when we first met her."

"Orianna?" Iona asked.

"An Unseelie that we met during our recent sojourn in Faerie," Lockwood said.

"Why would you have been associated with an Unseelie?" Iona asked. "Admittedly, I'm not expert on Faerie having never been invited—"

"Vampires are not welcome in Faerie," Lockwood said.

"—but I didn't think an Unseelie would cross the line to deal with you two."

"You seem surprisingly well-versed in the politics of Faerie," Lockwood said, raising an eyebrow at Iona. "And far more interested in this than most other topics, I note."

"It's because there's drama," I said. "And Iona likes to rub it in my face when I make bad decisions."

"You make so very many of them, though," Iona said. "And I'm not even counting Forehead in this, because I'm sensitive and wouldn't want to mention him as a terrible, terrible choice while he's ailing—oops." She puckered her lips. "Uh, Lockwood, why don't you tell me all about this Faerie adventure you two went on without even asking me if I'd like to come along?"

Lockwood rolled his eyes. But he told her anyway.

I sat in the back seat, only half listening to them, staring out of the window and up at the starry sky. It was way easier to see the stars out here. In the city, I could never see them. Back in my home in rural New York, I could see them all every night.

I hadn't realized how much I had missed it.

There was so much about my life that had changed, but to have something comforting like the presence of the stars over my head, along with some constellations that I recognized, sort of gave me the chance to mentally check out, and just let my mind wander and be lulled into a passive state.

It didn't last long, though. It never did, these days.

"Turn here," Lockwood said. I sat up with a jerk as we exited on a dirt road with a thump when the tires left the pavement. We bumped along through the dark, headlights revealing potholes as big as ones I would see after a harsh winter in the north.

"Where are we going?" I asked.

"To a place where the veil is thin between Earth and Faerie," Lockwood said. "Somewhere humans don't want to tread."

Well, that made it sound a lot more ominous than I would have liked.

"Couldn't people just walk onto this guy's property?" I asked, looking around. "This seems like a relatively normal rural road to me."

As we pulled up, swarms of gnats flittered around the swamp outside, visible in the streaks of moonlight that made their way through moss-covered trees. An owl hooted on a distant branch as I stepped out into the warm, wet air. The breeze was still this far inland, and I was already starting to itch thinking about the gnats.

It was a swamp, all right, just like I was told that all of old Florida used to be. Crickets and frogs chirped to each other. I could just make out the glint of starlight off the still surface of a pond, between blooms of algae. And rising up off a hummock in the distance sat a little wooden shack, bathed in moonlight.

Bubbles in the murky water made me leery. I had read

somewhere that alligators lived in every body of water in Florida.

"Oh, this is disgusting," I said, staring out at the little hut. "You can't be serious, Lockwood. Wait—this is a glamour, isn't it? Or an un-glamour?" I paused, searching for the word. "Whatever, this is an unglamorous a setting as I can imagine. There's really a fae mansion somewhere ahead, right? Not a..." I glanced at the shack. "...uh...whatever that is."

"No. He is...unconventional, for one of my kind," Lockwood said. "Let's just get this over with."

The air was sticky, even at midnight, and I swatted at the bugs that made a bee-line right for my face, with little success.

Lockwood snapped his fingers, and the bugs seemed to have suddenly lost interest in me.

"What'd you do?" I asked.

"Made you invisible to them." Lockwood said. "Or your scent, at least."

"That is just the nicest way of saying I haven't bathed since Faerie," I said. "Iona, you should take lessons in how to talk smooth from Lockwood."

"Hey, my manners are just fine," Iona said. "For example, I haven't once mentioned that you stink like a rotting cesspool." She was staring warily at a small barn on another hummock of earth in the swampy ground, surrounded by a rickety, broken fence. Several goats were outside, grazing on the swamp grass.

"Um...why does he have goats?" I asked as one lifted its head from the grass, chewing lazily.

"That's a question you probably don't want to know the answer to," Lockwood said.

"Something is not right here," I said, pinching my nose and trying to waft the smell away from me. Everything stunk of wet earth and animal feces.

"You don't even know the half of it," Lockwood said. And he started across the rickety bridge made of wooden two-by-fours tied together with zip-ties toward the little shack. With each step the boards shifted, sagging into the swamp water.

Every horror movie I'd ever watched started flashing through my mind, and all my instincts told me to run. I half expected some masked crazy person with a chainsaw to pop out from around the back of the shack and start chasing us, our screaming dying in the night air as the chainsaw motor drowned us out.

But I forced my imagination to chill and was grateful that I was between Iona and Lockwood as we made our way across the wobbly walkway, my shoes getting progressively wetter as we went.

We walked up to the door, steps squeaking under the pressure of our weight, and Lockwood knocked three times.

There was no answer.

I looked at Iona, who had folded her arms, almost like she was constrained by an invisible straight jacket. She looked mad enough to spit. If she knew something that I didn't, it'd be nice if she'd give voice to it.

Flickering light shone out of the windows. "Maybe he's not home?" I asked, more hopeful than not.

"No, he's here," Lockwood said. He rolled up the sleeve of his shirt, and the silvery star tattoo on his wrist signifying that he was a Seelie suddenly glowed. Lockwood pressed the underside of his wrist against the doorknob, and there was a soft click from inside. He pushed the door open, and I nearly gagged, covering my mouth with my hands.

"This place stinks of blood." Iona's nose wrinkled. She paused and blinked, a little furtively. "Do you think he'll have extra for a hungry guest?"

"He wanted to know my allegiance before allowing us in," Lockwood said, his face paling. "Come. Let's go." And he stepped inside.

Hoping to get a good gasp of fresh-ish, swamp air before the blood smell took over, I took a deep breath, held it, and followed him into the creepy shack.

Chapter 30

The swamp shack was tiny, cramped, and made up of one room and a closed door, which I realized was a bathroom. Rickety bookcases stacked to the ceiling with old, worn leather tomes. A twin bed was squeezed into the corner, the faded, worn blankets askew over white linens. A couple of black cats were curled up into tiny balls there, sleeping. Two others were grooming themselves on the patched couch that ran along the wall near the door, and another pair were hovering over their food bowls beside the black mini-fridge that was propping up a convection oven.

My eyes were watering as I tried to not inhale the smell too deeply. Blood? All I smelled was cat pee, and I debated about breathing through my mouth. A pile of dirty dishes filled the small washing basin beside the mini fridge, and I watched with disgust as little flies buzzed around them.

"Are you sure that's blood?" I asked. "I only smell a ripe litter box."

"Definitely blood," Iona said, moving a dirty pair of socks wadded up on the floor with the tip of her combat boots.

Lockwood was standing near the doorway outside as if he were ready to bolt, possibly after shoving me out first.

"What kind of blood?" I asked, wondering if there might be a dead body underneath the stack of old newspapers piled up in the overflowing trashcan.

"Animal blood," Iona said. "I'd take some, if offered. Any old port in a storm at this point, y'know."

"What kind of animal?" I asked.

She gave me a quizzical look and gave the air a sniff. "All kinds."

"All? Even zebra?" I asked.

"I'm sure if this psychopath could get his hands on a zebra, he'd probably sacrifice it, based on the level of stink in this place," Iona said.

There was a sudden, harsh laugh that rang through the silence as a back door that I had completely missed behind some hanging shirts banged open, and a figure stepped inside.

"That's funny. Sacrifice a zebra? What do you think this is, Venezuela?" He cackled. "But no, I would definitely sacrifice a zebra. If I could."

Instinctively, I reached up into my hair for my stake, but lowered it as the man behind the laugh stepped inside.

He had *wings*. Dark blue wings like midnight. And I could see them. I had known he was a faerie, but he actually looked like one. On Earth, no less. That meant that he didn't wear a glamour like Lockwood did. Hair as black as coal hung all the way to his shoulders, shaggy and untidy. He was wearing something like what Lockwood had worn in Faerie; a dark tunic, leather boots, and a wide, black belt. In his hands he carried a large, swollen frog by the leg.

"Zebras are so rare, though. It makes me wonder if the scarcity of the creature would have any effect on the magical properties…" His eyes were red like rubies as he lost himself in thought for a moment, then flashed us a wide, toothy smile as he closed the back door. The cats scattered as he made his way over to the sink, dumping the frog inside on the stack of soiled plates. It tried to leap out, but he grabbed it in midair. "No, no, friend. Your spleen is needed for the—"

He hesitated, and turned to stare at us as if it had just registered for the first time that we were standing there in his living room…bedroom…kitchen?

"Sorry, can I help you?" he asked. "I mistook you for spirits come back to complain about how wretched your afterlife is." He turned back around and slapped the squirming frog onto a wooden cutting board on edge of the sink. He waved his hand in the air and a knife appeared in his grip. He brought it down gently, obscuring his work at the cutting board with his body.

I swallowed heavily.

"We are sorry to disturb you, Nex," Lockwood said. "My name is Lockwood. I am—"

"I know who you are," he said with a wave of his knife, not even turning around.

I was glad that his back was to me and that he was blocking my view of whatever he was doing to that frog. Though the noises allowed my imagination to run wild in the worst ways. I hope that he had killed it first.

"I saw you all were coming," Nex said. "And promptly forgot about it in the midst of my little project." He tossed something through the air that landed on top of the old newspapers with a splat.

I forced myself not to look.

"But the divination failed to tell me more than the bare details. I don't know much about you, other than you're a goody-goody Seelie," Nex said, his shimmering red eyes turning to Lockwood, pointing at him with the end of the knife, which was dripping with...well. You know.

I held my breath, fighting back a gag.

"...And that you're a vampire," he said, his crimson eyes lingering over Iona. "And a rather unhappy one, at that. You've had a nasty little afterlife, haven't you?"

Iona's glower deepened, but she said nothing.

Nex looked over his other shoulder and met my gaze, red eyes aglow. It was like the first time I had met Orianna. A faerie's gaze was mesmerizing. Almost as if I could get lost in them forever...

"A human? Why did you drag her along? Is she your personal vending machine?" Nex asked, glancing at Iona.

"I wish," Iona said. "Do you have any non-frog blood you could spare? Maybe something from a pig? Or a gorilla, they seem pretty similar to humans."

Nex shrugged. "The most recent mammal I slaughtered was a couple days ago, so...no."

Iona's face fell. "You don't anything fresher than that?"

"What does this place look like to you?" Nex asked. "A

179

Whole Bloods Market?"

"Going by the outside alone, I'd say...Kmart," Iona said.

"That's hateful." Nex's smile vanished. He popped something into his mouth. I pretended it was gum to avoid vomiting.

Iona crossed her arms and glared at Lockwood. "Still think my choice was worse?"

Lockwood sighed.

Nex turned his back on us, dumped everything else from the frog into the overflowing sink and wiped his hands on his tunic. He brushed past me and sank down onto his bed, letting out a long, drawn out sigh as the cats all woke up in a hurry, hissed, and bolted to the opposite side of the shack. One of them retreated between my legs, making me jump in surprise.

Nex stretched out like a sultan on his throne, surrounded by dirty clothes and everything else covered in a layer of dust. "So, let's get down to this so I can get on with life. What do you want? Fortune telling? I do bone casting as well as entrails." He narrowed his eyes at me. "So...what is going on in your little, insignificant life that being friends with a vampire and a Seelie can't fix?"

I took a deep breath, balling my shaking hands into fists. "It's my boyfriend..." I said. "He's a vampire."

"Oh?" Nex said, sitting up a little straighter. His red eyes narrowed, and a smile stretched over his thin face. "A human and a vampire. So very *Twilight*. I like it. Go on." He urged me along with a wave of his hands.

"He's been hexed," I said. "By a witch."

"Earth magic," Nex said, glancing up at Lockwood. "Did you try cleansing the—"

"I've tried everything," Lockwood said in a sharp tone. "Anything that you would suggest, I've tried."

"Oh?" Nex said, a new glint in his eye. "What about—"

"Anything that a proper Seelie Paladin would try." Lockwood said, cutting him off. "Which is why we have come here." He stiffened. "I was wondering if perhaps there were some avenues...beyond the proper."

Nex chuckled. "Ohhhh, this is tasty. Some sort of irreversible, love-sick revenge spell?"

"Something like that, yeah," I said. "The spell was ordered by someone so powerful that I can't kill them. And it's the only way to cure the hex."

Nex rose to his feet, clapping. "Ooh, that's good magic. Yes, all right. Now you're speaking my language."

He raced over to one of the book shelves and started pulling tomes off the shelf, flipping them open, and tossing them over his shoulder. I ducked out of the way, the three of us moving to stand closer to the wall. Books were flying through the air, cats were spitting in rage, meowing angrily and seeking cover. Soon, a dozen shining eyes glowered at us from under the bed.

"This is blood magic territory," Nex said, tossing another book.

I leaned out of the way as it came barreling toward me, my heart skipping a beat.

"Obviously, you were right in coming to me," he said, skimming another book, this one with a moldy green coating on the edges of the pages.

"So…can I cure him without killing Draven?" I asked.

Nex looked up at me. "Draven? The Lord of the Tampa territory? He's the one who commanded the spell?" He dissolved into laughter, then snapped the book shut. "This just gets better and better." He replaced the book on the shelf and turned back to me, his arms open in welcome.

"Well, I have some good news for you, little human child. You can certainly cure your boyfriend."

Relief washed over me. "Thank you. How—"

Nex's eyes flashed. "All it requires…is for you to sacrifice your life for him."

"I'm sorry…what?" It felt as if he had yanked the carpet out from under my feet.

Glee was shining on Nex's face. "What I said. A sacrifice for a sacrifice." He set his mouth in a grim smile. "You must die in his place."

The crushing weight of fear came back just as soon as it had left. "But I thought—"

"You thought that because I was a fae that I could make all of your dreams come true with magic?" He fluttered his eyelashes at me, then laughed. "Blood magic doesn't work that way. There are always consequences."

"There—has to be another way," I said, my heart starting to race again. "I have gone everywhere—asked everyone. Someone has to help me." My voice fell to a whisper. "There has to be another way."

Nex was having a hard time catching his breath from laughing so hard. "To cure that curse? No."

"Come on, Cassandra," Lockwood said, gently touching my arm. "Let's go."

Iona had already turned to leave the dirty shack.

"Oh, please, like you didn't already know that was what I was going to say," Nex said, gaining some control over himself. "Magic like that is dark, wicked, and twisted. There isn't going to be some easy way to fix it."

Lockwood's jaw tightened, and he stepped protectively in front of me. "Thank you for your time, Nex. We will leave you now."

"Why did you even bring her to me if she isn't willing to hear me out?" Nex asked.

My mouth was dry.

"Her experience with magic is very limited," Lockwood said. "And has not been very good."

"Then you should have explained it to her," Nex said, anger starting to darken his voice, his eyes. "It's blood for blood. Her life for his. You knew this, unless you are a fool. Why give the poor creature any hope?"

Lockwood stood, defiantly, in front of me. "I suppose I fell to that most human of emotions—hope."

"That makes you a fool," Nex said. "There's nothing free in this magic. If she wants to save his soul, she must give hers."

"Yes," Lockwood said, "I suppose I am a fool."

"Then leave me in peace, fool," Nex said. "Fools, all of you. Go, then. Moan in your pity."

Fear coursed through me, chilling me, like ice in the veins, and I couldn't tell if it was from Nex's words or just simple desperation at being hit with this following that brief surge of golden hope.

"Fine, we're out of here," Iona said with a toss of her silvery hair. She opened the door and walked out into the darkness.

"Go find a zebra to amuse yourself."

Lockwood ushered me toward the door, and I was grateful for his closeness like I was when we were in Faerie. I had met some creepy fae when I was dealing in their world, but none of them ever made my blood run cold like Nex did.

"Or you could always kill Draven," Nex shouted into the darkness after us, laughing again.

I stumbled my way back over the rickety wooden bridge, nearly falling headlong into the swamp as the car roared into life, Iona already sitting in the driver's seat.

Nex's laughter followed me all the way, and still rang in my mind even after we were back on a paved road.

"I am sorry, Lady Cassandra," Lockwood said, glancing over the seat at me. "I shouldn't have—"

"It's all right, Lockwood, I'm not upset with you," I said.

"Magic is a thing of balance," he said, giving me a sad look. "I should not have given you hope when I knew better." He gave me another sad look before turning back to Iona, who looked ready to ream him out the same way he had done her about the Oracle. Neither said a word, though.

My thoughts dragged me from the car into their own place, whirling and quick. Magic was a thing of balance? I pictured myself on one side of a great scale, Mill on the other.

Give up my own life to save his...or toss Draven onto the scale in my place.

The latter was impossible. Draven had hundreds of vampires in Tampa. Maybe thousands. An army.

I had one vampire, one fae, a bunch of humans that couldn't fight worth a damn...

And me.

Face my greatest fear?

Throwing my friends into an impossible fight like that was a pretty damned big fear.

I cradled my head in my hands. Hopelessness washed over me in waves. I wanted to be alone, to curl up in the back seat and never have to see anyone else ever again. I didn't want to hear any questions, because I didn't have the answers. I didn't want to have to see Mill again because I didn't think that my heart could take the sight again, not when I already had enough horrific images of him lying there, dying, in my head.

There was a small part of me that was deeply ashamed that I wasn't willing to give up my life for his. Wasn't that the deepest form of affection? Did I care more about my own life than his? How could I face him again when I had the answers in my hand?

No. I couldn't go down that route. Blood magic. I'd read enough fantasy books and played enough games to know that sort of magic never worked out the way you wanted it to.

I sighed for the millionth time in the last week.

Once more, I didn't know what to do.

And no one had said, "I know someone!" that they could bring us to, which told me...

Everyone else in the car was just as lacking for answers at this point as I was.

Chapter 31

The drive back to Xandra's house felt like it was taking way longer than it had when we had left for Nex's creepy shack of horrors.

Iona and Lockwood had both fallen silent in their seats, apparently having reached a truce. Both were seething at the other for bringing us to dumb places, but I think I was on Iona's side on this one. Out of the two, I would have rather visited with the well-dressed Oracle than with the blood magic fae whose eyes were definitely going to haunt my dreams.

If I ever slept again.

"Hey," Iona said in a quiet voice.

I glanced at the rearview mirror and found her looking into the back seat at me. "Yeah?" I asked.

"Should we stop and get something to eat?" she asked. "You like McDonalds, right? Weren't you just telling me how you obsess over the nuggets?"

"Uhhh, maybe," I said, sitting up. "But Iona, you don't eat human foo—"

She didn't even give me a chance to reply. She turned into the parking lot, which was all but empty at this hour. Lockwood shot a quizzical look over his shoulder at me, and I shrugged. His guess was as good as mine.

"This will be good," Iona said. "Neither of you have eaten at all today." Her stomach rumbled, like a distant peal of thunder. "Which I can very much sympathize with."

"Yeah," I said as she pulled into a spot. There were more

cars in the drive-thru at this point. "But why…"

"That was a stressful life event," she said, putting the car into park, "and who knows if Xandra's mom will even be awake when you get home to whip you up something."

"I could make something myself," I said. "I'm not that incompetent of a cook."

Lockwood was staring at Iona like she had grown another head.

"Well, we're here already, so there's no need to chance you accidentally poisoning yourself," she said.

"I don't have any money—"

"Not an issue," she said and stepped fluidly out of the car.

"Interesting," Lockwood said, still in the passenger seat.

"Whatever," I said with a hollow laugh and followed her out. I wasn't going to deny that the smell of food was enticing. My stomach was growling, and I didn't mind the idea of some chicken nuggets. I followed her inside, and she gave me a smile as she held the door for me.

What was she up to? This was way out of character for Iona. Offering to buy me dinner? Involving human food?

We got in line, or the lack of one, and Iona stood there in front of the counter, staring up at the screens. She was studying the menu. The guy behind the counter looked like he was about to fall asleep and didn't seem to mind that she was taking her sweet time making up her mind.

This was really bizarre. Mill and I had been to cafes and other eating establishments, but he'd never ordered anything. Which took a little getting used to. Was he just strange? Was this thing Iona was doing more of a normal vampire protocol?

Lockwood stepped up beside me.

"I haven't been here in a while," he said. "I find the grease doesn't sit very well with me."

"Not enough magic?" I asked.

"Too much, if you can call heavily processed food magic," he said with a small wink.

"I'll try the number three please," Iona said. "With the French fries."

The guy behind the counter gave her a strange look. "So a combo, then?"

"Yes. That. Good. Okay. Thanks," Iona said, stepping aside.

Lockwood and I walked up to the counter together.

"I'll have a—" Lockwood started, but Iona cut him off.

"You can get your own. I've paid you in the past, so I know you have money. This is for the high schooler who can't afford to eat in fancy places like this without charity."

Ah, there she was. The Iona we all knew and loved.

Lockwood looked slightly taken aback, but pulled out a really nice leather wallet from...somewhere? Probably out of thin air, knowing him. Less chance of getting pick-pocketed that way. He took a step back behind me, waiting his turn.

"Cassie, go ahead and order," Iona said.

I stepped up and ordered my nuggets, resisting the urge to buy the biggest box like I normally made Dad spring for, and a cola. The food appeared on the counter on a black plastic tray, which Iona swiftly took out of my hands when I picked it up, thanking the cashier.

Lockwood ordered the same thing I did, and soon we were wandering through the completely vacant restaurant looking for a table. I followed Iona around the corner from the serving counter to a more private area of the restaurant. She picked a booth beside the window and slid into it.

I chose to sit across from her, and Lockwood sat down beside me.

Iona gave me questioning look, silvery hair contrasted against the darkness out the window behind her.

"What?" I asked.

She pushed the tray toward me. "Aren't you going to eat? That was the whole point in coming here."

I raised an eyebrow at her, but took my nuggets and fries from the tray, along with the ketchup and spicy buffalo dipping sauce I'd ordered along with it. I opened the little cardboard box and inhaled the fried, chicken-y scent. My mouth started to water.

Lockwood picked up his meal, too, and the two of us began to eat. Iona sat there across from me, hands knitted together on the table in front of her.

The chicken was hot and salty, and the cola was cold and sweet. It was hard not to shove it all in my mouth at once. It took a lot of restraint, but I forced myself to eat slowly. It was amazing how the most basic of needs, like food, could be so comforting when going through something so stressful.

Even Lockwood seemed to be enjoying himself. Tentatively at first, he started to lick the grease from his fingertips. Soon he was taking down fries a half dozen at a time.

What a sight we must have been. A faerie, a vampire, and a human all walk into a McDonald's…

Even Iona was attempting to eat what she had bought, which was apparently a fish sandwich. I never cared for those things, myself. She was taking small, nibbling bites, chewing with her mouth open, and then swallowing deliberately, nose wrinkling. "So…" she said, setting down her sandwich with about half a bite taken out of it, leaning forward when I was about halfway done with my meal. It was as if she'd run out of patience with this particular experiment.

"So…what?" I asked.

"By now, I've been around for a long time," she said.

I blinked at her. "Yeah. And?"

"And obviously I've lived through things, suffered my share of loss. Family, friends…entire fashion movements that really felt like they went before their time." She was staring wistfully out the window at the empty parking lot where her Beetle sat all alone. "I mean, why don't men wear fedoras anymore? It's such a shame…" She turned her attention back to me. "But we muddle through somehow. We make do."

"O…kay?" I said, taking another long sip from my soda. It was nearly empty now. I debated about going to refill it. Or bug Lockwood to do it for me since he was blocking my way. He was too busy trying to use the last of his French fries to mop up the rest of the barbecue sauce lodged in the corner of the tiny plastic container that it came in.

"And we hope that someday, the things that we love come back to us. Like hats. But not stupid baseball hats. Those are ugly," she said. She took another deliberate nibble of her sandwich, forcing it down almost painfully.

"You must love hipsters," I said. "They wear a lot of fedoras."

Iona gave me a very careful look. "Cassie, you are going to

lose people in your life." Her tone had changed suddenly. It was serious, soft. Gentle, even. "Consider yourself lucky that you didn't know him better. Imagine if this happened five years from now."

I stared at her. So this was why she'd dragged me into a McD's after midnight. It was to soften me up with food, and then have "the talk."

"Not knowing him for very long doesn't help as much as you might think," I said. "It still hurts. A lot." I pushed away the rest of my nuggets, my appetite fleeting as I thought about Mill.

"What do you mean?" she asked. "You don't think it'll be easier to deal with now than if it had been five years from now?"

"I don't know," I said. "It would suck then, and it sucks now."

"Of course it does," Iona said. "It all sucks. What I am trying to help you see is that it is going to suck less now than if it happened in the future."

"No, it won't," I said. "What would suck is the missed opportunity at everything that could have happened. You know? What sort of life would I have if he was still going to be in it?" My eyes stung, but I was too tired to cry.

Mill wouldn't want me to cry anyway.

Iona's eyes narrowed as she looked at me. "I don't understand. I'm trying to help you."

"Yeah, well, you aren't succeeding," I said, sitting back in the booth and crossing my arms. "I mean, do you even have emotions anymore? You're basically telling me to 'suck it up, buttercup'. That's not how this works. Not when someone you care about is dying."

I watched as she took another bite, and then winced afterwards.

"I thought vampires didn't like to eat human food," I said, my tone sharp, remembering what Mill had said about it.

"No, this fish is amazing," she said around another mouthful. "It's juicy, tender, and crisp. Everything someone would want from a sandwich like this. And only $3.99!"

Lockwood and I glanced at one another.

"Did you get that from a Yelp review?" he asked.

"Absolutely not," she said after she forced another bite down. "I don't even look at the internets. That place is a death trap for the soul."

"But—" Lockwood said.

"Shut up, Faerie boy. Can't you see that I am trying to be the consoling best friend here?" Iona said. She turned her attention back to me. "Cassie, I am sorry that this is happening. I know it's harsh, but you're going to have to pick yourself back up and move past this. It's the only way forward."

"Do you even remember what it's like to feel, Iona?" I asked. "You can't even possibly begin to imagine what I'm going through. You haven't felt the way a human feels in a very long time. And because of that, I don't feel like you're equipped to tell me how to feel about any of this."

Iona looked sadly around at all of our wrappers, empty, grease stained paper bags and cardboard boxes, and the little crumbs all over the table.

"So this whole dinner thing here isn't helping?" I could hear the sadness in her words, and then I saw it reflected in her eyes. She had tried so hard, gone out of her way to be kind to me. I was thankful for it. Thankful that she cared enough about me to try.

But I didn't have it in me to lie to her that it was helping. "No. It's not helping. Not really."

She forced a sad smile and nodded her head.

"I appreciate your effort, though, Iona. I really do. This was really nice. But…honestly, I don't think much of anything is going to help me right now," I said.

"Okay, well, then I'm done pretending," she said, and she spit out the bite she had just taken right into the napkin in her hand, shaking her head in disgust. "Let's get the hell out of this rancid rat-trap" she said, getting up from the booth, adjusting her jacket, and then starting to walk out of the restaurant. "I need some blood to wash the taste of fish out of my mouth. Blech. Who could possibly think this is tasty…?" She was still muttering to herself when she hit the door.

"Well, I suppose that was…nice?" Lockwood said. "I don't

really know what to say."

I started piling up our trash onto the tray as Lockwood slid out of the booth and stood to his feet.

"There really isn't much to say," I said. "Things are the way they are. Maybe she's right. Maybe all I can do is just accept it."

I dumped the trash into the trash can and we made our way back outside. The parking lot was quiet, the air warm and close, humidity beading on the windshield of the Beetle as Iona started the car.

"I wish there was something that I could say to help," Lockwood said as we walked through the dark.

"I appreciate the thought," I said. "You guys being here is what I need most right now, I think." I held that thought in mind as I got in the car, which was somehow even quieter than the empty parking lot, my mind once again dwelling on Mill, who was dying quietly, in agony, somewhere out there in the night.

Chapter 32

"You okay back there?" Lockwood asked after we'd been driving for a while. "You're being awfully quiet."

"I'm just thinking," I said, looking down at my hands in my lap. The Tampa lights were in the distance, the city once again on the horizon, suburban neighborhoods rolling past as we motored along. "I don't know what to do. Or think. I'm so afraid of all of this. Of getting back there and finding Mill dead already. I can't imagine how I would feel if I wasn't there when—"

"It's okay, Cassie," Lockwood said. I was surprised to hear him use my nickname. "We are here for you and will help you get through this."

I smiled at him, even though it was forced. "Thanks, Lockwood."

"Oh, crap." It was Iona who spoke, and the way she said made my heart skip a beat.

"What? What's the matter?" I asked.

She'd pulled into the driveway behind Xandra's dad's car. Laura's car was there, too. But she was pointing up at the front door to the house, which was slightly ajar. No one was out on the front porch, and all of the lights were on still.

"Someone probably just forgot to close it," I said. But my throat was tight, my heart beating in my eardrums. "Maybe they just wanted some fresh air."

Neither Iona nor Lockwood said anything as we got out of the car and made our way toward the house. I controlled my pace only with great difficulty, keeping to a walk. Funny how something as pedestrian as accidentally leaving the front door open could trigger what felt like heart palpitations in me. Haha.

Please, let it have been someone leaving the front door open. Not...something else.

As I walked up the path, Byron telling me about the night he was turned into a vampire stirred to mind. He talked about walking up to his house just like this...and finding a nightmare scene when he went inside. Blood painting the walls, dripping from the stairs, pooling on the floor.

There was a ringing in my ears, and the edges of my vision started to go black. My tongue tasted metallic, and I felt like I couldn't breathe.

One foot up the step. A second.

Iona and Lockwood were already inside. And they didn't call back to me to say anything.

I hesitated before crossing the threshold.

What was I going to find here? Was this image going to be burned into my brain for the rest of my life? Was I about to see something so horrific that I would never be able to sleep again without having nightmares of it?

"Cassie?" Iona finally spoke. It was steady. Cold. Inhuman. "They're gone. All of them."

Gone?

I stepped inside, and the silence pressed in around me. No sizzling sounds of cooking from the kitchen. No chattering from the television. No hair dryer going in the bathroom down the hall, four women sharing one mirror and producing the predictable results thereof.

Things were overturned, broken. Bookshelves were knocked over. The television had a wooden stake driven through it, cable news still playing around it. Plates and mugs, all broken, were scattered across the kitchen floor.

Iona and Lockwood stood among the mess, looking at each other for cues, then to me, though subtly at first. There was an unearthly quiet as we went room to room and found...

Nothing.

Because all of them, every last one of them...

Was gone.

Chapter 33

"What the hell…?" I asked, blood pounding in my ears. "It looks like a tornado went through here."

Xandra's dad's favorite couch had a large gash through it, exposing the yellow stuffing, and the floor was littered with books. Broken pieces of Xandra's mug collection were all over the place, the dust from them covering the grey carpet in a fine, white powder.

"Looks like they did not go gently into that good night," Iona said, walking to the kitchen table, avoiding spilled contents of the silverware drawer. "Good for them," she added in a whisper.

My heart lightened. "Maybe they ran away?"

"I…don't think so," Lockwood said. "The amount of things broken says otherwise, unfortunately. And before we left, I prevailed on Xandra to text me any updates."

As quickly as my hopes had risen, they sank again. "Well…at least they aren't dead," I said.

"As far as you know," Iona said, stepping over a side table that was on its side. Ironic. The lamp that sat on it lay in shattered ruins on the floor, the light bulb still burning brightly from the wreckage.

I unplugged it for good measure. No need to start a fire here, too.

"Perhaps we can find some clue as to what's happened," Lockwood said, starting to pick up some of the books and the curtains that lay on the couch where Mill had been. I watched, hoping perhaps Mill would magically appear from the thin space between cloth and leather when Lockwood picked up the curtains, but no such luck.

"It's obvious what happened," Iona said. "Draven figured out where we were and sent vamps here."

"But how did they find us?" I asked. "Without the witches—"

"It was only a matter of time before they tracked us down here, wasn't it?" Iona said. "Xandra is your friend, after all, and you don't have many. It couldn't have been that hard to figure out where you'd go."

"I did set up wards here, though," Lockwood said. "It appears they didn't conceal the home enough."

"How could they have broken through your magic?" I asked.

"I was somewhat limited in my options," Lockwood said. "I am sorry, Cassandra. My magic works differently here than it does in Faerie. There is only so much I can do. If I had used a different sort of barrier, or maybe a—"

"Zip it," Iona whispered, making a motion with her hand like a sock puppet snapping its mouth shut.

Lockwood did, and we all listened intently. There was a whimper from somewhere down the hall.

My eyes widened. Could it be Xandra? Or Laura?

Iona held a finger up to her lips, and then she was gone, disappearing in a blur of vampire speed. Lockwood followed, and I trailed behind, as quickly as my human legs would allow.

The sound came from Xandra's room, and I hurried down the long hallway. Lockwood entered just ahead of me, and I found Iona standing in front of the closet when I came in. She was peering at the closet, an angry look on her face, and threw the doors open.

There was a shriek, and inside the closet a boy ducked and covered his head. He wasn't very tall and was trembling from the top of his head all the way to his feet.

"Who are you?" I asked.

The boy turned to look at me, arms still draped over the back of his head. "You—you—" he said.

Iona yanked him out of the closet. "Come here, you."

"No! No, please!" he said, still covering his head.

He was wearing a black leather jacket, jeans, and a Twenty-

One Pilots T-shirt. He had dark hair that was buzzed close to his scalp and his green eyes were wide with terror. The weirdest thing about him, though, was the dark veins that raked up his face, his forehead, and his neck. They were prominent on the back of his hands too. It looked like someone had drawn all over him with a really fine pencil.

Iona threw him on the ground, and he cried out as he struck the carpet. Then he curled up into a ball.

"He's a fledgling," Iona said.

"A what?" I asked as the boy whimpered on the ground at our feet. The word sounded familiar.

"A baby vampire," she said. "How old are you, kid?" She gave him a swift kick in the leg with her boot.

He cried out in terror. "Seven—seventeen," he said.

"Not that age," Iona said. "How long since you were turned?"

"Six weeks," he said at last.

"Goodness." Lockwood frowned.

"What are you doing here?" Iona asked. He just cowered from her, shaking.

"What happened to my family and friends?" I asked. "Where did they go? Are they still alive?"

He shook his head over and over.

"Answer her," Iona said, lifting a fist over his head.

"Taken," the boy said. "Back to Draven."

My stomach squirmed painfully. Draven. He wasn't messing around anymore.

"Were they hurt?" Iona asked.

"N- no," the boy said. "Tied up and hauled out. They left me—me here."

"And what about the vampire?" I asked. "The sick one."

"Not moving," the boy said. "They dragged him out by his feet."

A fresh hatred for Draven started to bubble up in me. But at least everyone was all right.

For now.

He squeaked, and I saw one large, round green eye look up at me.

"I have—I have a message. From L- Lord Draven. For the

great and mighty slayer of vampires."

I blinked. "Um. Who's that?"

"Seriously?" Iona rolled her eyes and bumped me in the arm with her elbow. "He's talking about you."

"Okay, but why is he cowering on the floor?" I asked. "And why is he making fun of me, calling me great and mighty?"

"I don't think he's making fun of you," Lockwood said. "Ask him what he wants."

I stared down at the kid. Not even a kid. He was the same age as me. And he was terrified. Of me. "Um, okay. What does Draven want to say to me?" I asked.

The boy didn't answer.

"I'm not going to hurt you," I said after a few seconds of silence.

That made him quiver even more. What had he been through that traumatized him so much? The veins might have suggested an answer.

"Remember that Draven only just found out that you aren't a vampire," Iona said. "The game changed when they found out that you're a human killing vampires. And not just one. Lots of them. That makes you kind of scary."

The boy hesitantly lifted his head. "You—you really don't know?" His voice fell, hushed. "Vampires in Lord Draven's territory are afraid to even speak your name."

"Oh, please," I said. "This is like some cheesy horror movie—"

"Well, that and since Draven hates you, he probably doesn't even want to hear the sound of your name. Probably makes him a little crabby," Iona said. She moved to kick the boy again, but he scurried backwards until his back collided with the wall.

He stared desperately up at me. "I'm supposed to give you a message—" he said again, breathing heavily. A human reaction to fear. He didn't even need to breathe. I guess he hadn't forgotten yet.

"All right, let's hear it," I said.

He swallowed, licked his dry lips, and said, "'You will come to me. You will come to me immediately. You will surrender to me'."

197

My blood went cold. I looked at Iona and Lockwood. Like a blow to the side of the head with a bat, I realized that was it.

That was my greatest fear. Surrendering to Draven. Actually having to face him. I'd run for so long...

And the Oracle had totally been right. This was the only way to save Mill, and my parents, and Xandra, Laura, Xandra's parents...

This was the only way.

I looked down at the kid and knelt before him.

It wasn't his fault that he was put up to this. Who knows what they had done to force him to stay here? Or what he had experienced when he was turned? He could have been any kid at my high school. I wondered where his parents were. If they even knew that anything had happened to him yet. It made me think of Jacquelyn, and everything she had gone through.

"I'm sorry this happened to you," I told him as gently as I could.

He was staring at me with wide, unblinking eyes, his mouth slightly agape. He was kind of cute, too. I probably would have had a crush on him if he had gone to my school. All of the girls in my grade would have.

"All of this," I said, "I'm truly sorry." I swallowed past the lump in my throat, but I realized that all of the fear had gone.

I had been so afraid of finding out what my greatest fear was. I had been afraid of this moment where Draven gave me an all or nothing, because I had known from the beginning, from the first time I crossed him, that it would come to this.

Everything was leading to this moment.

And now that it was here, an eerie sense of calm had taken hold of me. My hands were steady, my breathing even.

That old song was right: the waiting really was always the hardest part.

"Tell Draven I'll be there soon."

"Tell him—" the boy said. "Tell him how?"

"By going to him, obviously," I said.

"But..." He gave me a wary look. "Aren't you going to..."

"To what?" I asked.

"Kill me?" His face twisted, as though he were holding off tears.

I stood up and dusted off my jeans. "No. I'm not going to kill you. I have no reason at all to kill you."

The boy seemed stunned. He sat there against the wall for a few seconds, staring up at me, dumbfounded.

I gestured to the door. "Seriously. I'm not going to hurt you. But my advice to you is that as soon as you tell Draven, get out of there. Run from him, and never look back."

The kid hesitated for only a second more before he was off at full vamp speed, sending my hair swirling in the wind he left behind.

"I survived!" I heard him shout into the night as he burst out the front door which clapped against the frame behind him.

Iona clicked her tongue in annoyance. "You know, I feel like I should take him out just out of general principle."

"Let him go," I said. "He didn't do anything wrong."

Lockwood sighed heavily, shaking his head. "That poor lad…having his life ripped away when he was so young."

I scowled. "This can't keep happening. Too many people are dying because of me." I looked at them both. "This is it," I said, and realized it sounded a lot more dramatic than I had intended it to. "One way or another, this ends tonight."

Chapter 34

"Nothing is ending," Iona said into the quiet of Xandra's room, motes of dust wafting through the air as we stood, the three of us, in the stark light of her single bulb. "We are not going anywhere near that penthouse, those vampires, or that crazy sociopath, Draven. End of discussion."

"Yes, we are," I said, turning to make my way out of the room. "Or at least I am."

"Cassandra, I understand that you are quite upset," Lockwood said, hurrying to keep up with me as I walked to the kitchen, "but you must see reason. To go to Draven would be to throw your life away."

I wondered if I would be able to compile a good supply of chopsticks. Maybe duct taping them together would make for a sturdy enough stake to use in a pinch. I ignored him as I started combing through a pile of laundry that had been scattered across the hall. Xandra had more than enough black. I should be able to find something a little more apropos to wear for a fight.

"You've gone insane," Iona said, laughing hollowly. "You've been so afraid of Draven all this time, have run from him constantly. Now some kid calls you a mighty vampire slayer and you suddenly change your tune?"

I didn't say anything. Didn't even look at her. I didn't care what she said now. It wouldn't change my mind.

"I do worry that the stress has gotten to you," Lockwood said as I pulled Xandra's backpack off the hook near the door, which was still open, and started tossing every chopstick I could find into it. Knives would be useless. Maybe she still had some of those bottles of holy water I had given her when I got back from New York...

Iona grabbed my shoulders and shook me until I looked at her.

"You listen to us," she said, her brow an angry line. "Lockwood and I are agreeing for the first time in recorded history. Draven is going to make you suffer. A lot. He is going to play with you and it is going to be *fun*—for him. Do you understand that? And it isn't going to be quick, or merciful, because those are words he does not have in his vocabulary." She frowned. "I mean, he probably knows them, on a literal level, but he eschews them in his non-life. Torture and misery are more his wheelhouse, and he's very good at them."

"Wasn't it always going to come down to this?" I asked as she dropped her hands from my shoulders. "No matter what I did, it was always going to this moment...wasn't it?"

Iona and Lockwood exchanged uneasy glances.

I shook my head. "I know. I've always known, deep down. All of this was going to come to a head, and I was going to have to face him eventually." I didn't have to say what that meant. "Consequences. For all my lies."

"What do you mean?" she asked, just as quietly.

"What happens when they drain you dry?" I asked. "Does it hurt? Do you become a vampire?"

Her eyes widened, like she couldn't believe that I had just asked her that.

It wasn't like I was eager to hear the answer. These were things I laid awake thinking about since meeting Mill and Iona. What had it been like when they became vampires? Would it ever happen to me?

Would any answer she gave be able to prepare me for what was coming?

"No. If they drain you, then you're dead," Iona said. "Same as if someone stabbed you thirty times. Your heart stops, then your brain, and then all your organs. And you die."

"What happens when a vampire turns a human?" I asked, voicing the next question I always wondered. "Is it like falling asleep? How do they do it?"

Iona looked over her shoulder at Lockwood for support, but he only shrugged, the look on his face suggesting he had no words.

"Cassie—" Iona said.

"I get that you probably don't want to talk about it, but I want to know in case…" Yeah, I really didn't want to finish that sentence.

It looked like Iona was really fighting with herself. "No, you have to drink the vampire's blood after they bite you. And the process isn't quick. Or painless. It takes time. And then…"

The idea was repulsive. I'd had my hand in enough of that hot, black, tarry blood to know that I wanted it nowhere near my mouth. But if Draven forced me…

"How do I know that I won't end up, you know…evil?" I asked her. "How can I be sure that I'll end up like you?" I had asked this of her, or Mill, at least a thousand times in my mind. I never thought that I'd actually be standing in front of her, asking for real.

"That's hard to say," she said. That masked sadness that she carried with her came back just then, in her eyes. Always in her eyes, though sometimes it disappeared for long stretches.

"What do you mean?" I asked.

"Saints and nuns that have been bitten have turned into the most vile, execrable vampires of all time. On the other hand, I've seen the worst criminals end up like Mill, vowing never to hurt anyone ever again."

I nodded. "So, there's no way of knowing?"

"Not that I can tell," she said. "I'm sorry I can't be more help than that."

I wondered about Jacquelyn. It hadn't been her choice to become a vampire. Had they hurt her? Tortured her? She'd hated me before all of this, but there was a blood lust in her now, one that I figured only killing me would satisfy. And maybe not even that.

"Well, if that's what Draven decides to do with me, can you find me and teach me to be like you?" I asked. "Help me remember…who I am?"

"This is stupid," Iona said, throwing her hands into the air.

"I can't even believe we're having this conversation right now. We need to run."

"You said they'll find us," I said.

She made a disgusted sort of sound. "That doesn't mean we just give up and march up to Draven for the slaughter."

"I need to be prepared," I said. "For whatever could happen."

"I wouldn't take the chance, if I were you..." Iona said. "Even though you seem determined to go through with this— this—this lemming walk."

"What am I supposed to do, Iona?" I asked.

"Anything but what he asks," she said. "You can at least try running. You don't have to sit here and take this. You don't have to walk into their jaws, letting yourself be gobbled up like a dumb sheep."

Lockwood lifted his head. "We could escape to Faerie," he said.

"I thought that option was out, too?" I asked.

"I could find a way to hide us from the Seelie," Lockwood said, "I have allies there that we could—"

"And do what?" I said, shaking my head. "Spend the rest of my days hiding in the skirts of the Winter Queen, *if* she would even have me, while everyone I know and love is killed because of me?" I shook my head. "No. This is where I belong. I don't want to run. I can't abandon everyone. Not now, not ever."

"Things change," Iona said. "New York was where you belonged not that long ago."

Her words rang in my mind, the truth like a punch to the gut. "Yeah, I did. But things in my life pushed me out of there against my will."

"What's so different about now?" Iona asked. "Cassie, you could have a *life* in Faerie. You could thrive. Be happy. Maybe find that you actually like it better there."

"Even if we just hand-wave away the danger of the Summer Court, who I'm pretty sure hate me," I said, watching Lockwood nod, "humans in Faerie for long periods of time see themselves become more like the shape of their heart. I saw through lies in Faerie, because I started to change there, becoming whatever a human liar becomes in that place. I imagine it's not good." I looked up and found Lockwood had averted his gaze from me. "What do you suppose a coward would become after a few weeks there? Some sort of chicken creature?"

"It would not be good," Lockwood said.

"Okay, that does sound bad," Iona said, "but here, you only have one outcome waiting for you, and it's death, Cassie. If you stay, this is the end of the road for you."

What she was saying was what I was already thinking, but it still hurt to hear it from someone else. I didn't want it to be true. "I have to at least try to save my parents. Mill. My friends."

"They're are as good as dead already," Iona said, voice rising and filling the whole empty house. "Do you really think that if you go now, Draven is just going to spare them?"

I licked my lips and opened my mouth to counter with a very weak argument, but she interrupted.

"Did you hear what I said, Cassie? Because I want it to be perfectly clear what you are walking into."

I knew perfectly well what was waiting for me, what sort of pain I was in for, how I was going to suffer, maybe physically, but definitely emotionally. Somehow, I had always convinced myself that they were still alive, even though I knew how unlikely that was.

Because if they were alive, then at least I had something to fight for. Something to get me there so I could look the Lord of Death in the face.

"I do," I said. "I know what's waiting for me, Iona." I turned to stare out into the night, wondering if this was the last night I'd ever see. The last time I'd feel the sticky, humid heat. The last time I would ever smell the salty air from the Gulf of Mexico. "Besides, if they're dead…" I turned back, forcing a weak smile, "what do I have to live for anyway?"

Iona turned and started away, toward the front door.

"You really don't understand, do you?" I called after her.

She turned and gave me a very sad, very pathetic look. "That's where you're wrong," she said. "I may be the only one who does." Then she turned and walked away, out into the sticky night.

Lockwood was looking at me sadly, too. We had gone through so much together, and such a short time ago. We had made it out of that alive, somehow. "Lady Cassandra, I..."

"You don't need to say anything, Lockwood." I smiled. "This is my choice. And I need to do it alone."

He nodded, once, tried to smile, and failed. I could feel the unease swirling in him, showing itself in the tense lines of his face.

I had run from this fate for so long, fought it so hard, made such a mess of...well, everything.

But now I felt...strange. I felt...

Free.

I'd run from fate as long as I could, but now, fate had caught me, as it always does. And now it was time for me to answer its call.

Chapter 35

It was still dark. The roads were quiet. All the streetlights were still on, casting pools of light onto the grey, sun-faded pavement of the highway. I was driving Xandra's mom's Toyota Corolla. It had all the bells and whistles, including a back-up camera, motion sensors so you didn't accidentally merge into another car. And a really great stereo system.

Not that I was using any of that, or cared about it, either. It was just easier to think about the features of the car I was driving than where I was taking it. Or where it was taking me.

I was driving by myself. Lockwood had volunteered to drive me, of course, but I'd flatly turned him down. "You've driven me everywhere these last few months," I'd said with a forced smile, "I'm not having you drive me to my death."

He'd balked at that, offering no more fight. Which was good, because I didn't have much fight left in me and I was saving it all for Draven.

The city skyscrapers were bright in the distance, and as I drew closer, it was like the buildings were growing, expanding, reaching up into the sky.

I heard a jackhammer somewhere along the highway, fixing a broken wall. At one point a loud buzz came from behind as a helmeted, suited motorcyclist shot past me doing a hundred.

I sighed heavily as I drummed my fingers on the steering wheel. This was taking forever.

It had been days since I'd last been alone, and I hadn't realized just how frightening the silence would be when I finally had a moment to myself. My brain had shifted into "worst case scenario" mode, playing image after image of the horrific things that might be waiting at the end of my journey.

There were so many things that I didn't know, so many ways in which Draven had the advantage. He knew the setting, had support, and the leverage of everyone I cared about in my life at his disposal.

I had...nothing.

Nothing but the stake in my hair and the will in my heart, the little spark of hope that somehow, some way, they'd still be alive when I got there. If I had to give up myself for them, then I would. Assuming Draven would honor the arrangement. Which was a poor assumption.

But if he did...my life for theirs. That wouldn't be so bad, right?

Mill would hate it. So would my parents. The grief I'd be leaving them would be far worse than if they were to die, in a way. The grief that I would suffer if I left them to die would be unbearable. Which was part of why I was doing this. Going out together seemed a more favorable alternative to the mental torture of knowing all my days that I was a coward and let them die horribly while I slunk off to hide. There would always be a lurking fear, too, behind every door, always over my shoulder, wondering if Draven would get to me that day, or the next.

I didn't want that fear. If Draven was a smart guy, he'd know that killing them all in front of me then turning me would be the worst torture. Of course he'd know that. Jacquelyn would have told him all about me, about what I feared.

Jacquelyn must have been loving all that Draven was putting me through. She'd made it clear she was out for my blood from the beginning. That she blamed me for everything that had happened to her. She wasn't wrong, but I didn't appreciate the sheer amount of hate that she was throwing around at me.

Would Draven let her be the one to take my life? I suppose that would be fair, and probably what she would want. But why would he let her be the one, when I'd been peeing in his bloody cornflakes for months?

No. He'd kill me himself when the moment came. He

wouldn't let anyone else have that honor.

I took the exit ramp off of the highway into downtown, slowing at the bottom for a red light.

Lockwood had driven me to Draven's place the first time I'd been there. And the second time I'd been here, I hadn't actually gone inside, but had a nasty fight with Roxy and her posse out in front of his condo building. Iona had dragged her by the hair into the sunlight when dawn came, just in time to watch her burn.

I'd thought I was going to die that night. But I had help.

I wasn't alone.

But I was alone now. The silence pressing in around me from all sides was a potent reminder. Crying wouldn't change anything. And I didn't think I could at this point. I'd shoved all my fears behind a wall of shock these last few days, just doing what I had to do.

I was getting closer to his condo, my skin crawling, palms getting slick. My heart was pounding in my ears, my head, a thundering bass note only a little quieter than the Corolla's stereo could have produced. I glanced down at the clock as I put the car in park in front of the condo building. It was just after six thirty in the morning.

I stepped out into the humid darkness, slamming the door shut. It echoed through the quiet streets.

Was this the last time I would ever drive a car? I didn't bother to lock it, and I left the keys on the front seat. Maybe, if I was successful, my parents and my friends could find the car and use it to get out of Tampa.

But that hope, faint as the fading night and just like it, probably wasn't even going to last until dawn.

A group of vamps was standing just underneath the portico, the very same place where Roxy had been the last time I'd been here. One of them took a step toward me, dangerous smile flashing across her face.

And I held up my hands into the air in surrender as they came to take me to my fate.

Chapter 36

I hit the floor of the lobby, the vampires manhandling me without any mercy. My shoulder tweaked as I slammed against the tile, stars flashing in my vision. I looked up to see the opulently appointed entry to Draven's condo. It was the same as I remembered it. Gorgeous, brilliantly lit with chandeliers…

And filled with vampires.

I winced as I got to my feet, dusting off and looking around. A dozen or so vampires surrounded me in a circle, faces impassive, a couple bordering on gleeful.

There was no escape.

A snort of laughter drew my eyes to the shortest vampire present and I realized as my vision cleared from the hard landing, it was Jacquelyn. She stepped forward, came so close to me that when she looked up at me, the tip of her nose almost touched my chin.

"You made it," she said with a smirk. "I was starting to worry you'd bail. Like you did in New York."

I just looked at her. "I don't bail on the people I actually care about."

Her eyes flashed with menace. "I'm going to enjoy this." Her breath smelled like blood. "I've been looking forward to this ever since I realized that you had been lying again, parading yourself around like you were some kind of badass vampire." She turned around and paced a few steps away. "You wanna know something?"

I didn't answer.

"He *laughed* when I told him the truth. He sang my praises and told me how wonderful I was, how he was going to make all my wildest dreams come true." Her lips split into a wide grin, and I could tell she meant it. "I told him all I wanted was revenge on you…for doing *this* to me…" she said, baring her teeth. I could see the gleam of her fangs.

I hung my head. "I wouldn't have chosen this fate for you, Jacquelyn."

"But you did," she said. "You haven't changed a bit, have you, Cassie? Lies, lies, lies. You'll hurt anyone in your way. You'll lie to get what you want, to get yourself out of trouble. Everyone else be damned."

"You don't know what you're talking about," I said.

"I'm the only one here who does," Jacquelyn said. "The only one—even among your so-called friends, your parents—who actually knows you. Knows what you're capable of." She sneered. "It's going to be nice to be here for the end." She snapped her gaze to one of the vamps behind me. "Let's go. I'm done looking at her stupid face."

Impossibly strong hands seized me and shoved me toward the elevators, pushing me inside after Jacquelyn. Someone pushed the button for the penthouse and the doors slid closed.

"You know? Your mom was pretty brave," Jacquelyn said into the quiet. "She told Draven they weren't going to give you up, no matter what he did to them. Draven laughed at her and told her that it wouldn't matter. That you'd come to him. I had my doubts. But look how right he was."

"I thought you knew me." My blood was boiling, but I figured I'd transfer a little of that rage to her while I was fighting the urge to wrap my fingers around her throat. It wouldn't do anything now, anyways. No breath to choke out of her. As I looked at her, my anger faded, just like it always did. "Jacquelyn…"

"What?" she snapped, her face darkening. As if I would even dare to address her at all. Maybe I was getting to her.

I looked up at her and hoped that she could see the truth on my face. "I really am sorry about what happened to you. About what I did, about everything that happened before I moved. I'm sorry that you were turned because we ran into each other by accident in town. It's all my fault, and I wish I could go back and fix everything."

Jacquelyn studied my face and for the briefest moment, I thought she had actually heard me, had understood.

But then her smooth, stoic look broke, and she snorted, laughing out loud, throwing her head back. "You want to apologize? Now?" she asked with a wicked smile. "That's rich. Kind of late, don't you think?"

I tried to swallow the lump in my throat. Part of me wanted to keep trying, see if I could break through the fake laugh and façade she was putting up for my benefit, see if there was hurt and sorrow beneath the rage and hate.

If I kept pressing, kept pushing…but we were only seconds from the penthouse. I wouldn't have time to convince her. Especially not with all of these other vampires with us.

The elevator dinged, signaling that we had reached our destination.

Time was up.

The door opened, and all my waiting, my wondering, all my fear…came to an end.

Chapter 37

The penthouse was different from how I remembered it. It was a large circular room with an opening in the middle of the room that revealed a balcony on the second floor above. But instead of dancing vampires, pulsing strobe lights, and a sick bass line throbbing through my bones, it was like walking out onto a quiet stage, and the audience was a large group of jeering, snickering vampires.

The main party area overlooked the eastern part of the city, but I couldn't see the breathtaking view because the windows were all covered with thick, velvet curtains. They were an interesting alternative to Byron's shutters. They were probably closed tightly during the day then thrown open at night, which is what I had seen the last time I had been here.

My heart caught in my throat as my eyes fell at Draven's feet. My friends and family were all kneeling in a line, facing me, their heads were being forced down by vampire hands clasped at the back of their necks. It looked a little like a firing line, but without a single gun in sight.

Mom's usually neat bun was askew. Dad's glasses were gone. Xandra had a gash across her cheek, and I was pretty sure that Laura was having a hard time staying conscious, the way her head was lolling. Xandra's parents were there, too, bedraggled and trembling, but alive.

I had almost convinced myself that they'd already be dead. The image of myself losing it, knowing they were gone and I had nothing left to fear, wielding the stake in my hair, had lingered in my thoughts on the drive over. I'd pictured lashing out at Draven, only to be struck down, one last, glorious spit in his eye before I went out. I wouldn't have cared at that point.

But since everyone was still alive, it gave me a surge of fresh hope. This wasn't over yet.

I looked a little closer, and saw Mill was sprawled out at Draven's feet like some kind of hunting trophy. The sick feeling in my stomach returned.

"Here we are…" said the man sitting above him, perched on a luxurious throne.

Draven.

It was padded in red velvet, adorned with gold filigree and intricate, polished woodwork, and massive to match his enormous frame. His face, papery white, looked almost transparent. The same dark veins that covered the face of the fledgling we'd found in Xandra's house were visible at his temples, his throat, on the backs of his hands. His eyes were so dark they were black, and there were no irises.

The sneer he wore on his face was mocking, confident…disgusting. I'd seen his face too many times in my nightmares the last few months, looking almost exactly like this.

Vampires surrounded Draven like groupies around their rock star. They broke into applause when Jacquelyn shoved me out of the elevator. I stumbled and hit carpet, listening to the laughter and clapping. They were everywhere, around me in every direction. Someone flicked my arm as I rose to my feet. Someone else yanked on my shirt sleeve. A third gave me a shove.

"Go on," Jacquelyn breathed in my ear. "He's waiting. Take your walk of shame."

"No, no," I said, trying to stand tall in spite of the jeering going on around me, "the walk of shame is what you're going to do with him later, as you slink out of—"

She shoved me again, but I caught myself before tumbling over. The message was clear: go. I didn't need any more motivation, so I pushed on toward the throne, toward the people that I cared about most in my life and held my head high. I was not going to let these bloodsuckers see me tremble with fear.

I was going to be strong. I had to be. For them.

Draven tucked his leather boot underneath Mill's belly and shoved him over, sending him sprawling like a big doll. Mill's eyes were closed, his mouth slightly open.

I kept my face blank, but my heart was beating quickly, and there was a roaring in my ears.

"He is still alive, if you're wondering," Draven said, his smile growing as I drew closer. "I had to keep him going for as long as possible. He was no good for you if he was dead, right? Oh, wait. What am I saying? He was dead already."

That drew a peal of laughter from the vampires in attendance. Someone tossed something at me, and my right arm was suddenly wet. A metallic smell filled my nose, and my stomach churned. Blood. And not fresh. They'd hit me with the vampire equivalent of a rotten tomato.

"A human and a vampire…how unorthodox," Draven said. He looked down at Mill as if he were nothing more than a rat. "Even if I didn't care for this one's betrayal, anyone with our blood is still too good for cattle like you."

I stayed quiet, taking one step after another. I couldn't decide if he was aiming his words to spur me or rile up his faithful. Probably both, but for my part, I wasn't eager to give him what he wanted, so I kept my expression neutral. Playing to a crowd? That was a kind of lying I was very familiar with.

Draven held out his hands to quiet the room.

"Look here, brothers, sisters. I give you the dreaded, unstoppable vampire slayer that has haunted your days, stealing your rest." He let out a small laugh. "Look at her! See how small she is. How she quivers."

I steadied myself. Hell if I'd quiver before him.

There was an awful lot of clapping and cheering going on, some wolf-whistling. Their celebratory mood oddly reminded of a football game. *Yay, our team is winning! High fives and chest bumps all around!*

"This is the one who killed Theo, one of my greatest servants." Draven's pale, long face lost its mirth. "He was like a son to me. And he was taken from us by this pig who thought she could walk upright, thought she could act like one of us, could enter my humble home and spit right in my eye."

His look became dangerous, his eyes as black as pitch.

"She has a long string of insults to our brethren," he said. "Killed many of us. Many...loyal servants."

That let some of the celebratory atmosphere out of the room, as a more suitably morose mood settled over them. I guess it was harder to be cocky when he was reminding them I took down the entire squadron of vampires that he sent after me in New York. Same for Roxy's little gang.

"But her lying days are done." Draven said. "Now... Search her. Make sure she's not carrying any of her little party favors."

Rough hands grabbed at me and I couldn't help but wince. I closed my eyes as they jeered and snickered, one of them gnashing their teeth in my ear. It sent shivers down that side of my body. They checked every pocket, as invasive as the TSA but maybe a little more gentle.

"She's got a cell phone," one of the vamps said, lifting it high to show Draven. It was Xandra's. I'd grabbed it with the keys to her parents' car. I hoped they wouldn't turn the screen on. If they did, they'd see I was in the middle of a call.

"That just proves she's a human teenager," Draven said. "They don't go anywhere without those these days."

The vamp put it back into the pocket of my sweatshirt. Well, at least something was going right.

"That's it," a female vamp said in a low, throaty voice, "she's clean."

I felt a little dash of hope. The stake was still in my hair. Maybe—

"Wait," Draven said, eyes narrowing. He pointed a boney finger at my head. "What is that in her hair?"

Jacquelyn appeared in front of me and yanked the stake out of my bun, not caring that it scraped against the side of my head as she pulled it free. I cringed but didn't yelp. It stung.

She dangled it in front of my eyes as if she had discovered a dirty secret of mine, then tossed it over her shoulder. It clattered on the floor at Draven's feet, just inches away from Mill's limp form.

Draven knelt over on his throne, picked up the stake

between his thumb and forefinger, and held it up.

And then he grinned. "Were you planning to kill us all…with this?" He twirled it between his fingers, then snapped it in half as if it were a pencil.

"Do you feel powerless now?" Draven asked, resting his chin in his hand. "You should. You, like all humans, are but a meal to us. You mean nothing at all. We are superior to you in every way, and in your heart, your tasty, beating heart," he smiled so wide, long canines poking out, "you know it to be true. You stand here, a sheep in the midst of wolves. And it is only my word that's keeping these hungry predators at bay, preventing them from tearing you and your family apart." He gestured to me like a king condemning one of his subjects. "Do you see the truth of this specter you feared? Look at her, trying to keep from crying. She's pathetic. She's so…*human*."

Another buzz ran through the crowd, a series of laughs and jeers that rang in my ears like they had during the Great Winter Formal Incident of last year, where all my lies had come crashing down on me. I remembered my cheeks burning, the humiliation stinging like knives in my flesh.

And just like that, I was done listening.

"Yeah, I'm a human," I said, surprising even myself by how steady my voice was. How was it that I managed to play it so cool in these kinds of situations, when inside my head, I was screaming like a lunatic? "…But you were too stupid to realize that until someone blabbed it, weren't you?"

That shut everyone up after another little ripple of shock ran through the crowd. Apparently, you didn't insult Draven in his own living room. For his part, Draven was glowering at me with an icy hatred that I could almost feel in my bones.

I stared up at him defiantly. "You know what else comes with being a human? And a teenager of 'these days', as you put it?" I waited to deliver the coup de grace and caught a flicker of unease in Draven's eyes. "A Netflix subscription."

That spurred a nervous laugh from a vamp to my right, and I shot him a cool look that cut his laugh off like I was a substitute teacher that had just pulled a gun on an unruly class. I guess my vampire slayer rep wasn't completely destroyed by Draven's little scene here—yet.

"Do you guys have Netflix? Or something like it? Bloodflix, maybe?" I just kept riffing, waiting to see if anyone bit on any of my ridiculous lines. "No? Anybody?"

Xandra raised her head; the vampire who'd been pinning her down was too focused on me, his long fangs bared in confusion. It took all my strength not to look at her. Definitely didn't want to wink.

"Yeah, you guys are probably too busy doing the whole 'YOLO—but eternally' thing," I said, watching Draven's reaction. A cold fury was emanating from him at being upstaged, but he seemed too riveted to try and shut me up, probably curious about where I was going with this. I doubted many people stood in front of him with as much sheer chutzpah as I was displaying. Especially since he'd marshaled his entire territory here to see me humiliated. "It's funny you guys don't watch movies. Because the thing that you'd know if you watched movies is that when the villain starts spouting off about his plans and how stupid the hero is…it's called 'monologuing'."

Draven's eyes narrowed to dark slits, and his jaw was clenched. He was like a cat, all wound up and ready to leap at me.

I met his gaze evenly. No fear here. "You know what happens when you monologue?"

The room had fallen silent. No one was moving. No one said anything. No one even breathed. Not that many of them needed to breathe.

A *ding* from the elevator behind me came, loud as a bomb going off, and I smirked.

Every head turned to look as a stir ran through the room. Confusion, terror, it all rippled through the crowd. There was a sound of metal sliding loosely across metal, and the elevator door opened—

217

Chapter 38

—and it was totally empty.

Crickets.

Draven and the whole gang stared past me, and when they realized that the elevator wasn't filled with a tidal wave of holy water, or a stake-launching machine gun, they all looked around at each other, a little murmur of confusion mingled with relief running through the crowd.

Draven smirked at me, his confidence restored, mirth clear on his face. "You were saying something about my monologue?"

That prompted a round of laughter that turned into hilarity as some of the vamps bent double laughing it out, hanging on to one another as if it were the greatest joke they'd ever heard.

Mom had lifted her head, and I made the mistake of meeting her eye. The look on her face was fear, sorrow and defeat all wrapped up in a smorgasbord of a perfect Mom expression.

Draven's laugh was low, deep, and maniacal. Between that and the monologuing, he really had committed to the villain thing.

Despite the laughter that was making my skin crawl, I was patient. It felt tense waiting as everyone laughed at me. I just kept standing there, head held high. The seconds were ticking by slowly. I was aware of every single one of them as they passed. Draven seemed to think that whatever I had planned had failed, and therefore, he had won. The triumph was obvious on his long face, his jaw wide as he laughed.

I noticed after a few seconds that there was lack of familiar laughter from behind me. I turned to see Jacquelyn standing there, looking at all the rollicking mirth with her brow knitted tightly together. As soon as I turned, she locked eyes with me, staring me down.

I smiled back at her.

Her eyes widened, lips parting in surprise, and she turned her attention to the rest of the crowd. "No, listen—She's doing something!" Jacquelyn shouted.

No one was listening to her, though.

I stood there and watched her wave her hands over her head, trying to make herself heard over the endless laughter.

"Listen to me. I know this look. She's planning something, we can't lower our—"

Whether anyone heard her or not, it didn't matter.

Because at that exact moment, a figure dressed all in tight, black clothing, wearing a black motorcycle helmet with the visor shut came barreling out of the "empty" elevator with a fluffy, white blanket draped over her shoulders like a poncho.

It was Iona, and I couldn't keep in the grin that spread over my face. I wasn't sure that I had ever been so excited to see her in my life.

Iona had ridden on the top of the elevator car up to the penthouse, sliding down through the hatch once everyone was busy being distracted by me. She had stakes in each hand and launched herself at the vampires who were nearest to the door. She staked three of them before anyone got out a scream.

The laughter died, albeit slowly. The scream was short and sharp, and barely overcame the noise in the cavernous room. When it did start to die down, Iona tore the blanket from around her shoulders and whipped it in a circle over her head like a lasso before tossing it high.

That was my cue.

While the vampires around me started to succumb to the surprise that came with watching your laughter die and horror spring up to replace it, I dove past Jacquelyn, reaching for the blanket as it started to come down.

I managed to snatch it out of the air, the fabric smelling like Xandra's laundry detergent and perfume as it wafted down and I yanked it over my shoulders, covering me like a cape.

I caught that blanket like my life depended on it…because it kind of did.

I yanked it off in time to see Iona throw herself into a squirming pile of the vampires closest to her. It looked like a riot had broken out near the elevator bank, screams and chaos busting loose as the vamps tried to climb over one another to get as far away from her as possible, not caring if any of their brethren got in their way. It got brutal fast, a veritable war to escape the staking.

So much for unity in the vampire clans.

Pulling the blanket from around me, I tore across the room toward Draven's throne, where Mill was sprawled on the floor. He hadn't moved since I got here. He hadn't even stirred when I was speaking.

The vampires that had been holding my friends and family down were gone; apparently too scared of Iona or me to stay where they had been.

I skidded to a halt on my knees beside Mill.

Draven didn't seem to notice. He was half standing, unfurling his flagpole-like frame, pointing and shouting orders to those nearest him. I couldn't hear his words over the din.

My hands were trembling as I tossed the blanket over top of Mill, trying to tuck it in all around him. Was I putting a blanket over a dead body? I didn't know. I couldn't check for a pulse, and his skin was cold on the best of days.

All I knew was that Draven was still alive, or at least undead. As long as he was still standing, Mill was going to keep suffering.

The vampires were reacting with a herd mentality. I hadn't seen this much shoving and stampeding and climbing over everything—in this case couches, chairs, and the melting, dead bodies of their compatriots—since that time I'd ventured out on Black Friday. It was as if everything that Draven was saying earlier about me, minimizing what I had done, tearing me down as a source of fear, hadn't taken hold in the collective vampire psyche. From their reaction, it was clear that everything the messenger from Xandra's house had said about me was true.

They were terrified of me, and my actions had become a

nightmare to them.

It was strange, seeing them all scramble away from the elevator, from one single vampire. I wasn't even trying to help her. She was doing it all on her own, slashing and twirling, taking them out with ease.

No one was fighting back. If they'd tried, they would have been able to overwhelm her, easily. A hundred vampires against one, and she was taking them out in droves because they were running, not fighting. Pained screams filled the air, along with the acrid smell of vampire blood. Puddles of black goo cascaded onto the tile floor as the crowd broke in places, avoiding the twirling black figure at the center of the panic.

"You!"

I looked up, trying desperately to finish covering Mill fully with the blanket, unsure if I was succeeding or not.

Draven was staring down at me, his fangs bared, a nasty grimace on his face. "What is this?"

I smirked at him, my body draped over Mill's. "There's something else that you need to know about villains, Draven," I said. "The good guy always beats the bad guy. No matter what."

"You are not going to win," he said, holding up his long fingers. "You are here in my hands. That little traitor that you brought here to kill my people? She's going to die screaming while you watch. And then I'll start on your friends and family. Then your boyfriend. And finally. you. Did you hear me? You cannot win."

"Here's the other thing you missed, Draven," I said. "A tiny little oversight that anyone could've made—if they hadn't read the Evil Overlord checklist of things you shouldn't do. Because right at the top—don't build your evil lair on a volcano."

"What do you mean?" he asked, standing in front of the thick, dark curtains that ringed the entire room.

I just grinned at him. He was right where I wanted him. "You didn't think I showed up right at dawn because I was running late...did you?"

Draven's face faltered.

I lifted the cell phone out of my pocket, glancing down one

last time. Mill was as covered as I could make him. I touched the screen and it flared to life, my call still ongoing, the time ticking up as I spoke. "Lockwood," I said, "Now."

A loud crash of breaking glass echoed through the room, followed by the sound of fabric ripping. In the same moment, blazing sunlight broke through as Lockwood tore through the curtains behind Draven, a shadowed form trailing cloth behind him like streamers as he pulled down every inch of shade from the eastern facing of the room.

Light burst in, finding every corner of Draven's immaculate, penthouse, bringing in the burning dawn.

And then there was chaos. Chaos and screaming.

Draven had tried to reach me and I hadn't seen him, his blurry speed erasing him from my sight until the sunlight caught him. He was inches away, maybe less, his hand outstretched, ready to wrap his long fingers around my throat.

He stopped as the light caught him, though, playing over his pale, delicate, veiny skin like a camera flashbulb. He was frozen for a moment in time as his skin started to brighten, then sizzle...

Then burn.

Draven's face lit like a match run across a striker, bursting into flame. "Curse you!" he screamed. And his fingers flared to fire inches from my nose.

"If only you had Netflix, this could have been avoided," I said as he burned, jerking and spasming, dropping to his knees. Around us, every vampire in the room was on fire, a sea of flaming people adding their voice to a chorus of screams, a hideous counterpoint to their earlier laughter.

There was a good minute or so of quiet. Of little or no motion. Of me counting each heartbeat, reminding myself that they weren't my last.

I lifted my head from where it lay on Mill's body and looked around.

Iona stood across the room, a figure in black surrounded by piles of the tarry goo the same color. Beneath the stairs were eyes staring back at me, human ones—

My parents. Laura. Xandra. Her parents.

They were all fine.

I forced myself to breathe through my nose. Ash hung in the air, suspended in the beams of sunlight.

I heard furious clicking as someone pounded their finger against the button in the elevator. I whipped around, ready to call out to Iona for help—

Jacquelyn was standing inside, shrouded from the sun by the elevator box. She was glaring at me from its shadow, but there was fear in her eyes, too.

I half thought about stopping her, but I didn't. It was run after her or stay with Mill.

The elevator dinged, and the doors slowly swept closed.

My decision was long made.

I was going to choose Mill every time.

Chapter 39

"Are you all right?" Lockwood fluttered to the ground beside me, his wings catching the sunlight that was streaming through the window.

"Are those wings?" Xandra had crawled out from under the stairs and was struggling to her feet. She was covered in dust and ash, and her blue hair was askew, hanging in her eyes. "Wow." She was full-on gawking.

Lockwood was breathing heavily, and I saw streaks of bright, shining silver flowing down his arms from where he'd crashed through the glass. He smiled tightly at her.

"He really is a faerie," came Laura's voice from the shadows beneath the stairs.

Lockwood moved toward the stairs as I watched and pulled out a thin knife with a blade that was as clear as glass, but green like an emerald. He sliced through the bindings on everyone's wrists, one by one. Mom didn't even say anything, just offered her hands to the man with glittering wings and stared at them with dull eyes as he cut her free. As soon as she was loose, Mom ran over to me, practically tackling me over onto Mill's prostrated form, still covered by the thick blanket.

"I was so worried," she choked out. Dad joined her a moment later, a little slower, enfolding us both in a gentle hug.

"I'm fine." I said, pulling free. "Really." I would say you could color them skeptical, but they were more sunlight-colored at this point, orange dawn shining in through the whole place. "It's okay. We made it."

"Barely," came Iona's voice, muffled by her black helmet. She was standing in the shadows near the elevator, blackened stakes on the ground at her feet.

A fresh dribble of Lockwood's silvery blood drew my eye as it dripped down his arm. "We need to get you patched up," I said.

"I'll be fine," he said.

"You crashed through hurricane-rated glass," I said. "That's no small feat. I'm surprised that you didn't get shredded like lettuce on a taco."

The corner of Lockwood's mouth turned up in a smile. "There might have been magic involved in that."

"Thank you," I said, hoping he could see the gratitude in my face. "Seriously. I know that my plan was crazy—"

"Insane, actually," Iona called, still lingering by the elevator.

I glared at her. "Yes, okay, it was insane. Nevertheless, thank you for helping me."

"Wait, this was your plan?" Xandra asked. "Rip down the curtains? This wasn't you trying to die nobly and these two coming in to save you at the last minute?"

"Uh, yeah, this was the plan," I said. "Why do you think I waited as long as I did to show up? Can't burn vamps without sunlight."

"Wow, Cassie," Mom said, blinking away surprise. "This was surprisingly well thought out."

I almost fell over. "Thanks, Mom. Is everyone okay, though?" I peered at Xandra's mom and dad, still hanging back by the stairs. They didn't answer, but they seemed fine.

Laura stepped, ash streaking her pretty face. "No, they didn't hurt us. They made sure to keep us healthy so that when you got here, they could...well, you know."

I shuddered, thinking how close we'd come to actual disaster. "Well, he didn't get the chance," I said, ignoring that squirming feeling in my stomach at what might have been if I'd failed.

"This was incredibly risky, Cassie," Dad said, voice soft, a little shell-shocked.

"I know," I said, "but what else could I have done?"

He pulled me into another tight hug. "I'm just glad you're all right." He looked around. "That everyone is."

There was a moan of pain, and movement from underneath the blanket beside Lockwood. I'd gotten so used to Mill being still that it spooked me, and my heart jumped.

"Whoa, whoa!" I said, dashing across the room and pinning the blanket on him as he moved beneath it. "There's sunlight out here."

"Yes, please keep your massive forehead covered given all we just went through to save it," Iona said.

"What…what happened?" Mill asked, halting his motion, voice muffled beneath the thick cloth.

I lay flat against the blanket and felt his shape beneath it, my eyes welling with tears. The relief that I felt at hearing his voice was so strong that it nearly made me giddy. "You're alive. Or as alive as you are normally."

He shifted under the blanket. "Cassie? Are you…lying on me?"

"Of course I am, you idiot," I said, clutching him like my life depended on it. "How else am I supposed to show you how happy I am that you're all right?"

"Oh." I heard a low chuckle, and then a deep, barking cough. "Ugh, I feel like hell. Where am I?"

"Draven's penthouse," I said.

"What?" he asked, his body stiffening.

"It's fine, he's dead," I said, and then I froze.

Draven…was dead?

Mill froze, too. "Beg pardon?"

"He is, indeed, dead," Lockwood said, dabbing at one of the cuts on his arm with a handkerchief.

"Draven had those witches cast a blood magic spell on you that would only break if he died," I said. "So…I kinda made sure he did so."

"I'm sure there's a long, involved story about how that all came about," he said, sounding pretty tired, "but can we just get out of Draven's penthouse? Dead or not, I don't really want to be sitting here blind, under a blanket."

"Yeah, the vibe in here is really grim," Xandra said. "Let's bounce."

"Yes, it'd be a real shame to survive all that and then get

charged with breaking and entering," Mom said.

"Well," I said, "you're not wrong." And I watched Lockwood help Mill, still covered by the blanket, to his feet with care.

Iona clicked the elevator door button in the exact same way Jacquelyn had, repeatedly pressing it.

"I knew you were going to show up," Xandra said, falling in beside me as we made our way over to the elevator.

"You did?" My brow furrowed. "How did you know I'd be able to do anything?"

"Because it's you, Cassie," Xandra said with a shrug. "You're like the wonder slayer or something. These vamps were like…legit afraid of you. All of them. Even Draven, regardless of what he acted like."

"I don't know about that…" I said. "I was probably more afraid of him than he was of me."

"He was wrong, though, wasn't he? In the end, you got the better of him," Xandra said with a smile as the elevator dinged open.

She was right.

I filed in with the rest of them, huddling tighter, bumping against Mill in his blanket as Lockwood led him in beside me. "How do you feel?" I asked.

"Like I'm in a crowded elevator with a bunch of human space heaters," Mill said, and I could see the outline of his head through the blanket. "You?"

"A little dinged up, but otherwise okay," I said, repressing a fierce desire to hug him. Oh, screw it. I threw my arms around him and hugged him anyway.

Mill didn't say anything. I felt him wrap his arm as best as he could around me. It was an awkward hug, but I couldn't stand to wait anymore.

He was safe. He wasn't dead. And Draven was gone. I could have tackled a hundred thousand vampires then and taken them all alone, that's how good I was feeling.

When we broke off, Iona cleared her throat, then smacked me in the back of the head.

"Hey, ow," I said.

"Idiot," she muttered under her breath as she pulled off the helmet. "You go through all this for him and settle for a hug?" She shook her head at me, then pulled the helmet back down as the elevator dinged and the doors opened on the lobby. I looked around for Jacquelyn, but the place was quiet, not a single person in sight.

We strolled out through the main doors under the portico and into the streets of Tampa, which were starting to come to life. Mill walked at my side, Lockwood leading him along like a gothic ghost.

"Mill needs to get back to his house as soon as possible," Iona said. "He's going to need rest and darkness. And blood." She smacked her lips together beneath the helmet. "Actually, so do I. I swear, hanging out with you is exhausting, even worse than spending time with normal people. I'm always hungry and tired and haven't slept for days after one of our little adventures."

"I brought the limo," Lockwood said, letting go of Mill once he saw I had taken him by the arm, "wait here just a moment."

"I'm going to get my motorcycle," Iona said, pointing over her shoulder by the portico. I could see it parked over there. "You're just lucky they weren't actually watching my house so I could go get this bad boy. No way was I mounting a daylight rescue wearing all this motorcycle gear without actually having a bike to ride. I'd look like an idiot." She glanced at Xandra. "Like her. Blue haired and not even a grandmother yet."

Xandra just rolled her eyes. "Learn a trend, biker chick."

Lockwood pulled up and Xandra opened the door. I pushed Mill into the dark interior, the tinted windows almost black, and climbed in after him. The others were getting in now, too, but I hustled him up to the front and sat him down on the bench.

"Can I come out from under the blanket now?" Mill asked.

"For a second, yeah," I said, my heart racing. "Lockwood, don't open the divider. Mill is exposed."

I caught my mother's flinch at that. And I didn't care.

Mill pulled at the fabric and shortly after, his dirty blond head appeared, and I found his dark blue eyes blinking at me.

"It's good to see you," I said, almost breathless as someone slammed the limo door. For a minute, it felt like we were the only two in there, sitting on the backward-facing bench together.

He leveled a half smile at me. It was obvious he was not feeling his best, still. Dark veins stood out on his cheeks and forehead, and his skin still looked near transparent, a little Draven-y for my taste, but...

But I didn't care. I threw my arms around his neck, unable to stop myself, and kissed him. I'd thought that I'd never get the chance to do that again, to show him how much I cared about him. I squeezed him tightly, throwing everything I had at the kiss.

He almost fell off the seat under the force of my embrace, but eventually, and easily, he wrapped his arms around me and lifted me off my seat.

I didn't think that I would ever be able to tell him how scared I had been. How much I had missed him. How guilty I had been. How important he was to me.

So I just tried to make it clear with my kiss.

"Oh, for..." I heard Xandra say. "Could you like...not? At least not here?"

I broke from him with a laugh. "Yes. Yes, I can...'not'." I caught Mill smiling at me, weary but mischievous. "For now." And I settled back against the seat, his fingers interlaced in mine, and just enjoyed the ride.

We'd made it.

Chapter 40

"It doesn't look all that bad," Xandra said, standing beside me on the walkway up to my house. "Not really."

It was early afternoon the day after everything went down. The air was warm. Duh. It was Florida. The air still smelled of charred wood, but there was also a sort of musty odor. Like ozone before a rainstorm.

Xandra wasn't wrong. The roof seemed to still be intact, and the whole left side of the house, where the bedrooms were on the second floor, seemed undamaged. The living room and kitchen, however, had giant holes where the windows had been, scorch marks that stained the grey stucco walls on the outside.

"I guess not," I said, "the fire inspector says it's not a total loss, that they can rebuild." That made me smile, because it was kinda...sorta...maybe a little bit...

Starting to feel like home.

Xandra snorted. I noticed that she still had a butterfly bandage under her eye. She was wearing it proudly, though, like a badge of honor. "You know, Cass, I noticed something different in you through this whole mess," she said, folding her arms, squinting against the bright sunlight through the trees.

"Oh, yeah?" I said. "What's that?"

"You were honest. About everything. And to everyone."

I gave her a sidelong glance.

"I mean, you were the serial liar, right?" she asked, not

tiptoeing around my feelings. "So why not lie your ass off to Draven? To Jacquelyn? Hell, even throwing some little white ones your parents' way during this process would have made your life easier."

I sighed, staring into the dining room window. I could just barely make out the dining room table where I had been sitting with Mom, Dad, and Mill the night I had come back from Faerie. Mill had sort of started the process, but I was the one who wanted to see it through.

"No, it wasn't because I had no other choice." I said. "I'll tell you about it later, but the short version is that in Faerie, I think I finally got the point about just how detrimental my lying could be. What it could really affect."

Xandra nodded, brushing a few stray blue hairs from her eyes. "I get it. I hope you don't mind if I don't join you in total honesty town, though. Because while my parents are okay, they're not exactly eager to hear about vampires and faeries and whatnot. So last night's dinner was super quiet." She looked over at me. "Probably like how it was for your parents the first time they were kidnapped."

I sighed. "Yeah, they aren't exactly sanguine about that happening again. Mom's even wearing garlic, even though I told her that it wouldn't work." We shared a smile. "You know, I think if Draven would have asked me what I was planning, I would have told him exactly what I was going to do. He would have thought I was crazy, sure. But I would have told him."

"I mean…maybe lying, just that once, would have been okay," Xandra said. "He was too cocky anyways, though, wasn't he? He really thought we were just cows for him to eat, didn't he?"

"Strongest argument I've heard yet for vegetarianism," I said. "Making me feel for the cows."

"Eat a burger, you'll forget about empathy for tasty creatures," Xandra said. "How's Iona doing?"

"She's good, I guess? Keeping her distance, probably waiting for my trauma to wear off." I reached up into my hair, and remembered that Draven had taken my last stake, snapping it in half. I was still trying to get used to not sleeping with it underneath my pillow. "I think secretly she was happy to have had the chance to slay those vamps. She didn't like them very much." I thought for a second. "I feel like she's a Viking in disguise."

"She does give off that vibe, yeah," Xandra said. "Like she would bathe in the blood of her enemies."

I snickered.

"So, um…shifting to the uncomfortable," Xandra said, kicking at a stone on the walkway. "How's Mill?"

My cheeks burned, but I smiled. "He's fine. Better, definitely. As good as you can be without a heartbeat."

She smirked.

"Lockwood helped get him the blood he needed, and he's resting. We haven't had a lot of time to talk since Mom and Dad and I moved into that hotel. But he's okay. That message has gotten through clearly."

Xandra gave me an appreciative smile. "So…you kinda killed every vampire in Tampa, didn't you? Or, all the bad ones, at least?"

"I don't know, really," I said. "I can't imagine that they all were there that night. But yeah…probably a lot of them are dead. At the very least, the Lord of the region is, which Iona said could lead to some problems in the future, but I'm having a hard time giving a care." I shoved my hands deeper in my pockets. "He and Byron were the bane of my existence."

"And he was the top of the food chain, right? Like, there won't be anyone who will step into his shoes and come after you for vengeance on his behalf?" Xandra asked.

I shrugged. "I don't know. Iona doesn't think so, and Mill seems to agree, so that's good news." But the knot in my chest wouldn't ease, no matter how much I wanted to believe it was true.

Maybe it was still the shock of it all. In time, that would probably fade. My body was still too eager to jump into fight or flight mode.

"You know what I want, though?" I asked. "I want to go to the beach. You know, do some normal Floridian lifestyle things. What do you guys do down here? Because if we're going by my experience it's all fighting vampires and riding around with fae and running with Amish werewolves."

"That's a definitely a side of Florida that most don't experience." Xandra shrugged. "I mean, I don't know what other people do, but me...eat noodles? Watch anime?"

I sighed with happiness. "That sounds like heaven to me right now."

Her eyes got wide, and then she laughed. A goofy expression appeared on her face, and she lifted her fist to her mouth, as if she were holding a microphone. "So, Cassie Howell," she asked, in a fake, overly dramatic, deep voice like a TV anchor, "you've just killed almost every vampire in the Tampa region. What are you going to do now? Keeping in mind Disney is totally an option, because it's like a two-hour drive."

I turned and stared up at the house, a stark reminder of everything that I'd lost since all these paranormal shenanigans had begun.

But this could very well be where that madness all ended. My life from here on out could be very different.

It *would* be different. Draven was gone.

Mill was safe.

My parents and friends were all okay.

"You know what? I think I'm going to finish out my last two weeks of school...and then just sort of go wherever the road takes me," I said.

"Then I hope your road takes you to many noodles, and much anime," Xandra said, still in her silly, croaky TV anchor voice.

I laughed. "Sounds good to me." And we turned our backs on the house for the warm sunlit walk back to the car, headed for an afternoon of yummy food, couch napping and being...

Normal.

Huh.

What a funny word.

Yeah. I could get used to a normal life.

Cassie Howell will return in

HEIR OF
THE DOG
Liars and Vampires
Book 6

Coming November, 2018!

Author's Note

Thanks for reading! If you want to know immediately when future books become available, take sixty seconds and sign up for my NEW RELEASE EMAIL ALERTS by visiting my website. I don't sell your information and I only send out emails when I have a new book out. The reason you should sign up for this is because I don't always set release dates, and even if you're following me on Facebook (robertJcrane (Author)) or Twitter (@robertJcrane), it's easy to miss my book announcements because...well, because social media is an imprecise thing.

Come join the discussion on my website:
http://www.robertjcrane.com!

Cheers,
Robert J. Crane

ACKNOWLEDGMENTS

Welcome to Lewis Moore in his first foray into editing my works, and hopefully this will be the first of so many of my endless, error-laden manuscripts he'll be fixing.

Proofing by Lillie of Lillie's Literary Service (https://lilliesls.wordpress.com) and Jo Evans of Raj of India.

Cover by Karri Klawiter (artbykarri.com).

Co-authoring by Kate Hasbrouck.

Formatting by Nick Bowman (http://www.nickbowman-editing.com)

Sanity NOT by Robert J. Crane's family. But I love them anyway.

Other Works by Robert J. Crane

The Girl in the Box *and* Out of the Box
Contemporary Urban Fantasy

Alone: The Girl in the Box, Book 1
Untouched: The Girl in the Box, Book 2
Soulless: The Girl in the Box, Book 3
Family: The Girl in the Box, Book 4
Omega: The Girl in the Box, Book 5
Broken: The Girl in the Box, Book 6
Enemies: The Girl in the Box, Book 7
Legacy: The Girl in the Box, Book 8
Destiny: The Girl in the Box, Book 9
Power: The Girl in the Box, Book 10

Limitless: Out of the Box, Book 1
In the Wind: Out of the Box, Book 2
Ruthless: Out of the Box, Book 3
Grounded: Out of the Box, Book 4
Tormented: Out of the Box, Book 5
Vengeful: Out of the Box, Book 6
Sea Change: Out of the Box, Book 7
Painkiller: Out of the Box, Book 8
Masks: Out of the Box, Book 9
Prisoners: Out of the Box, Book 10
Unyielding: Out of the Box, Book 11
Hollow: Out of the Box, Book 12
Toxicity: Out of the Box, Book 13
Small Things: Out of the Box, Book 14
Hunters: Out of the Box, Book 15
Badder: Out of the Box, Book 16
Apex: Out of the Box, Book 18
Time: Out of the Box, Book 19
Driven: Out of the Box, Book 20
Remember: Out of the Box, Book 21
Hero: Out of the Box, Book 22
Flashback: Out of the Box, Book 23* *(Coming December 2018!)*
Walk Through Fire: Out of the Box, Book 24* *(Coming in 2019!)*

World of Sanctuary
Epic Fantasy

Defender: The Sanctuary Series, Volume One
Avenger: The Sanctuary Series, Volume Two
Champion: The Sanctuary Series, Volume Three
Crusader: The Sanctuary Series, Volume Four
Sanctuary Tales, Volume One - A Short Story Collection
Thy Father's Shadow: The Sanctuary Series, Volume 4.5
Master: The Sanctuary Series, Volume Five
Fated in Darkness: The Sanctuary Series, Volume 5.5
Warlord: The Sanctuary Series, Volume Six
Heretic: The Sanctuary Series, Volume Seven
Legend: The Sanctuary Series, Volume Eight
Ghosts of Sanctuary: The Sanctuary Series, Volume Nine
Call of the Hero: The Sanctuary Series, Volume Ten* *(Coming Late 2018!)*

A Haven in Ash: Ashes of Luukessia, Volume One *(with Michael Winstone)*
A Respite From Storms: Ashes of Luukessia, Volume Two *(with Michael Winstone)*
A Home in the Hills: Ashes of Luukessia, Volume Three *(with Michael Winstone)*

Southern Watch
Contemporary Urban Fantasy

Called: Southern Watch, Book 1
Depths: Southern Watch, Book 2
Corrupted: Southern Watch, Book 3
Unearthed: Southern Watch, Book 4
Legion: Southern Watch, Book 5
Starling: Southern Watch, Book 6
Forsaken: Southern Watch, Book 7
Hallowed: Southern Watch, Book 8* *(Coming in 2019!)*

The Shattered Dome Series
(with Nicholas J. Ambrose)
Sci-Fi

Voiceless: The Shattered Dome, Book 1
Unspeakable: The Shattered Dome, Book 2* *(Coming in 2019!)*

The Mira Brand Adventures
Contemporary Urban Fantasy

The World Beneath: The Mira Brand Adventures, Book 1
The Tide of Ages: The Mira Brand Adventures, Book 2
The City of Lies: The Mira Brand Adventures, Book 3
The King of the Skies: The Mira Brand Adventures, Book 4
The Best of Us: The Mira Brand Adventures, Book 5
We Aimless Few: The Mira Brand Adventures, Book 6* *(Coming 2018!)*

Liars and Vampires
(with Lauren Harper)
Contemporary Urban Fantasy

No One Will Believe You: Liars and Vampires, Book 1
Someone Should Save Her: Liars and Vampires, Book 2
You Can't Go Home Again: Liars and Vampires, Book 3
In The Dark: Liars and Vampires, Book 4
Her Lying Days Are Done: Liars and Vampires, Book 5
Heir of the Dog: Liars and Vampires, Book 6* *(Coming November 2018!)*
Hit You Where You Live: Liars and Vampires, Book 7* *(Coming December 2018!)*

* Forthcoming, Subject to Change

Made in the USA
Middletown, DE
14 October 2020